The Secret of Berry Brae Circle

E M McIntyre

The Secret of Berry Brae Circle

Book 2: The Red King Trilogy

United States of America

ISBN-13: 978-0-9988993-2-9

ISBN-10: 0-9988993-2-1

To those who believed in me along the way, many thanks.

You gave me strength.

Book 2

The Red King Trilogy

1

*A*bby opened her eyes. A blinding white mist engulfed her. She could see nothing through the haze. She squinted, her eyelids fluttering until she grew accustomed to the light. A hollow feeling inside gnawed at her gut—something wasn't right. *Where am I? Where are the others?* Abby panicked when she realized her companions were no longer present. It seemed only minutes ago Finlay used his special powers to teleport the group from deep inside the mountain. *What if those creepy faerie brothers escaped and captured them again? Please let this be a dream.* She called out into the oppressive barrier, "Mom? Sage?" Whirling her head around, she continued, "Rory? Finlay? Agatha?" After several moments of quiet, she called for Finlay with her mind. *Finlay? Can you hear me? Where are you?* When no answer came, she wanted to run, to break free from the mist. *I have to find them!* She broke into a sprint but realized she wasn't moving. Sensing no solid surface beneath her, Abby looked down into the mist and searched with her fingers. *What the...where are my feet?* Her heart raced. *Where are my legs?* Abby straightened and brought her hands in front of her face. She sighed with relief upon seeing them. *I'm not going crazy, I'm just disoriented by this stupid mist.* Abby stretched low again to verify her feet were there. When she felt nothing for the second time, she gasped, straightened up, and reached for her face. Again, her fingertips felt no sensation. *This isn't possible. I must be dreaming.* Placing her hands in front of her face again, Abby attempted to calm herself. *Get a grip, Abby. Freaking out won't help anything.* She held her hands still while watching the mist swirl. Abby drew a sharp breath as the haze curled around, and then through, her fingers. *No way. I, I'm invisible or something? What the heck is happening?* As she stood bewildered, a distant, ethereal voice called out to her. Abby craned her neck and listened, hoping the faint sound wasn't her imagination. An eternity passed before the voice repeated itself. "Amaray, find your way home."

Who's Amaray? Battling her confusion, Abby called out. "Hello? Who's there?"

"Amaray, all will be lost without you..." The wispy voice trailed off into the distance one last time.

Abby contemplated the strange words. *Sure seemed like she was talking to me. Hate to disappoint though; no Amaray here. At least, not that I can see.* Abby snorted. *Speaking of seeing, what's the deal with this mist? I'd like to know where I am so I can get out of here.*

As Abby further inspected her surroundings, a familiar, rough accent made its way to her ear. "A-by?"

Her heart skipped a beat. *Is that Rory?* His voice beckoned to her again. Abby was certain he was not far.

"Rory!" She called out with fervor. "Rory. Where are you? Can you see me?" She spun around in search of her companion, her Red King. Because he now believed in the power coursing through his blood, confidence welled within Abby. He could help her find a way out of this void.

Rory called to her again. This time Abby swore he was standing right next to her. "A-by. A-by. Wake up."

Abby paused. *I knew it. I'm dreaming. But this mist looks so real. And that woman's voice.* As Abby called out again, she felt an unusual tugging from inside her belly button. The sensation strengthened, turning into a pinch. "Ouch!" Abby reached for her stomach, still surprised when her hand passed through her midsection.

"A-by. Come back to us." Rory's voice was full of emotion.

"Rory, I'm..." The tugging ended with a final, harsh pull that swept Abby from her feet. A wave of blackness washed over her as the misty prison disappeared.

✳✳✳

Abby felt a gentle hand stroke her forehead. "A-by?"

Abby opened her eyes. Her head throbbed. "Wha...What happened? Am I awake now?"

Rory's fiery braids brushed Abby's neck as he leaned over her. "Aye, A-by." Concern filled the young Scotsman's eyes. "Ye gave us quite a scare. Ye've been lost to us from the moment we arrived in yer time."

"Are we really back?" Abby sat up with Rory's help, unaware of those gathering around, watching her. Her mother held back tears as she shared hugs with Agatha and Mrs. MacTavish. Abby rubbed her face. "How long was I unconscious?"

Sage stepped forward and held a hand out to pull her younger sister to her feet. "Long enough for me to ride your bike back to the shop and grab Mrs. MacTavish and the car."

Abby stood, rotated the kinks from her neck, and smoothed her clothing. Combing her fingers through her chestnut curls, she surveyed her audience with a warm smile until her eyes fell upon her massive, white Irish wolfhound. "Finlay!" Abby flung herself at her furred companion and sank every bit of her being into his soft coat. Realizing she no longer needed to bend to wrap her arms around her white warrior's neck, Abby was certain the faerie's magic must have constrained him. It appeared to her Finlay experienced a generous growth spurt, even in the short period since escaping the faerie's oppressive cave that trapped so many innocents for so long. She reached out to Finlay with a flurry of thoughts. *I couldn't find you, or anyone. It was pretty scary. I figured Mavis and Tavis broke free. And then there was this voice calling out for someone named Amaray. And then...*

Finlay pawed at the ground and snorted. *Hush, young one, it seems you were in the midst of a bad dream. Calm yourself and start over.*

Abby drew in a deep breath and relaxed her mind. *Okay. Well. I thought I was dreaming, but it seemed so real. A bright, white mist surrounded me and I couldn't see through it. When I called out for everyone, there was no answer. And the most bizarre part was I couldn't feel any of my body and I swore the mist floated right through me. But then I heard this strange, female voice calling out for someone named Amaray, telling her to come home or all would be lost. After that, I heard Rory saying my name. I couldn't see him, but it sounded like he was standing right next to me. I tried calling out to him, but something pulled me backward...and now here I am. Awake. Right?* Abby tittered while running her fingers through Finlay's coat. *Yup, feels real.*

Finlay curved his head to the side and nudged Abby's midsection. *Yes, Lass. You are awake. Now may I suggest you give a proper greeting to the group? You had everyone worried. They were certain you hit your head.*

Abby released her grip on the wolfhound. *Alright. Back to reality. But let me say, fuzzball, you'll be as big as a stallion soon if you don't stop growing. What's up with that?*

Finlay turned to face Abby, and with a playful snort, retorted. *I'm just as I should be; it is of no concern for the nosy, young woman.* With an exaggerated wink, he added, *And all the easier for the fuzzball to make a snack of you, in case you've forgotten.*

Abby giggled and stuck her tongue out at the dog as she turned to observe her surroundings. The sun was announcing itself—hues of pink and blue stretched across the horizon, only to be lost behind a spattering of old forest. Abby pictured the grand expanse of trees from Rory's time. Shock and disgust overwhelmed her; so few remained now near the impressive mountain. Finlay had transported the travelers to the base of Caledonia, near the desolate visitor parking area. *That's right. I left my bike there when I went exploring. Good thing no one stole it.* The image of her older, taller sister riding her bike percolated to a more serious thought. "Hey, Sage. Why didn't you bring Dad back here with you too?"

Sage rubbed their mother's back while responding, "He's not home yet. You didn't really expect him to be back so soon from his latest literary expedition, did you?" Sage turned her focus to Victoria. "Don't worry, Mom, he should be here any time."

Victoria reached for both daughters' hands and gave them a gentle squeeze. "No worries, my sweets. I waited thirteen long years to get back home. I imagine I can manage a few more days before seeing Jonathon." Victoria turned to beam at Mrs. MacTavish. "Besides, I've just reunited with my dearest of friends." With a chuckle, she added, "I think that will tide me over for a bit."

Mrs. MacTavish dabbed her eyes with her kerchief as she pulled Victoria into another embrace. "Oh, heavens. I knew in me bones ye were still alive. And such a tale ye've told." The squat woman then drew Abby into a loving hug. "And to think our Abby saved ye all." Mrs. MacTavish released Abby, and stepping back, took the teenager's hands in her own. The shopkeeper's face shined, "Yer a true heroine, Lassie!"

Abby blushed as she let go of the old woman's hands. "Na, I'm no heroine." Abby motioned to the rest of the recent arrivals. "We all played a part in locking up those obnoxious faerie brothers. In fact," Abby paused and pointed to Rory, "has anyone introduced you to Rory yet? He's the reason we're no longer trapped, or worse."

Mrs. MacTavish nodded, "Aye, but only in brief, Lass. We were all a wee bit concerned about ye at the time to be makin' pleasantries."

Rory stepped forward, bowing as he introduced himself. "Good morn', Mrs. MacTavish. Me name is Rory MacKay of the clan MacKay, just and true descendant of the Red King." With careful precision, Rory pulled his sword from the makeshift scabbard on his back and held the weapon across his chest. He smiled at the shopkeeper and added, "At yer humble service."

Mrs. MacTavish fanned her face with her kerchief. "Oh, dearie me. It's true then? The old prophecy passed from generation to next in me family?" The old woman paused, a realization forming in her mind. She grasped Rory's free hand and exclaimed, "Ye are me kin!"

Rory squeezed her hand in return. "Aye, it is so. I am honored to meet ye."

Abby stepped close to the pair. "Mrs. MacTavish, how come you never mentioned anything to us about your bloodline?"

The old woman lowered her head and sighed. "Honestly, Lass, I never thought anythin' important of it.

The tales of me ancestors—Enya Myst and her mysterious beau with the fiery red braids—were always told as just that, tales. Seems this old goat thought wrong!"

Abby gave the shopkeeper a one-armed hug. "You're definitely not an old goat, Mrs. MacTavish. It's okay." Abby's eyes grew large as a thought came to mind. "Hey." She pointed to the hilt of Rory's sword. "What about this? Do you recognize that jewel?"

Mrs. MacTavish shuffled closer to Rory and adjusted her bifocals as she peered at the handle of the sword. With surprise, she replied, "Oh my." The shopkeeper again fanned her face. "I dare say that is me family's amulet. The one I passed on to Victoria. How did it end up in the sword?"

Abby stood straight, shoulders back. "That's the golden drop of the prophecy. It was the key to everything, though it took a while to figure it out."

Mrs. MacTavish continued to stare at the sword, her eyes big. "Tell me, Lass, how did ye come to know of the Prophecy of Myst?"

Abby appeared stupefied as she searched her surroundings. "Has anyone seen my backpack? I know I had it on me when we left the cave."

"Over here," Sage called as she sauntered toward their father's blue, compact car. "I tossed it in the back seat while you were still out."

Abby sprinted to the vehicle. *Guess it's a good thing Dad always insists on leaving the car with us when he goes off on his crazy book hunts. This would have been a long walk for Mrs. MacTavish.* Abby reached the vehicle as Sage pulled the bag out and handed it to her. "Thanks, Sis," she said as she rummaged through each pouch until her hands wrapped around the now-familiar scroll. *Phew. Was afraid I left it behind.*

Abby darted back to Mrs. MacTavish, holding the scroll out as she approached. "Here. I found this scroll in a secret spot on the mountain. It's the prophecy, but I couldn't read it. I was on my way to bring it to you. I figured you'd be able to read it. But, I got a little, ah, sidetracked." Abby nudged Rory with her elbow. "Rory translated it for me." Rory grunted in response as the shopkeeper unrolled the scroll with care and studied its contents.

As Mrs. MacTavish stood silent, her cheeks hinted of red. She looked back to Abby, "May I keep it, Lass?"

"Of course," Abby replied, adding with a snort, "let that be the last scroll I ever see."

The old woman smiled in return, though her eyes showed remorse. She tucked the scroll into the pouch of her shop apron. "Aye, Lass, I shall keep it in a safe place."

Sage interjected to catch the group's attention. "Speaking of safe places, isn't it about time we head to town? I'm betting Mom and Agatha would appreciate hot baths and a decent meal." She paused, giving Rory a once-over. "And if we don't want to draw attention, we'd better get Mr. Medieval to the shop. I bet some of Dad's clothes would fit him."

Rory sheathed his sword with a resistant grunt. Abby leaned in and gave a quick tug to one of his braids. "She's right, Rory. If you want to live in our time, you must blend in. I promise, it won't be so bad. Besides, you might like wearing something that isn't so itchy. I don't know how you stand that wool tunic!"

"Enough of the chit-chat guys, we can sort it all out later." Sage jingled the car keys while motioning toward the vehicle.

Abby rolled her eyes, "Okay, okay, but we all can't fit in the car. It barely seats four."

Sage inspected the group. "I'll take Mom, Mrs. MacTavish, and Agatha back to town. They're in no shape to walk that far." Sage looked at her sister with a playful smile. "You can have your dog take you guys back to the cottage." Her grin turned mischievous as she continued, "And while you're waiting for us, you should introduce Medieval to Dad's shower. He stinks!"

Rory stared at Sage. "Show-er?"

"Hilarious, Sage." Abby giggled at her sister before turning to Rory. "Never mind about that now, Rory. You are kinda stinky, but I'll explain the shower later."

Rory lifted the front of his tunic over his face and sniffed. Wrinkling his nose, he made a comical face at Abby and shrugged.

Sage chuckled at them as she ushered the women toward the car. Victoria paused and turned back to Abby. "Abigail, my sweet," she said as she hugged her youngest, "see you at the bookstore. I love you."

"Aw, love you too, Mom." Abby squeezed her mother's hand as she stepped away.

Victoria hurried to fall in line with the other women. When Agatha showed apprehension upon approaching the car, Victoria soothed her friend. Agatha hesitated before climbing into the vehicle, staring at it with amazement. Once everyone seated themselves, Sage started the engine and rolled the window down. "See ya there, squirt."

When the vehicle left the parking lot, Rory pulled his dirk and crouched into a defensive stance. Abby lowered his armed hand. "Whoa there, Rory." She held back laughter knowing this would be the first of many things to confuse, or frighten, the 14th century Scotsman. "It's okay, don't be afraid. Think of the car as a kind of improved wagon."

Rory eyed the disappearing auto and relaxed his shoulders. He stood, sheathing his dirk. "Aye, A-by. I will do better to remember yer promise to see me no harm here."

Abby smiled as she pointed toward the tiny town. "Come on, it'll take us a while to catch up. We should get going. Don't want to roll in when everyone is up and about." Abby considered her companions before adding, "Pretty sure you two might scare people at first glance." Finlay circled the duo several times, blocking their way as he sat in front of them.

Are you forgetting the resources at your disposal, Lass? I can have you there in moments.

Abby came to an abrupt stop and turned to Rory. "Finlay wants to take us."

"It's yer choice, A-by. Would be fastest, but I'll heed yer judgment."

Abby stood silent, her body tensing as she envisioned the mist-filled void she had just escaped. "No thanks, I'd rather walk this time."

2

*T*he trio avoided the road to town for most of their trek, following the River Corren as terrain allowed. The trees weren't as thick as Abby would prefer when trying to hide an over-sized wolfhound and medieval Scotsman, but the riparian woodlands offered just enough cover. Abby groaned when she glanced at her watch—6:30am. It was the end of May and the sun was already making a statement. Scotland's long days required Abby to adjust; little in her new home compared to that of Nebraska. Abby turned her attention back to her task. *No cars on the road yet. Should be able to sneak Rory and that sword of his into the bookstore without much problem.*

The river divided the village of Kinloch-Rannoch. To their benefit, Fletcher's Finds, the book store Abby's father owned, stood on the southern side of the river which they now skirted. She motioned for her companions to follow. "Come on, guys. Let's cut through this pasture to the road over there. The shop's a few buildings in." As the awkward ensemble made their way across the grassland, noises from the adjacent plot announced the waking of the community. Abby scanned the field to meet the inquisitive eyes of a local sheepherder. An elderly man wearing a heavy pullover and work pants stopped what he was doing to stare at the threesome. He stepped forward, adjusted the cap upon his head and rubbed his eyes. Abby assumed he was attempting to figure out what he was seeing, so she waved to the man, pasted a huge smile on her face, and clenched her teeth, all the while telling Rory to do the same. "Rory. Smile, wave, and keep walking. But don't stare!" Rory mimicked Abby's motions and continued to focus on the strip of small buildings paralleling the road ahead. The old man shrugged and lost interest in the spectacle as he continued about his morning business. Abby sighed with relief as they stepped onto the roadway. "Look," Abby pointed ahead to the little blue vehicle, "there's Dad's car. I wonder if everyone is in the cottage or the shop." After thinking about it a moment, Abby angled toward the bookstore. "We've been walking forever, surely they've had time to bathe and eat."

Rory groaned and placed a hand on his belly. "Need to catch us a kinnen, A-by."

Abby giggled as she pictured the rabbit Rory had last 'caught' for them at the Robertson's camp. "It was tasty, but there will be no more rabbit hunting, Rory."

Rory grimaced at her response. "Nae?" Standing tall, he grinned and continued. "Then I shall catch us a deer." He paused, realizing his limitation, "But I have no bow."

Abby looked at the ground and kicked a pebble, sending it skittering across the cement. "Yeah, sorry 'bout that." Abby recalled when they first met. Rory's bow was doomed when she fell on top of the Scotsman. *I should use some of my savings and buy him one of those fancy, compact hunting bows.* Abby glanced at her redheaded companion and said cheerfully, "But don't worry, you'll never have to hunt for food again."

Rory raised a suspicious eyebrow. "How do ye propose we are to eat then, A-by?"

Abby grinned. "Here in the 21st century, we buy our food from a grocery store. But sometimes you can have it delivered too." Abby's mouth watered as she pictured her favorite thick crust pizza: pepperoni, pineapple, and extra cheese. "Ooooo, I can't wait for you to try Domino's. It will blow your mind." Abby frowned upon a realization, mumbling to herself, "They probably don't have Domino's in Scotland, though."

Rory stared at Abby, dumbfounded by her ramblings. "What are ye sayin', Lass?"

Abby groaned and waved off his confusion. "Never mind for now, Rory. Mrs. MacTavish always has a tasty stew of some sort cooked up, so you don't have to worry. She takes real good care of us. I haven't had to cook a single meal since we moved here." Abby poked the Scotsman's rib cage and snickered. "She'll fatten you up though if you aren't careful. But that'd be a good thing. You could use a little more meat on them bones." Rory grunted in response as they continued along the road.

Finlay slowed his pace to trot next to Abby. *Do not tease the boy so, Lass. You should concern yourself more with what lays ahead, and less with mockery at any level.*

Abby rolled her eyes. *Yeah, yeah. He makes it sooo easy though. But you're right, I shouldn't pick on him. I'm sure he feels just like I did when I dropped into his time.*

Finlay snorted his approval. *Aye, young one. More thinking before speaking is all I ask. I sense you are destined for greater things. You must practice more discipline.*

Abby laughed aloud. *Um, yeah. Destined for a great big bowl of hot stew and a plate of Mrs. MacTavish's famous shortbread is what I'm thinking right about now.*

Rory smiled at Abby as she continued to laugh. "What brings ye such fits, A-by?"

Abby shook her head as she composed herself. "Oh, nothing. Finlay is just being silly." She halted and pointed to the bookstore. "We're here." Stand-alone buildings composed of gray, speckled bricks lined both sides of the street. White window and door trim accented the shops, and many displayed a burst of color from windowsill planters. However, her father's store always caught Abby's eye. The building's trim popped with a vivid red and Abby loved the custom-made sign her father had ordered. The wrought iron support bracket attached to the building incorporated a bow and arrow into its design. A weathered piece of wood in the shape of an open book hung from the bracket; the sign displayed the name Fletcher's Finds. Abby admired the elegant script before rotating and pointing across the street.

"Our cottage is that one over there." Wasting no more time with a tour, Abby opened the door to the shop and ushered Rory and Finlay inside. "It's kind of cramped in here, so please be careful."

Once the trio was out of public view, Abby shut and locked the door, flipping the 'closed' sign around in the window. Victoria and Agatha sat at the lone table in the back of the bookstore while Sage helped Mrs. MacTavish carry platters of food to the newcomers. "Ah, there ye are, child," said the shopkeeper, "we were beginnin' to wonder if ye'd ever show up!"

Abby shrugged. "Sorry to worry you. I felt like walking and decided it would be a good idea to stay off the road and follow the river. Guess it took a little longer than I expected." A familiar, tantalizing odor wafted its way to Abby, triggering her stomach to growl. "Please tell me you have an extra batch of stew, Mrs. MacTavish. I'm betting we're all famished."

Mrs. MacTavish chuckled, "Come then, both of ye fetch a bowl. There's plenty to be had for all." She eyed Finlay over the top of her glasses as he sniffed a leather-bound book displayed on a stand. "I reckon there's even enough for your grand friend. Ye may dish him a serving too."

Finlay turned his attention to the back of the shop and watched as the caretaker placed heaping bowls in front of Agatha and Victoria. Sage helped herself to some shortbread and leaned against a nearby bookcase as her elders ate. Trotting to Abby's side, Finlay lowered his head and nudged her hand with his nose. *This nourishment you call stew, the smell agrees with me.*

Abby reached up to ruffle his head. *I'm sure it does. And I'm betting you'll want it all for yourself once you taste it.* Abby grinned. *So mind your manners, fuzzball.*

Finlay rumbled playfully in response as Abby led Rory to the back of the bookstore. Rory waited while she prepared three bowls of the shopkeeper's savory smelling concoction. Abby glanced up mid-scoop to notice Rory's intense examination of the rows upon rows of books.

Shelves lined every wall of the bookstore from floor to ceiling; shorter units—perhaps four feet high—stood in even rows throughout the main floor area.

Abby placed a bowl on the floor for Finlay before motioning for Rory to join her at the closest short bookcase. She set the bowls down and handed him a spoon. "Dig in." Rory hesitated but soon understood this meant it was okay to eat.

The group indulged in silence, devouring several servings all around. Feeling satisfied with the contentment on every face, Mrs. MacTavish cleared the dishes. Abby collected the bowls she had filled and placed them on the platter Sage held out in front of her. "Thanks, Sage. I can take that to the sink if you want."

"No, no problem, I've got it." Sage wiggled her nose and winked. "Wouldn't want to take you away from your 'friend.'"

Abby rolled her eyes in reply. "You're a regular comedian, Sis."

"Thanks, I try," Sage said as she strolled to the front of the shop and out of sight.

The store consisted of the main sales floor and two side rooms, one at each end of the building. The extra room at the front of the shop provided comfortable living quarters for Mrs. MacTavish, along with an equipped kitchenette. The corresponding room in the back of the store served as storage for miscellaneous items and books Jonathon didn't want on display.

Abby patted her stomach. Leaning against the bookshelf, she stared at her mother thoughtfully. Sighing, she blurted, "I sure wish Dad would hurry." When Sage and Mrs. MacTavish returned to the main room, she continued. "Are you sure he hasn't called?"

Sage frowned and shook her head. "Pretty sure. And there have been no messages in the shop's voice mail."

"Hmm," Abby scratched her chin. "Well, maybe he sent me a text!" Abby grabbed her backpack and rummaged through its pouches. She stopped short as she pulled her phone out and pushed the power button. "Ugh. I forgot. The battery died when I was inside the Robertson's nasty hut." Abby shivered as she replayed the scene in her head. Having the flashlight app die after discovering the Red King's sword had done nothing to help the situation. She shook the memory off as she walked to the front counter and called over her shoulder, "Your charger up here somewhere, Sage?"

Sage nodded and hollered back, "Check the top drawer. It should be in there."

Abby located the charger with ease, plugging in the phone. "Maybe he's emailed the shop. I'll check." Abby strummed her fingers on the counter top after jiggling the mouse to wake the store computer. When the screen popped on, she logged into the shop's email account. Mrs. MacTavish maintained the email, so there were only a handful of new messages. Disappointed, Abby sighed when she didn't see the name Jonathon Fletcher listed. She glanced at the Spam folder—1 new message. *Well, why not, just to be sure.* The sender and visible message line were odd enough to cause Abby to pause before deleting it. The subject line read 'Bring me the Book of Shay. Or else'; the sender name was a nondescript combination of numbers and letters. *That's weird. Wonder what this is.* Abby opened the email and read its contents.

> Bring me the Book of Shay or the Librarian dies. Mr. Fletcher insists he's never heard of it, but I know otherwise. Respond to this email when you have the book, and I will give further instructions. You have until June 1st if you want to see him again.

Abby stared at the computer screen and reread the message, trying to digest its meaning. "Uh, guys," she called frantically, "I think Dad's in trouble!"

Everyone turned to Abby. The fear on her face spurred them to hurry to the front counter. Abby glanced over her shoulder to see Victoria squeezing through the group to stand next to her. Her mother stared wide-eyed and white-faced at the screen, mouthing the words to herself. Sage stretched to view the monitor straight on. "Well? What's it say, Abby?"

Abby cleared her throat and read the message aloud, choking on the last sentence. Her lips quivered. "Do you think this is legit? I mean, if someone did kidnap Dad, what a weird way to send a ransom note."

Silence enveloped the room as everyone looked to one another, unsure of what to think or say. Eventually, Sage observed, "If this is for real, maybe the kidnapper didn't want us to hear their voice," she twirled a strand of hair around a finger, "and, maybe they didn't want us to see their handwriting, so, they did the next best thing. They emailed it."

Abby nodded. "I guess that makes sense. Dad knows we keep up on anything electronic, maybe he assured his kidnapper someone would read the message." She glanced at the date on the task bar—May 30th—and sucked in a breath. "If this isn't a joke, we only have two days to find the book and email them back!"

Rory reached across the counter and squeezed Abby's hand. "Then we will find it, A-by. I promise ye we will save yer faither." He stood straight and looked around the group, his eyes ablaze. "Where do we start?"

Agatha dabbed her forehead with her kerchief as she surveyed the vast number of books in the shop. "Surely we shall find it here, what with this endless collection."

"Check the inventory file, Lass," Mrs. MacTavish motioned to Abby. "If the book lives within these walls, it shall tell us; however, I regret the name does not sound familiar."

Abby's eyes lit up. *Why didn't I think of that? Dad's particular about accurate accounting of his books.* She opened the inventory spreadsheet, hit ctrl-F, and searched the name 'Shay.' Her shoulders tensed when no matches appeared. "Nothing," she announced with a frown.

Victoria snapped out of her daze and straightened her posture. "Then we will check every book by hand. If it's here, we'll find it. If not," she paused uncertainly, "well, we'll figure it out when we get there."

"Right," Mrs. MacTavish said. "I'll start in the stockroom. Everyone else, pick yerself a shelf and please mind how ye handle the older books."

The group dispersed from the counter to begin their task. Abby watched as Agatha and Victoria pulled chairs over to the back wall, opting to sit while searching the lower rows. Sage tapped her chin, contemplating the best strategy. She then grabbed the step ladder to search the highest levels next to her elders.

Abby motioned for Rory to follow her to the front corner of the shop. "Sage will have to search the top rows because we only have one ladder, but you can work this area since you're a head taller than me," she said, pointing to a section well beyond her reach.

Rory replied with a quick nod, his face serious. "Aye, A-by." He laid a hand on her shoulder, giving it a gentle squeeze, "I will do me best for ye."

"Thanks," Abby said, her cheeks growing warm. She turned to hide her embarrassment, unsure what to think of the response Rory's touch always seemed to elicit. *Focus, Abby. There are more important things to think about right now.*

Abby stretched her fingers out to Finlay, who sat patiently nearby. She took in a handful of silky fur and called out to him with her mind. *I guess you'll just have to sit here and watch while we check all the books. Or, you could take a nap if you wanted. It will probably bore you otherwise.*

Finlay stood and snorted. *I should think it most efficient if all eyes searched, Lass. Time is essential if we are to find your father.*

Abby put a hand on her hip. *What? You're saying you can read?*

Finlay tilted his head. *That is so, young one. This should not be so surprising.*

She eyed her companion. *Are you kidding me?* Abby pulled a book from the nearest shelf and held it spine-first in front of Finlay. *Then what's this one called?*

Finlay stepped forward, sniffed the book, and focused on the writing. After a moment of low grumbling and broadcasting of garbled sounds Abby couldn't understand, he stated, *The Monks of May.*

Abby twisted the book toward her to read the cover. She rolled her eyes and returned the text to the shelf. *Ok, then. You can read.* She tapped her foot. *Any other secret talents you'd like to tell me about while we're at it?*

Finlay licked her hand and burrowed his head into her side. *None I'm aware of, Lass.*

Abby scratched Finlay's chest before stepping back to her chosen bookshelf. *You take the short case next to me. Just ask if you can't make something out.* Finlay weaved his way in between Rory and Abby, sat in front of the shelf, and wrapped his tail around himself. Rory watched, confused, as Finlay leaned in and squinted at the row of books. Abby caught Rory's expression from the corner of her eye. "If you're wondering whether he can read, the answer is 'yes.'" Abby shrugged. "I suppose it shouldn't seem so odd considering his other skills."

Rory grunted, then returned his attention to the case in front of him, scanning his finger over the spine of each book.

The group worked on in silence through mid-morning. There was no sign of the mysterious book; despair hung heavy in the shop. Abby and Rory reached the last of the bookcases. It was a stand-alone case toward the center of the shop, which doubled as a display stand for several old vases. Abby waved Rory off, "I can check these books real quick, Rory." She paused, attempting a smile. "Thanks for helping, even though it looks like we won't find the book here." Rory nodded in reply as Abby dropped to one knee to skim the book titles. *Please be here. I don't know where else to look.* Abby sighed after several minutes. A knot formed in her stomach when she read the last spine. Ready to announce their failure, she stood up to find Rory handling an intricately painted pitcher that had been atop the bookcase. Abby gasped, startling Rory. "Rory! Be careful with that. It's one of Dad's favorites, he says it's special. You'd better put it back."

Rory mouthed he was sorry and returned the pitcher to its rightful spot. When he stepped back from the case, a small pouch tethered to his waist came free and dropped to the ground. He groaned, leaning over to retrieve it. As his fingers wrapped around the bag, he crooked his head to the side to meet the eyes of Finlay. Rory jerked and pivoted away from the beast. Abby shrieked, "Watch out!" as the tip of Rory's sword contacted the relic piece he had just admired. The pitcher wobbled wildly, bumped the vase in the middle of the display, and dove off the shelf toward Abby. Rory stood upright, expecting the worst, but soon smiled when Abby held the pitcher up triumphantly to show it was in one piece. However, their relief was momentary; the vase in the middle had tipped on its side and was rolling toward the edge of the shelf. Slow to react, Rory watched with horror as the piece crashed to the floor. He cringed and braved a glance at Abby, who could do nothing but shake her head.

"Smooth move, Medieval," Sage said, who had made her way over. Rory grimaced and squatted to pick up the larger pieces of the vase.

Abby set the pitcher down with care, calling out over her shoulder as she walked toward the stockroom, "I'll go grab the broom and dustpan for the smaller pieces." After returning and making short work of sweeping up the debris, Abby hurried to join Sage and Rory.

Sage motioned for the Scotsman to place the bigger chunks of the vase on the front counter. The base, which had broken away from the body, split in two from top to bottom. Sage sighed and picked up half of the base. "What a shame. Dad was so excited when he found this one." She examined its plain design; except for a small tree with roots looping around the base and ending in a spiral, the piece was unimpressive. "Don't know why though; it's drab if you ask me." Setting the portion down, something peculiar caught her eye. "Hey," she said, looking at the open profile of the base, "there's a false bottom, and I think there's something in it."

Sage held it up for Abby and Rory to examine. They squinted, peering into the small crevice in unison before nodding agreement.

Sage rummaged through the top drawer under the counter, then looked up at her sister. "I need a pair of tweezers. You seem to have anything and everything in that backpack of yours. Think you can help me out?"

Abby grabbed her bag, and after a moment of rummaging, she pulled out her homemade first aid kit. "Yup," she said, holding up stainless steel tweezers as she stepped back to the counter. "Here you go." She smiled proudly, handing them off to Sage.

"Nice. Thanks," Sage said as she inserted the instrument inside the small cavity. Abby held her breath, curious what mystery would be revealed.

Victoria, Agatha, and Mrs. MacTavish gathered around as Sage continued to fish the contents from the vase. Finlay sat back to observe the group, his ears perking when, after several anxious moments, Sage exclaimed, "I've got a grasp on it! A little more wiggling and it will be free." With a final, gentle tug, she pulled the tweezers from the tight opening.

Abby groaned upon seeing the discovery. *Really? Another scroll?*

Agatha cooed at the find. "I dare say that's the smallest scroll I have ever laid me eyes upon."

Victoria reached forward to pluck the yellowed parchment from the tweezers. She placed the four-inch wide, tightly rolled scroll on her palm and turned it over. "Look!" She pointed to the section now facing up. "There's something written on it, but not in English." She held it up by both ends for Rory and Mrs. MacTavish to examine. "Can either of you read it?"

The two leaned in to focus on the tiny script. After several moments of examination, they turned to each other with wide eyes.

"Well," Abby urged, "what's it say?"

Mrs. MacTavish nodded to Rory. A silent void filled the room after a single word left his mouth. "Shay."

3

*V*ictoria worked to control the trembling of her fingers as she unrolled the aged scroll. Abby tensed with anticipation at what they might find. Would there be a map with a big, black 'X' marking the location of the mysterious book? Or, would there be yet another brain-wracking riddle leading them on a wild chase to places unknown? Abby shifted her weight from one foot to the other, impatient to learn the contents. Victoria laid the parchment flat on the counter, pressing on the corners with either hand. No one spoke as all eyes studied the exquisite artistry. A detailed tree dominated the bottom third of the scroll. Its grand trunk supported symmetrically placed branches spread wide with enormous, overlapping leaves. Its many roots snaked up the sides, meeting at the top of the page. There they converged in the middle to form a spiral. Four elegant stanzas filled the center. Abby crinkled her nose at the verses—like with the Prophecy of Myst, she could not decipher the strange language. She looked to Rory and Agatha, awaiting a translation. When one did not come, she elbowed Rory in the ribs. "Enough with the suspense, tell us what it says. You can understand it, right?"

Rory nodded with a grunt. "Aye, A-by. But I fear ye shall have many questions." The young Scotsman cleared his throat and read.

> Where the land and sky meet
> Among the ancient pine
> Near the faerie pool
> The Wolf's lair ye shall find
>
> And within his stone haven
> A sacred book doth dwell
> The secret it holds
> It shan't likely tell
>
> But hold no despair
> Do not doubt thine eye
> For the Rose of Shaeron
> Will show its true guise
>
> A treasure so grand
> Protected through time
> Until blood of like blood
> Reveals what's inside

Abby rotated her shoulders and rubbed her temples as Rory finished translating the scroll. She let out a long sigh; as tired of riddles as she was, her father's life could be in danger. They could rest when he was in the safety of their home. Abby stretched an arm over the counter, grabbing a pen and pad of paper. "We better write this in English so everyone can study it." Nodding her head toward Rory to show she was ready, Abby wrote the verses as he repeated them.

"Well done, Lass," Mrs. MacTavish said as she patted Abby's hand. "Give it here, and I'll print copies."

"Good idea." Abby smiled, relinquishing the paper to the old shopkeeper. Mrs. MacTavish walked behind the counter, started up their all-in-one, and printed six copies.

"No sense knockin' heads tryin' to read the same one," she said with a chortle as she distributed the riddle to the group.

Carefully, Victoria re-rolled the scroll and held it upright. "What should we do with the original?"

"How about we put it in a Ziploc?" Sage suggested. "But we should tie something around it first, so it doesn't unroll."

"I have just the thing." Mrs. MacTavish raised a finger and called over her shoulder while hurrying to her private room. Moments later, she returned with a small scrap of red ribbon. Sage rummaged through a drawer in hunt of a baggie while Mrs. MacTavish tied the ornament around the scroll.

"Now what?" Sage asked, holding the bagged scroll in front of her.

Abby shrugged. "Eh, I'll stick it in my pack. Never know if we'll need it handy again."

Sage mirrored her sister's body language. "Might as well add it to your collection, my little hoarder of a sister," she said with a grin.

Abby rolled her eyes as she grabbed the baggie and stowed it in an inner pouch of her backpack. She rejoined the group at the counter and scooped up her copy of the riddle. "Anyone have any ideas right off?"

"It appears there are two puzzles to solve," Victoria said with determination. When no one interjected, she reread the first section aloud.

> Where the land and sky meet
> Among the ancient pine
> Near the faerie pool
> The Wolf's lair ye shall find

"We can agree this describes a location," Victoria looked around the group, continuing after she received a unanimous nod, "and the second stanza tells us we will find a book there."

> And within his stone haven

A sacred book doth dwell

The secret it holds

It shan't likely tell

"Surely this refers to the Book of Shay. The book that will save my Jonathon," Victoria said, a tear welling in her eye.

Agatha rubbed Victoria's back. "Don't ye worry, my dear. We shall bring yer husband home soon enough."

"Yeah, Mom," Abby added, "don't worry, we'll find him." She scratched her forehead in contemplation. "Sure would be nice if we knew the secret of the book, why this mysterious person wants it."

"Aye," Rory said, "would be helpful, but shan't we focus on what's in front of us?"

"The boy is right," Agatha said, "let us discuss the rest of the riddle. I find it vexing, yet," she paused and stared at the phrasing, "something of the name 'Rose of Shaeron' pulls at me memories of long ago."

But hold no despair

Do not doubt thine eye

For the Rose of Shaeron

Will show its true guise

A treasure so grand

Protected through time

Until blood of like blood

Reveals what's inside

"Maybe the book has a treasure map in it," Abby said. "And... maybe only someone of the same bloodline as the person who drew the map," she reflected, "or hid the treasure, can find it. But, sounds like they'd need whatever that Rose of Shaeron thing is, too."

Agatha thumbed her chin, frustration evident on her face. "I must sit and reflect. I know this Rose of Shaeron is familiar. Imprisonment in that cave for so many years has dulled me mind I'm afraid."

Sage eyed the older women. "Perhaps the adults should rest up in the cottage."

Victoria protested, but Mrs. MacTavish stopped her short. "That's a wise idea, dear. I dare say I'm not the only one feelin' weary from the excitement. A quick nap will do us good. But before we go," she said as she walked back into her private area again, this time to rummage through a closet, "I have somethin' for me young ancestor." Mrs. MacTavish returned to the group and held out a worn, leather scabbard with straps. "Here ye are, Laddie. Ye need proper protection for such a sword. Protection for it," she paused, smiling at the boy as she continued, "and protection for everything around it."

Rory reached out and accepted the unexpected gift, running his hand along the scabbard. After examining the straps, he attached them to his waist and adjusted the scabbard to rest on his left hip. Rory stepped back from the group and removed the sword and makeshift holder from his back. "There are no proper words to thank thee, Mrs. MacTavish," he said as he placed the blade in its new home. "I have nothin' to repay ye."

The shopkeeper waved a dismissive hand. "Family needs no payment, Lad." She eyed the placement of the sword. "It's just as it should be."

"Well," Sage snorted, "now that there's no further chance of impalement, how about that nap?" Sage ushered the women to the door, glancing back at Abby. "I'll get them settled and hang out there. Why don't you and Medieval keep working on the riddle."

"Sure," Abby said. *But I have no clue where to start,* she thought as she bid her elders a pleasant rest and locked the door behind them.

As she turned back to face Rory, Finlay's gruff voice disrupted her thoughts. *Why not use that magic box of yours?*

Abby giggled. *Magic box? You mean the computer?*

Finlay pawed at the ground. *Aye, Lass. If that is what you call the thing that delivered the ominous message. Can it not tell you other information of value?*

Abby groaned at her absentmindedness. *Why didn't I think of that?* She beckoned Finlay to her, reaching up to ruffle the fur on his head. "Such a smart doggy," she said, tugging at an ear. "I'm definitely keeping you." After one last pat on Finlay's head, Abby motioned for Rory to follow her to the computer. "So," she explained, "Finlay called this our magic box, which, it is in some ways. I can't even explain how it works," Abby added with a snort, "but there's nothing magical involved." She shot Rory a glance, "Or nothing witchy either, so don't even go there," Abby ended with a giggle. Rory replied with his trademark funny face as she elaborated.

"All you need to know is we can ask it any question we want, and it will give us lots of possible answers to examine one by one." Abby paused to make sure Rory was following her. Satisfied he didn't appear dumbfounded, she continued. "But, the tricky part is knowing what to ask."

"Do ye talk to it, A-by?"

Abby stopped from answering with a laugh, reminding herself how foreign and confusing this must be to her new friend. "No, but good question." Abby pointed to the keyboard. "We can type the words using this. It's real easy." Abby slid her copy of the riddle in front of her. "Here, I'll show you." She contemplated the first stanza. "Let's try this," Abby typed keywords from the mysterious riddle into the search bar, "Scotland, ancient pine, faerie pool, and Wolf." Rory watched with amazement as Abby hit enter and the results page loaded.

"A book with no pages," Rory said.

"Yeah, kinda like that, but there's more to it we won't worry about, okay?"

Rory grunted as he stared at the screen, eager to digest all he could. "How do we learn its secrets?" he said, pointing to the first search result that read 'Faerie Pools of the Highlands.'

Abby wiggled the mouse and explained its function. "Simple. Left-click the blue text and it will take you to that page of the book, so to speak." Abby clicked the link and smiled when she noticed Rory's expression of wonderment.

Rory looked from the monitor to Abby several times before placing a hand on her shoulder. "Not only are ye brave and strong-willed, A-by, ye are wise beyond yer years to have mastered such a thing."

Abby shrugged with the faintest of smiles as her cheeks hinted of red. "Nah, it's no big deal. I grew up with this stuff. If you were born when I was, you'd find it just as easy." Abby deepened her smile, "Just like with you and your bow n' arrow—it's what you know and have practiced."

A low grumble intruded into Abby's mind. *The boy has strong feelings for you, Lass. Do not allow that to be a distraction.*

Willing her cheeks to ignore the dog's statement, a wave of embarrassment washed over Abby. *You're imagining things, fuzzball. And I won't be letting any boy distract me.*

You underestimate your own feelings. You may deny it, but I can sense the bond that builds between you.

Abby rolled her eyes before turning her focus back to the computer screen. "Anyways," she directed toward Rory as she scrolled through the site, "here's our first page to investigate. Hard to say if there'll be anything useful." Random pictures of serene settings with clear, blue pools of water as their focal point filled the monitor. The pair examined each picture and description to no avail. Reaching the bottom of the page, Abby read the last sentence aloud.

> For more images and detailed information, see 'Myths of the Highlands' by R. J. Welling.

Finlay's ears perked upon hearing the title of the book. *I have seen such a name in your father's collection, Lass.*

Huh. Abby turned to Rory. "Finlay says that book's here. I doubt it will have any clues in it, based on what we just looked at, but you never know."

Rory stared at the dog, baffled. "Show me," he said.

Finlay snorted, stood, and stretched his massive frame, then strode to the closest bookshelf. Circling several times, he plopped his hindquarters on the floor with a thud and bumped the spine of a book with his nose. Rory approached the dog with caution, pulling the book from the shelf only after Finlay returned to the front of the shop.

Abby shook her head at the dog, who took solace in a sunny spot near the main door. *You enjoy scaring Rory, don't you?*

Rumbling laughter flowed through her mind. *Aye, perhaps.*

Abby grinned at the creature. *I thought as much.*

Finlay laid his muzzle on his outstretched paws. *He has nothing to fear. I am only keeping your best interests at heart.*

Abby shook her head again. *Uh-huh.*

Rory approached the front desk, looking back and forth between Abby and the dog. He extended the book in front of him for Abby to take, a wide smile creeping across his face when she thanked him.

Abby laid the book on the counter and flipped through the glossy pages. It consisted of few pictures, which was what she was after, making its examination swift. Towards the end of the collection, Abby stopped and thumbed her way back to an image that caught her eye. A low-lying waterfall acted as a backdrop to a striking pool of water. To the side of the falls stood an impressive tower surrounded by tall, thick trees. The caption contained only one word.

Badenoch

"Hmm." Abby rubbed her chin, mulling over the first part of the riddle. "A lair is basically somewhere that something lives. So, a castle could be considered a lair, right?" She turned her head to look at Rory who nodded in agreement. "Whatever this Badenoch is," she continued, "this picture shows old looking trees, a pool of water, and a 'lair.'" Feeling hopeful, Abby grinned at Rory. "Maybe we're on to something! Let's search for Badenoch." Abby closed the book, pushed it aside, and searched the strange name. Her insides twisted when she read the top result. She pointed to the monitor for emphasis. "Look, Rory. The Wolf of Badenoch!"

Rory exchanged an eager glance with Abby. "Left-click it," he said awkwardly, "let's see what it shall tell us."

Abby giggled to herself as she selected the link. When the page finished loading, Abby sneered at its presentation. The portrait of a middle-aged man filled the left half of the screen while a collage of a castle, during its finest years and then in shambles, filled the right. The man's piercing and ominous gaze disturbed Abby. A jet-black beard framed his face and the corners of his mouth turned downward. A brief caption followed the picture.

Damien Stewart, The Wolf of Badenoch: 1349-1394

Below the images, text completed the page. Abby skimmed through the long paragraph, noting what seemed important. "Sounds like this guy wasn't very likable, with all the raping and pillaging he did. But what's interesting is it says he obsessed over collecting rare items." She paused, her demeanor hopeful. "Like a certain book?"

Rory grunted. "Aye, A-by. It could be so."

Abby's eyes shone. "We should find his castle and search it."

Finlay opened his eyes upon Abby's declaration. *I find it unlikely, little one, for the book to be there, even if he indeed had it in his possession.*

Abby placed her hands defiantly on her hips. "Rory, Finlay says he doubts the book will still be in the Wolf's castle. Granted, the castle is in ruins now, but we have to start somewhere, right? We have to rule it out." She shrugged. "Maybe it's buried there. I dunno."

Rory eyed the dog, then turned to take Abby's hands. "If ye feel such urgency to search the castle, I shall follow. I will see ye no harm."

Abby blushed when she found herself slow to pull her hands free from Rory's. As she did, a quick rap sounded at the front door. Abby peered out the window. "Ah, looks like everyone's done napping." She rounded the counter and unlocked the door, giving out quick hugs as the group entered. When everyone was inside and the door locked, Abby blurted out their finding. "Great news! We've discovered a clue."

Victoria held her hands to her heart. "How splendid, my sweet." Agatha and Mrs. MacTavish cheered Abby's revelation.

Sage appeared unconvinced. "Let's hear what it is first before we get too excited."

Abby wrinkled her nose at her sister. "It's legit, Sis. We think we know where to find the book." She reached over the counter to grab the volume by Welling. "There's this picture in here," Abby explained as she searched for the image, "that depicts the location described in the riddle." She opened the book wide and turned it for everyone to see. Abby pointed to the image. "See. Old trees, a pool of water, and a castle, or lair."

"There could be many places that meet those criteria," Sage scoffed. "What makes you so sure this is the right one?"

"Because," Abby countered, "the name of the place is Badenoch, and if you were to research it like we did, it'd tell you that ruler's name was the Wolf of Badenoch." Abby snapped the book shut and continued, her words determined. "The Wolf's lair. And 'within his stone haven a sacred book doth dwell.'" Confident, she straightened her shoulders and stood tall. "It's got to be the right place. We need to search it."

The older women looked from one to another, exchanging silent glances of agreement. "Well you've convinced me this is something we need to pursue," Victoria said. "Where is this castle located?"

Abby scratched her head. "Oh, ah, I need to check a map, but somewhere in the Highlands." Abby hurried to the computer and performed a quick search. "Castle Badenoch, or what's left, is located in the heart of Towie forest." Abby snorted. "This says a large area surrounding the castle is haunted, that only the bravest of thrill seekers visit the site."

"That's absurd," Sage said. "They probably say that to keep people from disturbing the ruins."

Abby shrugged. "Anyway, it's not far, about an hour northeast."

"We shouldn't waste any time then," Victoria said.

"Well we all can't go," Sage said. "Someone has to stay here to check the email, and we don't want to miss any calls. Plus, who knows, Dad might escape from wherever he's being held and make his way home."

"I have an idea about that," Abby said as she fiddled with the drawstring on her hoodie, "but Mom's probably not going to like it much."

Victoria gave her youngest a stern look, "Let me hear it then."

"Well," Abby explained, shifting weight between feet, "Sage is right that someone needs to stay here. Not only so we don't miss any further communication from the jerk that has Dad, but also to use the computer to figure out more of the riddle. That's a good job for Sage."

Sage looked up from examining her fingernails. "No arguments here. But what do you assume you will be doing then?"

Abby cleared her throat, looking at Rory as she spoke. "Rory and I will find the castle. And everyone else should stay here." She continued before anyone could object. "Mom and Agatha need to rest. After everything they've been through, they deserve it." Abby turned to smile apprehensively at the old shopkeeper. "And Mrs. MacTavish, well, no offense, but you shouldn't be out running around through a forest." Biting her lip, Abby looked at her mom. "So...what do you say?"

Victoria contemplated Abby's bold suggestion in silence. "When considering the things you've pointed out, there is logic to your plan." Abby became hopeful as her mother reached out to stroke her hair. "However,"

Victoria cupped Abby's chin in her hand, "I dislike the idea of my youngest going off on her own, again."

"But—" Abby interjected.

"And for all we know," Victoria countered, shaking her head "your father's kidnapper may be watching us. I could not bear it if anything happened to you."

Abby drew in a deep breath, releasing it slowly as she collected her thoughts. "Mom," she stated with poise, "I'm not a little kid anymore. I'll be fifteen in a few months. And don't forget that I helped save a cave full of women from a pair of magic-wielding faeries. I'm sure I'll be fine investigating a rundown castle. Besides," she added with a smile, "Rory will be with me, so technically I won't be alone."

Victoria sighed, "And you'll have your dog with you too, so I suppose you'll be able to take care of yourself."

Abby restrained herself from jumping up and down when a thought occurred to her. "Oh yeah, about Finlay." She beckoned the dog to her and ran her hand through his fur. "He probably won't like this either, but Finlay should go off on his own to search for Dad. He could smell one of his shirts and try to track him down. Like a bloodhound. You can do that can't you, Finlay?"

Finlay pawed the floor, his voice rumbling at the suggestion. *Aye, Lass. I am capable of that, but I should be by your side at the castle. I am hesitant to leave you.*

Abby stroked the dog's ears. *We can cover more ground this way. Plus, you can always meet up with us there. And Rory and I should wait until dark to go. You know, so no one will see us. You'd have a lot of time to search around beforehand. Who knows, you might even find him, and we can end this mess.* Abby reached for Finlay's muzzle, pulled his head to her, and touched her nose to his. *It will be okay. I promise. Will you do this for me?*

Finlay stared deep into Abby's eyes. With a snort, he stepped back and bowed. *It shall be so, little one.*

Abby looked to the others, her body tingling with excitement. "Finlay will search for Dad. He'll meet up with Rory and me later in the forest." She motioned to her sister. "Hey, Sage? Will you grab one of Dad's shirts or something for Finlay to sniff?"

"I'm on it," Sage said as she headed to the door, "there's nothing over here, so I'll have to get one from the cottage. Back in a minute."

As Sage walked across the street, Abby opened Google Earth on the computer to show Finlay where she thought the castle might be. *Here's us, and here's where we're going. You can't see much because of the trees, but do you think you can find us by looking at this?*

Finlay strode to the monitor, bumping Abby to the side with his imposing girth. He studied the image of the forest. *Aye, Lass. This should be sufficient to locate you. But you must promise me you won't enter the castle grounds until I am by your side.* Finlay turned his head, staring deep into Abby's eyes. *Do you understand?*

Abby blinked after a moment and shook her head fervently, breaking free from the dog's hypnotic gaze. *Stop that—that thing with your eyes! Yes, I understand. I promise we won't enter the castle without you.*

Feeling satisfied with Abby's response, Finlay lowered his head and rubbed against her side. *Very well, then. If you fear you are in danger before my arrival, call out and I shall find you.*

Abby crossed her arms. *What? Now you can hear me across vast distances? I called out to you when those creepy faeries dragged me through the mountain, and you didn't come.*

Finlay lifted his head and appeared to frown. *I regret my inability at that time. It was most unfortunate. But, something is different, now that I'm free from the faerie magic. I sense a strengthening in our bond. I do not know how or why. You must trust me with this.*

As Abby pondered the dog's words, Sage hurried into the bookstore with a blue and white, plaid button-up shirt. "Here," she said, tossing it over the counter to her sister. "Thanks," Abby said as she brought the shirt to her nose and inhaled deeply. She shrugged as she held it in front of Finlay. "Smells clean to me, but see if you can pick up a scent."

The dog buried his muzzle in the folds of the garment. After a moment, he stepped back and entered Abby's mind. *I have what I need to begin my search.*

Abby smiled and wrapped her arms around Finlay's neck. *Good luck, fuzzball. See you soon.* Before she could release her hold, a prickling sensation flowed around her body. In an instant, Abby's arms were empty. *Okay. That's a new one.* She turned to the group as she smoothed her hair. "So that's it then. Rory and I will leave at dusk."

4

*T*he car sat idle on a small pull-off, waiting to merge back onto the desolate motorway. Sage rolled the window down and popped her head out. "Promise you'll be careful, Abby. Dad would kill me if he knew I was leaving you here so late, and alone with a boy."

Abby waved goodbye. "There's nothing to worry about. I've got my phone, and my bag is full of supplies. We'll be fine, won't we, Rory?" she said, nudging the Scotsman with her elbow.

Rory feigned his most convincing stance. "Aye," he directed to Sage, "we shall travel unseen and endure no harm. Ye have me word."

Sage snorted as she pulled the vehicle onto the road. "Well, that makes me feel a lot better, Medieval. I'm holding you to that." Sage rolled the window up and gave a quick wave as she drove off.

Abby shrugged and turned toward the access point to a trail leading into Towie Forest. She pointed to a placard as Rory followed. "Let's see what that sign says." Taking a palm-sized flashlight from her hoodie pocket, she clicked the button on the end and directed the light to the top of the sign. Upon reading the first sentence, she frowned. "Let's hope no one sees us. We'll get in big trouble for being here after park hours."

Rory nodded, pointing to a map on the lower half of the placard. "Let us see what truths it shares."

Abby lowered the light to the bottom of the figure. The map displayed a network of trails stretching the expanse of the forest, with several points of interest marked along the main pathways, but her light found no castle. *Hmm. Where is it?* Moving the beam to the center of the map, she stopped on a small triangle. *Aha. Castle Badenoch.* Abby looked to Rory. "Well, there it is, about 3 miles in, but with no direct trails running to it."

After studying the map in silence, Rory pointed to a trail. "Here, A-by. We break from the path here," he said, sliding his finger along the line and stopping at a point due south of the castle. "Will be the shortest route."

"Good call, Rory," Abby said with a brief smile. She cringed upon reading the path's name. "Wailing Beast's Way." She cocked her head at Rory. "Sounds inviting, huh?"

Rory placed a hand instinctively on the dirk resting at his right hip. "No beast shall slow our way this eve, A-by, and no foulness shall touch yer soul." Rory frowned when Abby giggled. Confused, he asked, "Why do ye laugh so?"

Abby reigned in her laughter, remembering Finlay's lecture about thinking before speaking, or laughing in this matter. "Aw, I'm sorry Rory," she said, clearing her throat. "I shouldn't have laughed. It's just, you always seem so serious, and you're always so chivalrous. You talk like you think I might break, like I need a protector or something." Seeing a mixture of sadness and disappointment in his eyes, Abby added, "But, I don't mind. In fact, I guess it's kinda nice having someone other than family wanting to 'see me no harm.' It will just take a little getting used to having that person be a 14th century Scotsman who talks strange." Abby made a funny face, and when Rory smiled and returned one of his own, she pulled a second flashlight from her hoodie and handed it to him. "Come on," she directed, "we're wasting good hiking time."

Rory accepted the tool, examining it with wonder. "How do ye set the light free, A-by?"

Abby smiled, appreciating his innocence. "Just push the button on the bottom, but don't point it at your..."

Rory eyed the lens as he pushed the button. The beam of light engulfed his face. He jerked his head to one side, his eyes wide with surprise. "Aaaa, such strength it has."

Abby placed a hand on his flashlight and directed it toward the ground. "...face. Don't point it at your face, silly."

Rory grunted as he switched the light off. "We must save the second torch for only the most dire of moments, A-by. I fear our discovery with too much light. We must travel unnoticed if we are to find the book."

Abby considered her companion's words. "Yeah, you're probably right. Give it back then since you don't have pockets."

Rory nodded as he passed the flashlight back. "Let us go. Ye lead the way, A-by. I shall follow and take care that no one pursues."

Abby started past the placard but stopped abruptly, backing up to look at it again. "Wait," she said, pulling her phone from her back pants pocket. Opening the camera, she handed her flashlight to Rory. "Here, shine the light on the map. I want to take a picture of it in case there are no more signs," she looked into the darkening forest ahead, "or we plain miss them."

Rory stared blankly at Abby as he complied. "Picture?"

Abby groaned, realizing there was no clear way to explain a photograph to Rory, let alone one created by a cell phone. "Yeah, uh, you're just gonna have to trust me on this one, Rory." Abby smiled. "Nothing witchy here, I promise. I'm making a copy of the map with my phone, so we'll be able to look at it whenever we want." She snapped the shot and tilted the screen toward him. "See," she said.

Rory gave a brief nod and paused for a moment. "A-by?" he asked in a hushed tone.

Abby tucked her phone back into her pocket, then swung the flashlight toward Rory. Seeing his look of uncertainty, she stepped forward and touched his elbow. "What is it, Rory? What's wrong?"

Rory's forehead creased as he stood tall. With solemn eyes, he said, "Ye need no' be troubled further that I will think ye a witch." He fiddled with the pouch tied at his waist as he gauged Abby's response. "I am wise enough to know there will be many unusual and frightenin' things here that I will no' understand. I have accepted this to be so. Ye should feel no fear or grief in showing me."

Abby was at a loss for words. "Thanks, Rory," she replied, uncertain how to respond. "And, well," she continued, "that makes me feel a lot better." Seeing the faintest of smiles on Rory's face, she added, "And that was brave of you to say." A broad smile now stretched across his face. Abby wasn't certain, but his cheeks appeared to redden, visible even in the darkness. She smiled and giggled to herself. "Well," she said with a comical face, "now that I know you don't plan on burning me at the stake, let's go find that book."

The trees closed in on the cautious travelers as they made their way deep into the forest. Pine trees of varying size formed an endless canopy. While only random slivers of moonlight pierced through the cover, Abby had little difficulty following the trail. She kept her light trained to the ground in front of her in hopes it would go unnoticed by far away eyes. After a quarter hour of hiking, the terrain changed, taking them up a long, steep incline, and to a trickling stream. Five large, flat rocks acted as stepping-stones across the tiny waterway. Abby paused at the first rock, reaching behind her to catch Rory's hand. She took it firmly in her own and turned her head toward him. "What?" she asked in response to his goofy grin, "for better balance. The last thing we need is to slip on the wet rocks." She turned her attention back to the stream as she rolled her eyes. *You'd think he'd never had his hand held by a girl before.* Abby stepped from the first rock to the second and waited for Rory to plant his feet on the first. As she raised her foot to reach for the next rock, a distant noise on the far side of the stream gave her pause. She put her foot back down and whispered over her shoulder. "Rory? Did you hear that?" As the last word left her lips, the noise drew closer. Four quick steps, scarcely audible, a silent pause for several moments, then four more quick steps. In a panic, Abby turned her flashlight off as the unknown maker of the noise seemed seconds from them. Rory released Abby's hand and, without a sound, slid his sword from its sheath. Abby glanced back to see Rory in a defensive crouch. His blade giving off a faint red glow. She watched the light from the sword dance along the rippling stream and tried to swallow the tense lump in her throat. "What are you doing?" she asked under her breath. "Whoever, or whatever is there will see your sword, which means it will see us."

Rory brought a silencing finger to his lips. They stood frozen in place for several minutes, straining their ears for sounds of any kind. At last, Abby lifted both hands and shrugged her shoulders. Rory straightened up out of his crouch. But before he could return the weapon to its sheath, a thick mass of juniper rustled fifteen feet to their right on the other side of the stream, causing the duo to freeze. Abby held her breath. Her stomach threatened to intrude upon her throat when branches snapped and an enormous figure pushed through the undergrowth. Abby strained her eyes, desperate to discern the possible threat. To her surprise, the mysterious form snorted. Soft sounds of lapping water reached her ears. Abby dared to whisper. "Rory? Can you tell what it is?" she asked under her breath.

In response, Rory's sword roared to life. Flames danced along the clean line of the blade. The intricate symbols adorning the metal pulsed a deep red. Before Abby could protest, Rory sent a flame spiraling into the air. The surrounding environment illuminated an eerie red. What Abby recognized as a male deer looked up at the pair. Unconcerned by their presence, the stag resumed drinking. Abby wondered how it managed with the weight of its antlers. *Those things are outrageous. And I've never seen such a monstrous deer.* Abby chuckled to herself. *If Finlay were a deer, he might be jealous.*

The stag continued drinking as Abby and Rory watched on in silence. When it had taken its fill, it gave a curious glance toward its company before trotting downstream and disappearing into the trees.

Rory lowered his sword, his eyes wide. "I've niver seen a stag so striking, A-by," he stated, bringing his sword to a dull glow.

Abby nodded in agreement. "No kidding! And don't even think about trying to make him your 'denner,' mister," she added with a snort. "He'd probably skewer you."

Rory shook his head, dumbfounded by the suggestion. "No, A-by. One must revere a beast as magnificent as he. Some folk say the grandest of such animals have magical powers. I should niver think to take his life."

Surprised by his reaction, Abby paused and readjusted her backpack. "So are you saying you think that was a magical stag?"

Rory shrugged. "I can no' say, either way, A-by. Before meetin' you and the dog, I'd have said it was another fancy tale." Rory hesitated as he sheathed his sword. "But now I'd say most anythin' is possible," he finished with a grin.

Abby clicked on her flashlight and stretched her hand out to take the Scotsman's. Rory grinned, eager to oblige her request. "Good to know you're so open minded now," she said with a smile. Abby motioned ahead with her light. "Let's cross this stream before any other surprises show up."

Rory grunted as Abby led them from one slick stone to the next. Abby freed her hand from Rory's after crossing the stream. She turned her head, looking up at him as he stepped to her side "Ready?"

"Aye, A-by."

Abby smiled apprehensively while shining the light on the path. "Here's to no more spooky sounds in the night," she said, setting off onto the trail.

They traveled in silence, ever more wary of their surroundings. Dense trees continued to encompass them as they made their way down into a valley. When they reached the bottom, Abby stopped and scratched her head. "Hmm, which way to go," she said, contemplating a fork in the trail. To the right, the forest opened onto rolling hills. To the left, it transitioned to a thick, mixed woodland and the hushed darkness of its expanse loomed. Abby glanced at Rory as she pulled her phone from her back pocket.

"Let's check the map." Handing the light to Rory, Abby swiped the screen to unlock the phone, then opened her picture gallery. Due to the original size of the map, the image on her phone was difficult to read. "Here," she said, noticing Rory squint at the writing, "let me zoom in on it." Abby reverse-pinched on the screen and oriented the zoomed image to the trail-head from which they entered the forest. She followed the path they had traveled until spotting the split in the trail which stood before them. "I think we need to go this way," she guessed, following the left trail on the map.

Rory pointed to the image as Abby shifted it. "Aye, ye're correct, A-by. Look there," he said, calling her attention to a second fork in the path, "Wailin' Beast's Way."

Abby nodded and slid the image back to their current location. "Maybe another thirty minutes then," she said, tapping her chin.

Rory pointed to the screen again. "A-by, what's that?"

Abby zoomed further on the picture, examining a nearby spot just off the trail. "Looks like a circle of stones or something."

Rory contemplated her response. "I should like to see it, A-by," he said with passion.

"Rory, we need to get to the castle. We don't have time for sightseeing." She placed her free hand on her hip. "Don't tell me you forgot about my dad's life being in danger?"

"Me apologies, A-by," Rory groaned, "I was no' thinkin' properly." He looked to the ground and frowned. "It's just that..."

Abby relaxed her shoulders and softened her voice. "It's just that what, Rory?"

"Me faither once told me of a mystical stone circle said to hold great power. He was determined I learn of it." Rory sighed and continued. "He would no' tell me outright the secrets he believed it held, but he vowed to show me in the flesh."

"So what happened?" Abby asked when the Scotsman paused with a frown. "Did he take you to see it?"

Rory's shoulders slumped. "I regret no'. We had set elaborate plans to make a great journey to find it, but they niver came to pass." Sadness filled Rory's eyes, "This was no' long before I met ye."

Abby's stomach churned, realizing why he had learned no more of the mysterious stone circle. She pictured the scene Rory once described of finding his father cold, dead, and murdered in the forest near his home. "You don't need to say anything more, Rory," she whispered, reaching out to brush his arm. "I understand why it would mean a lot to you to see the stone circle here, but, you don't think it's the same one your dad told you about, do you? Did he ever tell you its name?"

"No, A-by. I have no knowledge of where the stone circle lies. But me faither had said to prepare for the passin' of many moons on our journey."

"Hmm, well, there's a lot of stone circles in Scotland. No telling which one it was." Abby reached out again and squeezed Rory's elbow. "But, if we're quick, I guess we can go check it out if you want."

The corners of Rory's mouth curled upright. "Aye, A-by, this would please me, but are ye sure?"

"You're helping me find my dad, it's the least I can do." Abby glanced down, shrugged, and slipped her phone into her hoodie pocket. "And I know it will be meaningful to you. You deserve it." She looked up and winked playfully while starting up the path, "Just no dawdling, we're on a mission."

Rory smiled and gave a quick nod as he followed Abby. She glanced over her shoulder and reached back mid-stride to motion for the flashlight. Abby aimed the beam to the right side of the trail as they continued forward, sweeping it back and forth, examining the path. "According to the map, a path should split off somewhere around here."

"There," Rory said, pointing to a spot the light had passed over.

Abby stopped and turned to face the tree line. "Where?"

"Back to yer right, A-by."

Abby oriented the beam at knee level and scanned back to the right. "I don't see it, Rory. You sure you saw something?"

Rory reached out, directing Abby's hand holding the light. "Here," he said, stopping its movement. Rory guided the beam to the ground, focusing on a small gap in the brush.

"Wow! Good eye, Rory. I'd never have found that." Abby gestured at his hand, still resting on her own. "Let me shine the light into the woods, see if we can see anything."

Rory nodded, releasing his grasp on the light. "Aye, best we don't go blindly into the woodland."

Abby stepped in front of the discreet split in the brush and shined the light at head level into the forest. The path was not evident, long covered by overgrowth, but at the furthest reaches of the light, Abby thought she spied the outline of something rounded and upright, jutting toward the canopy above. "I think I see something," she said, looking to Rory.

"Aye, A-by. I too see somethin'. Let us be swift yet cautious." Rory reached to take the flashlight from her with one hand as he stepped forward and parted the brush with the other.

Abby shrugged and handed over her light. "Your discovery, you might as well take the lead."

Rory led them along the hidden path with relative ease. He paused several times, extending his free hand palm-out behind him as a signal for Abby to stop. Each time he listened to their surroundings, and each time when he seemed satisfied with the apparent lack of danger, he gave the slightest of nods to continue forward. Abby grinned inwardly at the serious manner Rory approached most things. *He's sure not like any other 16-yr-old boy I've ever met.* Surprised by her own thoughts,

Abby turned her attention back to what lay ahead of them. She peered around the Scotsman and glimpsed an enormous, freestanding stone. *Whoa...*

"Rory," Abby whispered, "I'm gonna use the other light. Something tells me there'll be lots to look at."

The first to step into the vast ring, Rory grunted in reply, too enthralled to care.

Abby pulled her spare light from her pocket and switched it on. "Holy smokes!" she exclaimed after making a wide arc with the flashlight. Giant stones surrounded them, causing Abby to feel small in their midst. She followed Rory to the center of the ring and counted the megaliths. Twelve stood upright, each twice her height. One stone appeared to have toppled onto its side, or so Abby thought. *No, wait.* Abby walked closer to the overturned rock, discovering its symmetrical placement between the stones on either side, each end pointing to its neighbor. *I think they meant to do that.* She shrugged and continued exploring, shining her light at the nearest upright stone. Abby placed her palm flat against its cool surface and closed her eyes. She imagined the people from long ago who had placed it in its spot, the spot where she now stood. Disappointed to have felt no special energy, Abby opened her eyes and shined the light all along the stone's surface to its uppermost curve. *Huh. Weird.* Abby stepped back and raised her arm high, trying to shine the light parallel with the top of the stone. Aware she was far too short to achieve this, she turned to Rory. "Hey, Rory, c'mere for a sec."

Rory, half-sprawled upon the horizontal megalith, lifted his head at the sound of his name. "Aye, A-by," he said, straightening himself and readjusting his scabbard.

"Try shining your light even with the top of this rock," she said once he stood by her side, "I think there's a hole in it."

Rory raised his arm above his head and lifted onto the tips of his toes. "Aye, is peculiar, A-by. It seems to be as ye say."

"Keep shining the light, Rory," she directed, running to the back of the megalith. "I can see the light passing through it!" she said, coming back to join him. "The hole looks perfectly round. I wonder what made it." Abby glanced around at the rest of the stones. "Hey," she said, tapping Rory's arm with the back of her hand, "let's see if the rest have holes."

Rory nodded and set off in the opposite direction around the circle. Abby stepped to the next stone closest to her. After a moment of struggle to locate a hole, she realized backing further away from the stone gave her a better angle with the light. *Ah, there you are.* Pleased with her accomplishment, she moved to the next structure and found the puzzling hole with ease. The next stone gave

Abby pause—a chunk was missing from the top. *Huh.* She approached the stone, scanning the ground around it for the missing piece. Just behind the stone, she found it, no bigger than a beach ball, but heavy as evidenced by the depression in the earth. Abby inspected it with her light, coming to rest on the hole. She squatted low and ran a finger around the rim of the void. *So smooth. How the heck did they make it?* Abby attempted to roll the hunk with her free hand, but abandoned her efforts moments later. *Yeah, that's heavy. Wonder how it broke.* She shook her head at the thoughtless destruction and stood to move on. Meeting Rory at the last standing stone, they both nodded to one another. Twelve stones, twelve holes. As if reading each other's mind, they hurried to the thirteenth stone to inspect its surface. Abby walked around the far side of the giant slab. "I'll take this end," she said, "and check everywhere on your side, if it has a hole, it might not be in the same spot as the others."

Rory nodded, disappearing from Abby's view as he squatted. Abby did the same, searching every curve and crevice her hand discovered. Unsuccessful at finding any holes, Abby stood. "Nothing on this side. You find anything, Rory?" she questioned with a sigh.

Rory popped his head above the flat plane of the stone, looking discouraged. "Nothing," he said.

Abby scratched her forehead. "Hmm." She contemplated the circle as she hoisted herself up to a sitting position upon the rock and pivoted her legs around to face Rory. "So what makes this rock different from the others, besides the fact it's tipped over?" she asked.

Hopping atop the rock, Rory joined his companion. "Perhaps it is no' for us to know, A-by."

"Perhaps you're right," Abby said, echoing his sentiment. She ran a hand along the smooth surface, her fingers stopping to investigate a deep crevice. "I find the mystery of it exciting and want to know the answers. I hate not knowing the answers." Abby turned to look at Rory. "Kinda like aliens and Bigfoot, or..."

Rory met her eyes with a blank stare.

Abby snorted at herself. "Oh, never mind."

Before Abby could say more, a sharp snap sounded off to their left along the tree line. The duo jerked their heads toward the noise, their eyes scanning the trees. "Lights off," Abby whispered, clicking the button on her own flashlight. Rory hesitated to follow suit, determined to discover the source of the noise. He pointed his light toward the tree line, moving it first right, then back to the left.

"What are you doing, Rory?" Abby protested. She reached across his body, intent on muffling the lens with her hand. Just as her fingers passed in front of the light, she glanced at the tree line. Abby held her breath and lowered Rory's arm, having forgotten her initial goal. "Rory," she whispered, "did you see that? It looked like a pair of eyes reflecting the light."

Rory nodded hastily. "Aye, A-by." He groaned, switching his light off. "And would be a good guess to say we've been discovered."

Abby flipped her light on again. "Well, can't do much about that now. Let's see if it's still there." She pointed the beam toward the trees, sweeping it back and forth. When the light crossed paths with two glowing orbs, perhaps six feet off the ground, Abby clicked the power button. "Yep, still there," she said with a nervous giggle before considering their options. *Whatever it is knows right where we are. Even if we could sneak back along the path to the main trail, there's no way we could do it without turning on a light. Knowing me, I'd trip and break an ankle.* Abby chewed on her bottom lip while lost in thought. *Maybe if we hid behind this stone, it'd get bored with us and just go away.*

Rory nudged Abby with an elbow to catch her attention. Four soft crunches—the sound of fallen leaves and twigs giving way to the force upon them—followed by a drawn out snort caused Abby to grasp Rory's forearm. Her fingers stiffened as a wave of jitters washed across her body. She strained to hear what sounds would follow, praying it wouldn't be the call of a ravenous and angry animal.

As if to quiet her fears, a grand stag stepped from the trees and through a beam of moonlight, revealing its identity. Abby released her grip on Rory's arm, puffing out a breath held too long. "That's the same deer, isn't it?" she said, narrowing her eyes as she looked to Rory. Without waiting for a reply, she blurted, "Is he following us? I swear that's the same one as at the stream. No way there's two obscenely huge deer in this forest."

The stag lumbered into the stone ring as Abby and Rory looked on in awe, following it with their lights. The creature slowed to a stop and lowered its head to swipe a mouthful of grass. As it chewed, the deer swung its head to study its onlookers. After a powerful snort, the stag turned and strolled out of the circle. Just when Abby thought it would leave, the deer stopped, as if remembering something important. It circled to its left and approached the stone with the missing upper section. It sniffed curiously at the toppled chunk of rock before attempting to nudge it with its nose.

While the stag continued probing the stone, Abby leaned in close to Rory. "What do you think it's doing, Rory?" she whispered. "That's so weird."

Rory grunted in return. "Ye know as best as I, A-by." He shrugged as the deer continued to push against the stone hunk with its snout. "I agree its behavior is strange."

The stag quit its examination of the ancient stone and lifted its head to look straight into Abby's flashlight. Its eyes glowed yellow, blinking several times in response to the intensity of the beam. Deciding the creature bore no threat, Abby lowered her light. As she did, a wave of nausea washed over her. She grasped Rory's shoulder with her free hand to steady herself. Sensing something wasn't right, Rory wrapped an arm around Abby's back and cradled her close. "A-by, what's wrong?" he asked, searching her eyes for an answer.

Abby let her hand slide from his shoulder. "I, I'm not sure," she replied, raising a finger in the air to show she needed a moment. When the discomfort passed, she relaxed her arms and straightened her posture. "I felt like I would lose my dinner, but I'm okay now." Abby turned to smile at Rory. Assaulted with a new sensation, she dropped her light and pressed her fingers to her temples. "Ahhhhh," she wailed as a pressing force burrowed inside her head.

Rory brushed Abby's hair from her forehead. "A-by, tell me what plagues ye."

Able to give no response, Abby continued to groan. "Sweet A-by, I don't know how to help ye," Rory choked in a breathless whisper. "Tell me what to do."

As quickly as the invasion of Abby's mind began, it ended. She removed her hands from her head, let out a long, relieved sigh, and sat upright. "What the heck was that about?" she questioned to the night air, expecting no response. Her eyes grew wide as a distant and gruff rumbling directed itself at her. She looked to Rory. "Did you hear that?"

Rory tilted his head. "Hear what, A-by?"

Abby squinted and motioned for Rory to pass his flashlight to her. She scanned the tree line to their right, toward the trail they had followed to the circle, stopping when the light crossed paths with the stag. Her hand wavered as she focused the light at the creature's hooves. *I wonder...*

The stag snorted and bowed its head low, touching its enormous rack to the ground. A familiar tingling washed through Abby's mind, followed by a foreign voice. *Beware the howling specter.*

Abby whipped her head toward Rory. "Pleeaassee, tell me you heard that!"

Rory raised his hands, palm-up and shook his head.

"Ahh," Abby exclaimed. "That deer just talked to me!"

The stag raised its head, scratched at the ground with a hoof, and turned toward the trees with an exaggerated snort. Abby's mind tingled again as it disappeared from view. *Beware the howling specter.*

Rory watched his companion as she sat in silence, mouth agape. He nudged her with an elbow. "Are ye certain it was the beast, A-by?"

Abby turned to lock eyes with Rory. "Positive."

"Well, what did it say to ye then?"

"Four words. 'Beware the howling specter,'" she said, drawing out the phrase.

"Howlin' specter?" Rory repeated dubiously. "Why would it say such a thing?"

Abby hopped down from the megalith and retrieved her light. "No clue," she said, motioning for Rory to follow her. "But let's not stick around to find out!"

5

*A*bby removed her phone from her pocket, powering it on and pulling up the map in one swift movement. "Well," she said, "we should be near the split-off to Wailing Beast's Way." Pausing, Abby turned back to look at Rory, "I haven't noticed a sign yet, have you?"

Rory grunted and shook his head. "No, A-by, I have no'," Rory peered into the trees, parting the undergrowth with his hands. "Perhaps the brush has overcome it," he said.

"Good point, Rory. It wouldn't surprise me, given the overgrowth on the last trail." Abby stuck a boot out and parted the brush to the side of her. "Maybe we should slow our pace then," she suggested, having tucked her phone away.

Rory nodded. "Aye, A-by. If ye direct yer torch so I may see properly," he handed Abby his flashlight, then pull his sword from its scabbard, "I shall use me sword to search. We do no' know what waits in the brush." With a proud smile, Rory held the sword in front of him and admired the intricate carvings on its blade. As he did, a fiery glow traced its way along the symbols.

Abby agreed to the plan. "Okay," she said hesitantly, "but you'd better calm those flames. Forest fires aren't pretty. You're lucky one didn't start back at the stream with the way you flung that thing around."

Rory's smile disappeared, and the glow of his sword with it. He turned to Abby, soaking in her words. "Aye, A-by. Ye speak wisely. I am a foolish lad sometimes no' to always respect the power I bear." He lowered his blade to waist height and continued. "I swear to ye I shall be more careful here out."

Abby suppressed her urge to giggle at the Scotsman and instead gave him a stern eye. "Okay then," she said, imparting a nod toward the forest understory, "we should get going."

In minutes, the duo perfected a pattern of searching. Abby held a flashlight in each hand and pointed one at knee level and one at shoulder level. Rory focused his attention to the swath of light at knee level, parting the grass and brush with his sword, while Abby looked for a trail marker in the second beam of light. They moved along, scouring every inch of the trail.

Abby stopped. "There it is," she said, directing the beam at a faded sign. "Wailing Beast's Way." A foreboding feeling seeped into her stomach as she pointed the light beyond the sign. The forest was thick along this section of the path and threatened to swallow the beam.

Rory motioned for Abby to hand him one of the lights. With a nod of thanks, he aimed it low to the ground and used his sword to search for any sign of a footpath leading past the placard. "It appears no souls have traveled this way for many ages, A-by," he observed with a grunt. "I see no obvious path."

Abby frowned. "Well, I guess we'll just have to go slow and be careful where we step. Can't afford any twisted ankles or twigs to the eye slowing us up, especially when we're so close to finding the castle."

"Aye, A-by. Is best we move with caution," he said with a serious nod. "I shall lead the way and use me sword to clear any obstacles."

"Knock yourself out," Abby said, grinning.

Rory turned to stare at Abby, lifting an eyebrow. "Ye speak such strange things sometimes, Lass."

Abby snorted. "It's called slang," she replied with a giggle. "Maybe someday you'll catch on." She continued with a silly face, prodding Rory forward into the unknown, "But never mind now, we have work to do."

Travel along the dense path was far slower than Abby desired. At times, she was uncertain of their direction, but then they'd happen upon a random break in the grass and understory, which revealed the little used trail. And each time, the tension in Abby's shoulders subsided, and her confidence in finding the castle returned. After a long stretch with no hint they were on the path, Abby groaned. "We don't even know if we're still on the trail, Rory." She shined her light in a wide arc around her, hoping to find any sign they were traveling in the right direction. "We're lost," she sighed.

Rory stopped and turned around, determined. "Do no' think such things, A-by," he said firmly, "I shall see ye to the castle." He shoved his flashlight into the crook of his armpit and reached out to take Abby's hand. "I swear to ye we shall find yer faither." Rory squeezed her hand. "Ye have me word."

Abby began to respond when an eerie sound in the distance interrupted her. She released Rory's hand and stepped close. "Did you hear that?" she whispered.

Rory grabbed his light and pointed it at the ground. "Aye, A-by," he replied quietly. "Came from that way," he said, pointing in the general direction of the sound with the tip of his sword, which now pulsed red. Abby wondered if the sword reacted to his emotions.

As the pair stood silent, a wispy moan—closer this time—sounded from where Rory had pointed. Abby willed her stomach to stay in place as she exchanged nervous glances with her companion before turning off her light. Rory grunted softly and repeated Abby's action. With the only worthwhile light coming from the glow of his sword, Abby felt as if the forest were closing in on them. *I've about had it with creepy, unknown sounds in this place. And something tells me it's not that stupid deer again!*

Rory reached his right arm around Abby's shoulders and pulled her flush against his side. He tilted his head and whispered directly into her ear. "Be still and make no sound. I sense a great evil nearin' us." Abby nodded her head once as shivers danced across her body. *Where's my white warrior when we need him?* With little faith he would come, Abby called out in her mind with all the mental force she could muster. *Finlay! We need you!* Moments of silence ticking by, the only sound to fall upon Abby's ears was that of Rory's breathing. Disappointed, but not surprised Finlay did not answer her call, Abby focused on staying as silent as possible. Rory lessened his grip around her shoulders as the silence continued; the glow of his sword seemed to dim comparably. An instant later, a low growl disrupted the stillness. Abby thought it was from a dog, but could not be certain. The growl escalated in intensity and engulfed them. Rory's sword burst into flames. As if in response, the growl evolved into a frightening and ferocious howl. Every hair on Abby's body stood at attention.

"A-by."

"Y-yes?"

"Run!"

"Don't have to tell me twice!" Abby turned to her left and pushed through the brush as fast as she could, parting obstacles with both hands. She used the flashlight as best she could to guide her hurried steps, but still stumbled over unseen obstructions.

Rory followed close behind, having subdued the flames from his sword. "Keep moving, A-by. Do no' stop."

Abby's heart pounded, and her lungs burned as they continued scrambling through the forest at a fast pace. Oblivious to a downed sapling just in front of her, Abby's foot hooked the slender trunk, and she spilled forward. "Oof!" she grunted, falling face-first to the ground.

Rory skidded to a halt and hovered over her, shining his light on her head. "A-by, A-by, are ye okay? Please be unharmed!"

"Ugh," she replied, twisting around and pulling herself into a sitting position. She patted her body, brushed debris from her face, and pulled leaves from her hair. "I think I'm okay," she groaned, reaching for her light and perking her ears. Twisting her head in all directions, she waved for Rory to crouch beside her. "Can you see anything? Is it following us?" she whispered.

Rory listened intently. When he was sure he could hear no sounds, he motioned for Abby to stand. "It appears the beast has lost interest, A-by, but we should keep movin' nonetheless."

As Abby stood and flicked debris from her jeans, a wispy hiss swirled around the pair. Abby reached out to grab Rory's arm in response.

"Thieves," a drawn out, guttural voice whispered, appearing to come from all directions.

Abby's grip on Rory's arm tightened. *What the...*

"Murderers," the voice continued.

Abby scrunched her face in confusion and blurted, "I don't know who you think we are, but we are not thieves. And we aren't murderers, so leave us alone!"

The voice hissed in return, escalating into a piercing howl.

Abby cringed at the continued howling. *Keep your mouth shut next time, Abby!* She released her grip on Rory's arm but not before pulling him with her. "Time to go!"

Rory grunted agreement, plodding forward by her side. They maneuvered their way through the forest for a quarter hour, and no matter how fast they moved, low growls swarmed around them.

"Hey!" Abby yelled. "Maybe my eyes are playing tricks, but there's a clearing that way," she said, aiming her flashlight off to the right. The forest transitioned back to pine trees, increasing their line of sight.

"Aye! It appears to be so, A-by."

The duo angled to the right, picking up speed as they ran side by side. As they neared the clearing, Abby felt as if something were snapping at her heels. She ignored her fearful desire to scream and instead pumped her arms even harder, propelling herself into an open pasture of mixed grass and wildflowers. A strange sense of safety washed over her. She reached out to Rory, grabbing his tunic as she slowed herself to a halt. They both stood and turned to survey the forest. Abby leaned over and placed her hands on her knees. As she attempted to steady her breathing, a powerful howl pierced her ears. It was a different howl this time, mournful and defeated, and one that tapered off into the distance.

"I think we're safe now," Abby stated with confidence. She plopped down into the pasture, guided by intense moonlight. She slid her backpack off and tucked away her flashlight. Lying on her back, Abby spread her arms wide and sighed.

Rory sheathed his sword and copied her movements, handing Abby his light. "What do ye think it was?"

"I have no idea," Abby said with a half snort as she placed Rory's light in her bag, "and I don't want to find out!"

Rory watched his companion, unease in his eyes. "We should no' stay here long, A-by. I fear it may come back."

"Well if it does, we're going to need some help, I think."

Rory looked at Abby questioningly.

"I'm going to try something. Trust me on this."

Rory nodded in anticipation.

Abby sat up, drew in a deep breath, and yelled as loud as she could, "Finlay!"

6

*A*bby sighed after plucking the petals from a flower and tossing them to the ground. She stood and straightened her hoodie. "Let's go," she directed, scooping up her backpack. "I should have known better than to think the ole fur-ball could hear me from, well, wherever he is."

Rory jumped to his feet to walk beside her. "Why do ye think he would hear ye?"

"He said to call out for him if we were in danger, and he'd come," she replied as they descended into a shallow valley, "because our bond is stronger now that you freed him from the magical chains of Mavis and Tavis." Abby shivered upon saying the faeries' names.

Rory considered Finlay's declaration as they reached the bottom of the hill. "Perhaps," he offered, "if he can hear ye, it may take more time for him to hear what ye speak beyond the moment of the words passing from yer lips."

"Hmm," Abby nodded at the idea, "like, a delayed reaction. Well," she said with a nervous giggle, "if you're right, a little less delay and a little more reaction would be..."

Sounds of movement through the grass behind the pair stopped any further discussion. Whipping around to locate the source of the noise, Rory drew his sword and motioned for Abby to stay back. "It's movin' fast, whatever it may be."

"Yeah," Abby groaned, "and straight toward us!"

Rory set a defensive stance and willed flames to dance along the edge of his sword. With a flick of his wrist, he sent a spiral of fire into the air. It snaked out, following a multitude of unseen paths, and illuminated the environment around the young travelers.

In the distance, a large form plowed down the hill, taking no care for the racket it created. Abby tensed as it drew closer. Red hues from the flames reflected off a snow-white figure. "Is that..."

It is, child. And the boy is wise. Consider it a delayed reaction.

"Finlay!" Abby screamed with relief as she took off toward him.

Jogging after Abby, Rory called off the flames and sheathed his sword.

Abby flung herself at the dog, wrapping her arms around his neck and pressing her face into his coat. "I'm so glad you're here, Finlay," she said, her words muffled by his fur.

I answered your call as soon as I sensed your need. I feared the worst, more so after not finding you upon my arrival.

Abby continued soaking in the warmth of Finlay's fur. *Where did you land, or appear, or whatever you want to call it?*

Near a dense tree line, at the start of this grassy expanse. Finlay turned his head to nudge Abby's side. *Perhaps ten minutes travel from here with your insufficient legs.*

Abby stepped back to glare at her furry companion. *Ha-ha, funny.* She held the glare as long as she could before a fit of laughter overtook her.

"Why do ye laugh so, A-by?" Rory asked with a curious smile.

"Oh, Finlay made a joke," Abby said as she stifled her giggles and breathed deep. "I think he finds our mode of transportation inferior to his," she paused and pointed toward herself, "you know, only two legs, can't teleport oneself." Abby snorted, only to subdue another giggling fit threatening to overcome her. "Not bad," she said, turning to aim a hard stare at Finlay, "for a dog!"

Rory suppressed a small snort himself and tensed, watching as a realization came over Abby.

Abby motioned toward Finlay. "Hey, from what you described, you must have appeared at the same spot I called out to you." She stepped closer to the dog and wrung her hands. "Did you see it?" she asked in almost a whisper.

Finlay cocked his head, uncertain of the question. *See what, Lass?*

"The creepy monster in the woods, that's why I called for you. Sure seemed like it was out for blood!"

Finlay pawed at the ground. *No child, I saw no such thing. Describe this creature.*

Abby looked at Rory, recognizing it was impolite to exclude him from the conversation. "Finlay says he didn't see the monster."

Rory grunted. "And nor would he, A-by. If ye recall, we did no' see the beast. We only heard it."

Abby felt herself blush, realizing she misspoke. "Okay, okay, yeah, you're right," she directed at Rory. She turned to Finlay, put her right hand on her hip, and gestured with her left as she spoke. "So like Rory said, we didn't see the monster."

Finlay cut into her mind. *Tell me from the beginning, Lass.*

"Well, we were trying to follow the trail through the forest when we heard a scary howling." Abby's body stiffened as she recalled the encounter. "Honestly, I'm surprised I didn't pee my pants." She glanced at Rory. "It was creepy, right Rory?"

Rory nodded, his face serious. "Aye, A-by. Was a frightenin' sound. I sensed a great evil in the forest, Finlay. Was no' safe for us to be there a moment longer."

"Yeah," Abby agreed, "and so we ran, and for a minute I thought we'd gotten away from whatever it was." Pausing, she drew in a deep breath and added, "But then we heard a voice saying we were thieves and murders, and then more howling!"

"Aye, is true," Rory concurred, "and me thinks perhaps it could no' leave the woods."

Abby tilted her head. *Hmm, I hadn't thought about that, but I guess Rory could be right.*

Finlay strode close to stand between the two. *Why does the boy think this?*

Abby reached out to scratch behind Finlay's ear, then turned to the Scotsman. "Rory, Finlay wants to know why you think it couldn't leave the forest."

Rory straightened at the question directed to him. Clearing his throat, he responded, "For when we escaped the wood, the beast let out a final howl. A wailin' of resignation, me thinks. It was no' the same as when the creature stalked us. Then it wasted into nothin'. It has no' plagued us since."

Finlay grumbled and sat back on his haunches, contemplating Rory's explanation.

Abby continued to run her hand through Finlay's fur. "Yeah, I'd say Rory's right, now that I think about it. That thing didn't sound happy about us running into the pasture." Prickles crept along Abby's spine as she relived the experience in her mind. "You know, the way it howled reminds me of werewolves I've seen in horror movies."

Rory screwed up his face. "Were-wolves? And what are mo-vies?"

"Ah, never mind," Abby stifled a nervous laugh, "it's not worth explaining, just a bunch of made-up nonsense anyway." She leaned into Finlay and pressed her head onto his chest. *What do you think it was?*

Finlay lowered his head, twisting it back to nuzzle Abby's armpit. *This, I am uncertain of, child. I have no knowledge of any creatures roaming the forest in this region. What matters most is you and the boy are unharmed.*

Abby mushed her face into Finlay's thick fur. *Yeah, I suppose you're right. I'm just glad you're here now.*

Finlay nudged Abby's side, then stood to his impressive height. *We must squander our time no longer, Lass. We have a book to find.*

Abby stepped back from the dog and suppressed a yawn. "The book," she said, turning to Rory. "Of course. We'd better get moving if we're going to find the book by daybreak." Abby paused, realizing she forgot something important. "Hey," she said, looking at Finlay, "did you find any clues about where my dad might be?"

Finlay swayed his head. *Alas, young one, I can say I only know where not to find him at this moment. I found no trace of his scent in my search.*

Abby looked at Rory and frowned. "Finlay says no luck in his search." She set aside the memory of the scary moments in the woods, and Finlay's lack of success, and shouldered her backpack with renewed determination. "The sooner we get back to the shop with it and email the kidnapper, the sooner we'll rescue my dad."

"Where do ye suppose we go from here?" Rory asked as he surveyed their surroundings. The trio stood at the base of the narrow valley; tall pines surrounded them on both sides.

Abby ran a finger through her curls. "Well," she said nervously, eying the forest, "if we don't want to deal with the trees, our only choice is to continue up the hill through the grass."

Finlay circled the duo and sat heavily in front of them, halting their movement. *What of the riddle, Lass? It hints where we shall find the castle.*

Abby groaned while palming her forehead. "Of course. Why do I always forget the obvious?" She glanced at Rory. "Finlay just reminded me of the verse on the scroll. That should give us an idea where to look now." Sliding her backpack around to her chest, Abby searched one of the zippered pockets and pulled out the copy Mrs. MacTavish made of the riddle. She cleared her throat and read the first two verses aloud.

> Where the land and sky meet
> Among the ancient pine
> Near the faerie pool
> The Wolf's lair ye shall find
>
> And within his stone haven
> A sacred book doth dwell
> The secret it holds
> It shan't likely tell

"Well," Abby said, rubbing an earlobe, "we are definitely among ancient pine, so we got that part covered." She looked to Rory. "Any ideas about land meeting sky?"

Rory settled a hand on the hilt of his sword and gazed toward the crown of the hill. "Aye, A-by," he repliedthe surrounding forest, "let us first make our way to the top."

"After you then." Abby swung an arm wide toward the hill.

A proud smile stretched across Rory's face as he strode forward. Abby fell in line behind him, with Finlay striding next to her, adjusting his pace to hers. Abby looked up at the clear night sky. She studied the stars as they hiked, wondering if her father could see them too. After a short time, Rory crested the hill and disappeared from view. When Abby made it to the top, she found Rory standing motionless, staring straight ahead. Looking past her companion, she gasped at what laid in front of them. *The faerie pool?*

In the distance, a serene pool glistened in the moonlight. A rocky outcrop jutted into the night sky, acting as a backdrop. Small waterfalls at the base of the rocks fed the gleaming body. Abby wondered about their source; perhaps unseen crevices in the boulders. To the right, the forest opened to a plateau spattered with wildflowers and low-lying shrubs. Abby followed the gentle roll of the plain and strained her eyes toward the furthermost curve of the pool. "Do you guys see that?" she asked, looking first to Rory, then Finlay. When both failed to respond, she raised a finger and pointed. "There, where the water seems to end, and the forest cuts back in toward it." Abby cinched her backpack and took off in a sprint. She called over her shoulder, "The castle ruins. The wolf's lair!"

Rory groaned in response to Abby's action and dashed after her. "A-by! We must approach with caution," Rory urged, as he caught up. "Please," he pleaded, grasping her arm, "ye must slow down."

Finlay bounded ahead of the pair with ease, his swift, long strides carrying him forward. He slowed to a stop and barred Abby's way. *The boy is correct, child. You are acting with haste. We have no knowledge of what awaits us.*

Abby stopped and frowned. "Ugh," she said, catching her breath. "Okay, you're right." She wrenched at the straps of her backpack as she looked down, embarrassed by her propensity to act first and think later. "Guess I'm so focused on finding my dad I've forgotten to be smart about it," she said, raising her eyes to stare at the moon.

Rory placed a hand on Abby's shoulder. "No worries, A-by," he said with kind eyes, "I understand. We shall find yer faither, I promise." He let his hand slide to Abby's and gave it a gentle squeeze. "Let us be off now."

Finlay snorted, turned to the horizon, and trotted off at a moderate pace. After a brief period of quiet travel,

Abby sensed a hesitation consuming the dog. *What? What is it? I can tell you're itching to tell me something.*

Finlay glanced over his shoulder and grumbled. *The boy.*

Abby rolled her eyes at his lack of forthcoming. *Yeah. What about him? And he has a name, you know.*

The dog's grumbling intensified. *He indeed fancies you. I am certain of this now.*

Butterflies danced in Abby's stomach at the words. *Eww. Whatever!*

Abby considered the statement as she looked at Rory from the corner of her eye. She attempted to suppress the idea, that perhaps just a little, she might fancy him too.

I heard that, child.

Abby groaned and glared at the dog. *Don't you have an off switch?*

Her response was rumbling laughter followed by a loud snort.

Abby marched forward to walk next to Finlay. *Very funny, fuzzball.* She stuck her tongue out before breaking into a smile. *So what? What if he did? Which he doesn't. But what if he did?*

Finlay tilted his head and blinked. *If he did, which he does, I approve.*

Abby scrunched her face and glanced back at the Scotsman. *Well, okay then. But still. Eww.*

The group walked on in silence, slowing as they approached their target. Beyond the faerie pool, between the high wall of rock to the left and intruding line of trees to the right, lay the remnants of a once great stronghold. The walls of the castle were no more than three feet high, having not withstood unknown abuse over the centuries. Stones were strewn haphazardly—piled here and scattered there—making for a chaotic scene. Abby tried to imagine what the castle once looked like and what could have brought the wretched Wolf of Badenoch to his knees. As the trio absorbed what they saw, a piercing howl shattered the night's silence. Abby and Rory looked at one another. Finlay whipped around toward the howl. His tail stiffened and his hackles rose. Directing his ears forward, he let out a low and menacing growl, unlike anything Abby had ever heard.

Abby's knees quivered. "That's what we were talking about, Finlay," she whispered.

A second howl echoed through the pine, closer this time, yet still in the distance, prompting Rory to draw his sword.

Finlay swiveled his head to glance at Rory. *Tell the boy to clear his head and remain calm.* Finlay then turned to stand in front of Abby. He lowered his head to her level and gazed into her eyes. *Stay here, young one. Do not move.*

Abby protested. "But, wha…"

Do as I say, Lass. Stay here. Allow the boy…Rory, to protect you.

Before Abby could say another word, the spot Finlay had stood moments ago was now barren.

Rory shook his head, confused. "Where'd he go?" With a look of frustration, he added, "Why'd he go?"

Abby sighed, looking around nervously. "Guess he thinks he can find whatever that is, scare it off, or maybe even kill it." Abby attempted not to blush as she continued. "Finlay said I should let you protect me. Guess he also thinks I can't take care of myself." Seeing a hint of a frown on the Scotsman's face, Abby put aside her pride. "But, you're the one with the magical sword, so by all means, protect away."

Rory stood tall, a goofy smile now stretching across his face. "Will be safest if we keep the trees to our front, the ridge to our back."

Abby nodded agreement as she stared into the dark forest, wondering what was happening. A third howl sounded in the distance. After a moment of silence, a deep baying answered in return. Abby stiffened. *That had to be Finlay. I wonder if he found it.*

Repeated howls and growls filled the air, echoing throughout the valley and across the plateau, sending chills across every inch of Abby's body. She set her backpack on the ground and leaned against the rocky barrier behind her. "I don't like this, Rory." Abby fiddled with the drawstrings on her hoodie. "What if," she said, tensing her brow, "that thing hurts Finlay?" Abby choked on her next thought. Her voice strained, "What if he doesn't come back?"

Rory shook his head and propped on the rock next to Abby, sinking the tip of his sword into the ground. "Nae, A-by. Do no' think the worst." He reached out and took Abby's chin in his hand, turning her eyes to his. "Finlay will see no harm." Rory smiled before continuing. "And as much as I may dislike sayin', he is brave and powerful." He squeezed Abby's chin before removing his hand. "He will be back, A-by."

Abby looked at the ground, trying to hide the blush she sensed flooding across her cheeks. "You're always so positive, Rory. I don't know how you do it." Clearing her throat, she looked up at the Scotsman. "But I suppose you're right. He's smart enough to zap himself out of the way if he thinks things are too dangerous."

"Aye, Lass," Rory said with a grin. "Now yer bein' sensible."

Abby smiled and pushed off from the rock. She shouldered her bag and distracted herself from her worries by inspecting the castle ruins. *Any minute and he'll be back. Might as well look for the book.*

Rory kept close to Abby's side, his sword at ready. The howls and growls continued sporadically; then all was silent. Abby and Rory stopped and looked at each other when they heard no more. Before Rory could give Abby a calm reassurance, Finlay appeared at the edge of the tree line. "Finlay!" Abby and Rory exclaimed in unison. The dog trotted toward the castle remains, bowing his head to Rory and blinking his eyes in acknowledgment. He turned to Abby just as she threw herself at him.

I was beginning to worry. I thought maybe...well, I was worried. She buried her face deep in his coat. *I'm so glad you're back.* After reveling in his return, Abby stepped back from the dog. "So what happened?" she asked. "Did you kill the monster?"

Finlay grumbled as he plunked his hind end to the ground. *On the contrary, child. I laid no bite to the beast. In fact, neither did I lay eyes on it.*

Abby recoiled in surprise and looked to Rory. "Finlay says he didn't even see the monster!" Rory grunted as Abby turned back to the dog, confused. "But, we heard all kinds of howls and mad-dog sounds. I thought you were fighting it."

Finlay swayed his head. *No, Lass. As you described, I only heard the creature, at no time could I see it. Several times I sensed it was close. It even spoke, as it did to you, and called me a murderer.*

Abby leaned toward Rory while keeping her eyes fixed on the dog. "Finlay says it called him a murderer too! Makes no sense."

Aye, Lass. I find this curious. Regardless, I believe the mysterious creature understands it is not the dominant one in these woods tonight. You should worry no longer as we begin our search here.

"How's that?" Abby asked, puzzled.

I've laid my claim to the trees surrounding us.

"Laid your claim?"

What you humans would call marking territory.

Abby processed Finlay's statement for a moment and crinkled her nose. "Oooh, that kind of claiming. Yuck." She broke into a fit of giggles. "Remind me not to go hugging any of the trees. Bleck."

Finlay growled playfully in response. *Are you finished, child? We have a book to find.*

Abby composed herself and turned to Rory. "We won't have to worry about the monster. Finlay claimed the surrounding forest, so we can search for the book in peace."

Rory tilted his head, and after a moment, a look of understanding filled his face and he nodded. "Let us search then, A-by."

"Maybe the flashlights will help," Abby said as she swung her pack to her front and dug through a pocket. "Here," she said, handing a light to Rory. She faced the ruins and contemplated the task. "Let's each search an area alone to cover ground faster," Abby pointed to the highest section of wall left standing, "and meet up there in the middle."

Agreeing with the suggestion, Rory and Finlay set off to opposite edges while Abby searched the area in front of her. For a painstaking hour, the group investigated the rubble. As Abby neared the middle of the ruins, she stopped at one last pile of stones. With a grunt, she pushed a rock from the top of the pile and squatted to peer inside a crevice with her light. She groaned, standing up. "There's just a bunch of nothing here!" She looked up to see Rory and Finlay walking toward her. "Anything?" she asked Rory, a hint of hope in her voice.

"Nae, A-by. I have found no book."

Abby sighed. "I don't get it. The riddle says we'll find it here."

Finlay lowered his nose and sniffed wildly at the pile of stones Abby last inspected. He shoved his muzzle into the crevice, snorted, and raised his head with a shake. *I sense there was once a book here, Lass. It smells similar to your father's bookstore.*

"Rory, Finlay says he smells a book, but there's nothing there," Abby said, pointing to the crevice.

Rory shined his light at the spot in question and scratched his chin. "Hmm."

"What? What are you thinking?" Abby asked.

"Well, Lass, if the scroll speaks truth, we shall find the book here," Rory indicated by jiggling the light over the area. "If yer dog indeed smells it, then it simply isn't here now."

Abby pondered what the Scotsman said, repeating his words. "Isn't here now." Recognition of what Rory meant diffused across Abby's face. "We'll find it here, just not now." Abby turned to Finlay. "We have to go back in time!"

7

*F*inlay circled the pile of stones, his nose to the ground. After several moments of intense sniffing, he raised his head, first looking to Rory, then directing his mesmerizing gaze toward Abby. *He...*Finlay paused and grumbled as if clearing his throat. *Rory is correct. His assessment is wise.* Finlay turned toward the Scotsman and nodded before swinging back to look at Abby. *Someone has removed the book. We must find our opportunity to take it before they do.*

Abby stared at the dog. *You make it sound so easy. But how do we do it without getting caught?* Frustrated, she turned to Rory. "Finlay says your idea is smart and agrees we should travel back in time to find the book." Rory directed a curt nod toward the hound while Abby tapped a finger against the ridge above her lips, deep in thought. "Well," she said, "if I remember, that website said the Wolf died in 1394," Abby paused, frowning. "But, it didn't give an exact date."

"Aye, Lass, yer memory is correct," Rory said, sheathing his sword. "But we should no' assume 1394 is where we shall find the book."

"True," Abby replied, drawing the word out, "but it's probably a good guess that until he died, he kept it close to him, or well-guarded at least. I mean, if the book is as special as it sounds, you'd think he'd keep it protected, wouldn't you?"

Rory nodded. "Aye, A-by, yer thinkin' is sensible."

Finlay pawed at the ground. *Yes, child, your thoughts are enlightened. May I suggest we start after this Wolf died and work our way back to when he still lived?*

Abby bobbed her head in agreement as she relayed Finlay's thoughts to Rory. "So," she said, gesturing toward the dog, "Finlay agrees with me too and suggested we start a little while after the Wolf died, then work our way back in time." Abby looked from Rory to the dog, "So, like 1395?"

Rory grunted in affirmation but raised a questioning finger. "How is it Finlay controls where he is goin'," he paused, trying to find the right words, "when he uses his power to change times?"

Abby began to reply, but stopped short, scratching her temple. "Huh," she responded. "You know, I've never actually thought about that!" Abby turned to Finlay, running a hand through his coat. *I can't believe I haven't* asked you about this, fuzzball. You going to tell us your secret?

Finlay nipped playfully at Abby's hand as she reached up to rub behind his ear. *There is no secret to share, young one. In fact, I have no idea how I control said power.*

Abby's expression showed her disbelief. *Oh, come on. Surely you have to know how you can do what you do.*

Finlay grumbled as Abby continued to scratch his ear. *I speak the truth, Lass. All I can say is I envision where I need to be, using whatever information I have, and then I am there. It's quite straightforward.*

Well, if you say so, Mr. Easy Peasy. Abby chuckled at the dog. *I suppose it doesn't matter how you do it, just so long as you keep doing it!*

Abby giggled, making a funny face at Rory. "Finlay said he doesn't know how he controls the time travel. Lucky for us it works right every time!"

Rory nodded, looking nervous. "Let us wait no longer," he said.

Recognizing his unease, Abby took his hand. "No worries, Rory," she said with a smile. "We got this."

Finlay stepped forward to stand in front of them. Bowing his head low, he entered Abby's mind. *You know what to do, Lass.*

Abby shoved her flashlight in her hoodie pocket and threw an encouraging glance at the Scotsman. "Ready?" she asked.

"Aye, A-by."

Still gripping Rory's hand in hers, Abby reached out with her free hand and wove her fingers into the fur upon Finlay's crown. A tickling spark flashed across her body, replaced moments later by a black void. Unlike Abby's first experience in the cave on the desolate mountainside of Caledonia, she felt her feet stay in place and maintained control of her body. She wondered if she might be acclimating to the process of time travel, but found herself looking up at a crisp, full moon before she had a moment longer to contemplate. Releasing her hands from Finlay and Rory, Abby blinked, taking in the change.

Castle ruins still lay before them, familiar, yet different. Two outer walls stood erect, blocking Abby's view of the forest. The inner makings of the stronghold struggled to stand upright. A handful of walls were as tall as Abby, but the rest yielded to what must have been a violent attack. Abby took the scene in with amazement and whispered to her companions. "Wow. The Wolf must've been an awful person if his castle is already destroyed." She turned in a slow circle. "I wonder who did it."

Rory leaned in to respond, his eyes darting in all directions. "Let us not stay long enough to find out, A-by."

"Good point," Abby said, pulling out her flashlight.

Just as Abby switched her light on, a frightening howl far off in the forest caused her to jump. She looked to Rory. "No way!" she exclaimed, dumbfounded. "There's no way that thing followed us!"

A rumbling emanated from deep in Finlay's chest. *I am as perplexed as you how it could have followed us, but I shall drive it off again, young one.*

Abby stomped her foot. "Uh-uh. Nope. No! Don't you dare leave my side this time, Finlay." Abby switched her light off and stuffed it back in her pocket. "Look," she said, lowering her voice to a whisper again, "the quicker we search the castle, the quicker we move on."

Finlay snorted, then agreed with reluctance. *Aye, Lass. If your wish is for me to stay by your side, I shall abide.*

"Okay then," Abby said with relief. She gestured toward Finlay's nose, "The fastest way to search is by smell."

Rory cocked his head at Abby, prompting her to think back to her favorite science class. "Well, a dog's nose has hundreds of millions of olfactory receptors—probably forty times more than our noses, so we should search by nose and not by eye."

Rory sighed, confusion obvious in his eyes. After a moment, he nodded. "Aye. If Finlay shall smell the book before we see it, he should lead the search."

Abby smiled. "Right," she said, turning to Finlay. "Turn your sniffer on high, mister. You have an important job to do, so you better get going."

Finlay swung his nose toward Abby and drew in a deep breath. *My olfactory receptors detect a presumptuous veil around you. That will not do.* The dog licked Abby's face from chin to temple, overemphasizing the act with a loud slurp. *There, you smell appropriate now.*

"Eeew. Gross." Abby wiped her face on her sleeve. "Okay, I get it. Don't be so pushy. You still have a job to do, though," she directed with a giggle.

Finlay headed into the ruins. *Follow me and stay close, Lass.*

Abby motioned for Rory to follow. "Let's leave our lights off; there's enough moonlight to guide us." She surveyed the fallen stones. "Just be careful where you step."

The group picked their way through the maze of debris. Finlay stopped periodically, sticking his nose to the ground and in, and around piles of stone, snorting disappointment after finding no clues. The search stretched longer this time, limited by the lack of powerful noses, though Abby and Rory did their best by eye. When they reached the far side of the ruins, Abby leaned against one of the remaining outer walls and groaned. "This is pointless. It's clearly not here, or you would have smelled something already."

From just beyond the wall, a ghastly shriek rang out. Abby's eyes widened as she leaped away, landing between Finlay and Rory. The travelers stood motionless, staring anxiously at one another. Moments later, a familiar howl filled the air. Abby grabbed Rory's arm and pulled him close. Her heart pounded, her mind filled with confusion. *It's impossible, it couldn't have time jumped with us. It'd have to be touching Finlay!*

The creature's guttural voice surrounded them. "Murderers," it hissed.

Abby secured her hold on Rory and stretched an arm toward her white warrior, grasping a handful of fur and squeezing her eyes tight. *Finlay. Go. Now!*

✳✳✳

Abby opened her eyes. They stood in a stone hallway with little light. "Where are we?" she whispered.

"Inside the castle, A-by," Rory replied as he attempted to remove himself from her frightened grip.

"Oh, sorry," Abby said, releasing her tight grasp around Rory's arm and flexing her fingers to relieve their ache.

The hallway afforded little room for the three to move side by side. Abby released the handful of fur she held with her other hand and stepped back, rotating her neck and shoulders. "So now what?" she pondered. "We're making progress, but we don't even know where to go."

Finlay swiveled his head back to eye Abby, then puffed a gentle stream of air in her face. *We follow the nose, of course.*

Abby pushed Finlay's muzzle playfully away from her face. *Duh. Lead the way then.*

Finlay lifted his nose and sampled the air. After several sniffs, he paused. *Someone is baking bread. That way.* He motioned with his head. *It would be wise to follow the path behind us.*

Abby leaned toward Rory. "Finlay says we need to go the other way. The kitchen is probably that way," she said, pointing ahead. As she lowered her finger, a portly woman carrying a basket of bread rounded the corner at the end of the hall. Hair pulled back in a braid, and an apron covering her generous hips, she stared at the stone floor as she scooted along, humming a sweet melody, oblivious to the travelers.

Abby's eyes grew wide, knowing the woman would discover them at any moment. She grabbed Rory's arm and pointed toward their unexpected visitor. She pulled him with her as she edged her way toward Finlay.

Lost in her own thoughts, the woman drew near as Abby reached forward. With fingers inches from grasping a handful of fur, Abby sucked in a silent breath as the woman lifted her head and locked eyes with the dog. The woman skidded to a stop, moving her gaze to Abby, then Rory, and back to Finlay.

Abby pulled her hand back from Finlay and waved. "Um, hi."

The woman, who Abby thought to be in shock, gave the slightest of nods in return, dropped the basket, and retreated with a yelp back around the corridor as fast as her stubby legs would carry her.

Abby groaned as the woman's screeching continued. "Great. I'm sure she's off to find a guard." Abby followed through with her original intent and sunk her hand into Finlay's coat. "Better get out of here while we can." After a moment of thought, she continued with emphasis, "Maybe stick us at the other end of the hallway this time!"

Before she could signal to Finlay, Rory wiggled from Abby's grip and squatted to grab a flat piece of bread. As he stood, he tore it in half and stuffed a large chunk in his mouth. Abby rolled her eyes. "Really, Rory? We're in the middle of a serious mission, and you're stopping to shove bread in your mouth?"

Rory shrugged and grinned, offering the other half to Abby. "Ye need to eat," he mumbled as he moved to stand by her side again. "It's good, but no' like that of Mrs. MacTavish," he mumbled through a full mouth.

Abby sighed. "Okay, one bite, but we have to go then," she replied, accepting the piece and popping it into her mouth. Looping her arm through Rory's, she nodded to him and readjusted her handhold on the dog's coat. *Go now before someone decides he wants the whole basket!*

✱✱✱

Abby blinked, shocked by the speed of transition to their new destination. She questioned if they had even moved but realized they appeared to be at the other end of the same, or similar, corridor. Drawing in a deep breath, she noted no smell of fresh baked bread, except for the final chunk Rory popped into his mouth with a goofy grin. Abby giggled and shook her head as she gained her bearings. Random torches illuminated the passage, flickering along the stone.

Rory put a finger to his lips, signaling for Abby to stay still, and crept forward while hugging his back to the wall. Rory peered around the gentle curve in the passage. After a moment, he straightened up and waved his hand for the others to join him. "I see no servants," he whispered when Abby approached. "Let us proceed quietly, keepin' to the side as best we can."

Abby nodded agreement and fell in line behind Rory, with Finlay at her heels. Rounding the curve, they saw that the passageway straightened out into a long corridor with no end in sight. Torches lined the hall at regular intervals, unlike the earlier passage. It appeared to Abby there were several doorways along the left side, the first not more than twenty feet ahead of them. Tugging on Rory's sleeve, Abby pointed to the first door. Rory nodded and slowed his pace, stopping every few steps to listen for voices. Once satisfied with their safety, Rory approached the door and placed his ear upon it. "I hear no sounds," he breathed.

"Should we open it?" Abby questioned, looking between Finlay and the Scotsman.

"We should no' be so fast to do so, A-by," Rory whispered. "What if someone were only sittin' quietly. We'd be sure to be discovered then."

Finlay stepped forward and snorted. *Rory speaks wisely, Lass. Let us use our best resource. Stand aside and allow me to smell.*

Abby pulled Rory off to the side of the door. "Finlay says you're right. He wants to see if he can smell anything."

Rory grunted approval, making way for the dog.

Finlay approached the door, his nostrils twitching. Sniffing along the crevice between the door and the wall, he stopped with an abrupt snort. *Someone sleeps here.*

Abby relayed the statement to Rory and turned back to the dog. *Are you sure?*

Aye, Lass. I can smell the meal they last ate with each exhale they make. And I detect no book. We must move on from here.

Abby motioned for Rory to move to the next door. The group continued as before, staying close to the wall and taking care to make no noise. After several minutes of slow, cautious travel, they stood before a deep-red wood door trimmed with ornate carvings. The hairs on Abby's arms jumped to attention; she could hear faint voices coming from the far end of the hall. "We have to hide!" Abby hissed under her breath.

Rory darted his eyes first one way, then the other, searching for a means of escape. He motioned toward the door in front of them. "We must enter at once lest our presence be known."

"Finlay," Abby urged, "can you smell anything? Is it safe?"

The dog sucked in a long, deep breath and rumbled. *There is something there, Lass, but I do not think it lives.*

Abby turned to Rory. "Finlay thinks it's safe. Good enough for me," she said, pushing on the handle. "It seems to be unlocked, but it's heavy," she grunted, unable to move the grand door.

Rory stood behind Abby, stretched his arms on either side of her head, and placed his hands several inches above hers. With his added effort, the door swung open without a sound. The travelers filed into the room, and the door shut behind them with a gentle thud.

Abby's stomach lurched as she thought about what might lay ahead of them. There were no torches to guide them, and only a sliver of light from the corridor found its way under the massive door. *Time for some light.* Abby held a nervous breath, pulling her flashlight from her pocket. She flipped it on and aimed the beam low, scanning the floor. Wide stone blocks, laid in a circular pattern stemming from the center of the room, formed the barren groundwork. The chamber appeared to be devoid of furniture—and residents, to Abby's relief.

"We need more light," Rory declared, pulling his sword from its sheath. He raised it high and commanded flames to life along its sharp blade. Abby stifled a scream at what the enhanced light revealed. Not two feet to her left were the mummified remains of someone consumed by pain in their last moments. The corpse leaned against the wall as if propped up for display. *Great*, she directed to Finlay, *we've hidden ourselves smack in the middle of a mausoleum!*

The dog growled. *I smell evilness throughout. This is not natural. We must leave this place at once.*

Abby cringed, stepping back from the lifeless form as she shined her light on it. *Well, we can't go back into the hallway yet; we'll probably get caught. Maybe there's another way out of this disgusting place.*

Rory began his own search of the room, waving his sword in a wide arc. To his distaste, there were six bodies placed symmetrically around the chamber, each with its own horrified expression. "This is no' right, A-by," he spat, "the work of a beast, no doubt." Rory stopped at the sixth corpse, revolted by its appearance. "Looks like this poor soul had its throat ripped out," he lamented, shivering at the thought.

Abby stepped close to Rory and whispered. "We need to see if there's another way out of this creep show." She pointed her light toward the wall opposite the door.

"Maybe there's a secret passageway," she suggested, turning to Finlay. *There'd better be a hidden door. There's always a hidden door, right? Don't know how we'll get ourselves out of this one, short of time hopping again.*

Finlay strode toward the back of the room, raising his muzzle high. Abby followed and motioned for Rory to stay close. "Finlay's checking for another way out," she said in hushed tones, "before we go jumping around in time again." Abby concentrated on the dog's movements. "If we aren't thorough with each stop, we'll never find the book."

Rory's face tensed as he nodded in agreement. Stepping back toward the entrance, he placed an ear against the door. After several moments, he tiptoed back to the area of investigation. Leaning into Abby, he whispered, "I can still hear the voices, A-by. They move close." Peering over his shoulder at the door, Rory continued, "If Finlay is goin' to lead us out, now would be a fine time."

Finlay snorted in response and worked his way along the wall toward the middle of the chamber, avoiding each corpse as he continued sniffing. *There is something here, Lass, but it evades my eyes.*

Abby glanced at the Scotsman. "Finlay says there's something here, but he can't see it."

"Somethin' other than these wretched bodies, I pray," Rory replied, trying not to look at the corpse nearest him.

"Finlay?" Abby questioned. "How can we help? Any idea yet what you think you smell?"

Aye, child. I do not wish to cause false hope, but I believe the book is near. If I am correct, it lay beyond this wall.

"The book?" she replied excitedly, realizing her voice may have carried. Abby took a deep breath to calm her nerves. "The book, Rory," she whispered, "Finlay smells the book behind this wall."

Rory approached the wall nearest the giant hound. He ran his sword along the surface of the stone, searching for a sign of any kind as the flames illuminated even the smallest of cracks. He sighed, stepping back. "I see nothin' unusual, A-by."

Abby rubbed her temples. "Okay," she said with a slow exhale. "Finlay, why don't you show Rory where you think you smell the book," she directed, continuing to massage her head. "Then Rory," she added, "use your sword to inspect the spot. Maybe there's a brick that'll come loose."

Rory nodded but eyed the dog as it made its way past him to the wall.

Finlay tested the air again, snorting in deep breaths high and low along the stone surface. He stopped, bringing an abrupt silence to the chamber. His nose wavered four feet above the ground. As quickly as he stopped, he sniffed the wall again, this time focusing on individual blocks, following the outer edges of each stone, which led his nose to trace an imaginary square filled with nine blocks. He stopped and blinked at the wall before resuming to follow the imaginary line full circle a second time, then snorted and pawed at the surface, scratching at the block in the center of the imaginary square. *Here, Lass. We will find it here.*

Abby approached the wall and ran her hand across the cool, smooth stone. "Finlay says the book's here, Rory," she said, turning to the Scotsman. "See if you can pry the block loose."

Finlay shifted his mass to the side, allowing room for Rory to stand in front of the block in question. Rory nodded and stepped forward. He examined the stone, directing the flames from the sword first to one side, then to the other. The corners of his mouth turned down when he could find nothing. After a moment, with a glint in his eye, Rory pulled his dirk with his free hand. Holding the sword off to the left, he attempted to slip the blade of the knife into the crevice between the stone and those adjacent. He worked his way around the perimeter, frowning at his lack of success. He looked at Abby with a grimace as he sheathed his dirk. "Sorry A-by, it will no' give."

Abby returned the frown, but then something caught her eye. "Hey," she said, pointing to the upper right block in the imaginary boundary Finlay's nose had identified, "there's a little divot in the outer corner of that stone." She reached out to touch the spot. "Hmm, I wonder." Abby pushed against the divot with her thumb. A soft grating sounded as the stone inched inward at the point of pressure. Abby jerked back, surprised by the movement. With the release of her finger, the stone grated outward, again creating a flush wall. Abby looked at her companions before repeating her prior actions, only to find the same result. She sighed with frustration. "So the stone moves a little, but nothing else is happening. We're missing something," she groaned.

Rory tugged on Abby's arm. "A-by. Look," he whispered excitedly, pointing to her left. "The stone opposite bears the same mark."

Abby followed the perimeter of the imagined square with her eyes, stopping in the lower left corner. "You're right," she said, "it's the same indentation." After a moment of contemplation, she continued. "Push it. See if it does the same thing."

Rory nodded, pressing on the divot. To Abby's satisfaction, the stone grated as it slid in and leveled itself when Rory drew away. Abby frowned when all was silent again. "It must be a puzzle of some kind. I don't get it though."

"Perhaps press them together, A-by," suggested Rory.

Confused, Abby questioned, "What, you mean at the same time?"

"Aye, Lass."

Abby shrugged. "Might as well. You push the left one, and I'll do the right."

Rory nodded and placed his thumb on the indentation. "Press when I say, A-by."

Abby readied her hand. "Okay, say when."

"Now."

In unison, they pressed the corners of the stones, and together the blocks grated inward. "Okay," Abby said , feeling hopeful, "let's pull our fingers off at the same time too and see what happens."

Rory nodded. "Aye. Ready," he said, pausing. "Now."

Excitement tingled throughout Abby's insides upon seeing a different reaction. Both stones remained tilted inward after pressure from the pair's effort ceased. Abby sucked in a breath. "Come on, come on," she urged, "do something."

Not a moment later, a deeper grating stirred a flurry of butterflies in Abby's gut. The center stone of Finlay's imaginary square slid inward. The harsh sound of stone on stone echoed throughout the chamber. Abby groaned to herself. *Sure hope no one hears that!* To her relief, the stone relented and silence soon filled the room. Abby leaned over and peered into the dark hole. Grunting, she pulled her flashlight from her hoodie pocket and shined the light into the deep void. "Hmm," Abby muttered, glancing up at her companions. "It looks like something is sticking out from the sidewall of the hole, maybe a half-foot in on the left side." She motioned for Rory to look as she focused the beam into the void again. "Do you see it?"

Rory commanded the flames of his sword to retreat to a safe intensity and squatted to the side of Abby. He bobbed his head around, finding the best vantage. "Aye, A-by. I see it. But I'm uncertain what it may be."

Finlay bumped his nose against Abby's backside. *Let me inspect, child. We must be cautious.*

Abby straightened her posture and motioned to Finlay. "Rory, he wants to look too. You should probably step out of the way."

Rory stood, sidestepping to the left and pointing to the cavity with a hand palm-out and pointed down. Lifting his sword high, he bid the flames to illuminate the chamber.

Finlay bowed to the Scotsman, sauntered forward, and lowered his head. Turning his muzzle to the right, he leveled his left eye with the hole. Abby crouched to the left side of the dog's head and aimed the light into the blackness, adjusting the angle until the mystery object fell into view. "There. See? Sorta looks like a handle."

The dog snorted, raising his head. *I believe one would refer to it as a lever, Lass. If I am correct, we stand before a hidden door.*

Abby stood, flipped the flashlight off, and shoved it back in her hoodie. "Finlay thinks this is a secret door," she stated to Rory. "And that thing sticking out is probably the switch to open it." Abby reached toward the hole. "Maybe if I pull down on it, the door will open."

Finlay nipped at Abby's arm, grabbing hold of her sleeve. *Do not rush so, little one. Were it a trap, I would rather your arm not be the victim.*

Abby tightened her lips at the dog. *So you're saying you don't want me to get hurt, but it'd be okay if it were Rory instead?*

Finlay released Abby's sleeve and shook his body. *Well. Aye. If we're being blunt about it.* The dog paused with a sigh. *I do not wish harm upon the lad, but your safety is imperative. Always.*

Abby rolled her eyes. "Rory, Finlay doesn't think it's safe for me to stick my arm in the hole, in case it's a trap or something."

Rory stood tall and straightened his shoulders. "He is right," he replied, nodding to Finlay. "Step aside, and I shall examine the openin'."

Shrugging, Abby backed away from the wall. Rory turned his right side toward the stone surface while holding his sword out in front of him. He squatted and reached inside the hole. "Found it," he said after a tense moment. "Seems it's made of stone too."

Abby clasped her hands together. "Well, will it move?"

With determination, Rory attempted to push up on the handle. "Doesn't go up," he replied with a grunt. Abby watched on as she shifted her weight from leg to leg.

Readjusting his grasp, Rory pulled down on the stone shaft. The lever slipped free with a loud clunk. Startled by the sound, Rory pulled his arm free and tumbled back from the wall.

Abby felt the floor vibrate as a low rumble emanated from the stone barrier. A section of wall, three-foot-wide and six feet high swung open in silence. "Finlay, you were right," Abby whispered. "And thanks for sacrificing your arm, Rory," she said to the Scotsman as he stood.

The group stared at the now open entrance, looked at each other, and back. Darkness consumed the entryway, even with the flames dancing from Rory's sword. "Looks spooky in there," Abby chuckled nervously. Remembering the inhabitants of the chamber they stood in, she added, "But I guess it can't be any worse than this!"

Rory strode toward the threshold, holding his sword high. Intense flames roared to life, jumping and snaking their way into the blackness, revealing the silhouette of a barren hallway. Entering the hall, Rory motioned for the others to follow. They advanced, allowing the flames to light the way. With no curves or turns, the hall seemed endless as they continued.

Without warning, a door appeared in front of the group. They stopped in unison to stare at the new obstacle. Rory crept forward and placed an ear to it. After several moments, he returned to his companions. "All is silent," he whispered.

Abby tugged on Finlay's coat. *What do you think? Safe?*

Finlay raised his snout and filled his lungs. *Aye, Lass. And the book is near.*

Abby squeezed Rory's elbow. "Finlay says it's safe. And I think the book is behind that door."

Rory nodded and strode forward. Placing a shoulder against the barrier, and holding his sword out from his side, he leaned in with all his weight. To his surprise, the door opened. Stepping back, he directed the sword through the opening, waiting for its flames to illuminate the unknown. Looking back, he motioned for Abby and Finlay to follow.

A single stone step led them down into a tiny, square chamber. Wooden torches, not yet lit, lined the walls. In the center of the room stood a stone pedestal with a recessed top, the sole adornment of what felt like a small, stone cell to Abby. "Rory, I bet you could light those torches," Abby suggested, stepping into the room. Rory grunted agreement and walked the tight perimeter of the chamber. Tongue-like flames licked out and kindled each torch as he passed. Soon, ample light filled the room, allowing Rory to sheath his sword.

Abby looked around the barren room and walked toward the pedestal. As she drew closer, she realized an unopened book lay hidden in the recess of the platform of the pedestal. She rushed around the pedestal to look straight on at the book. Finlay and Rory joined her on either side. They all stared in amazement.

The Book of Shay beckoned; its impressive cover dared one to touch its surface. "I can't believe it," Abby exclaimed as tears formed in her eyes. "I mean, I knew we'd find it," she choked, "but finally seeing it...we will get my dad back now, won't we?"

Rory placed a gentle hand on Abby's shoulder. "Aye, A-by. I promised ye we would save yer faither. And that we shall do."

Abby smiled, composing herself. "Thanks, Rory."

Looking at the book, Abby studied its cover. A tree, resembling the one on the scroll they found, adorned the lower half. The title, calligraphed elegantly, filled the upper center of the space. Tree branches wove around the perimeter of the cover encompassing the title. The words were a deep red, and the tree a glistening gold. Abby reached out to open the book, but a rage-consumed howl echoed throughout the passageway, causing her to freeze. Looking up, she drew a sharp breath. An enormous man, his face framed by a jet-black beard, stood in the entryway.

8

*H*atred flooded from the man as he clenched his fists rhythmically. His biceps threatened to rip through the sleeves of his golden hued tunic. A low growl emanated from deep within his heaving chest. "Thieves!" he roared. "If ye try to touch me book, ye shall meet a certain end."

Abby gulped; she recognized the man from the drawing on the Internet. She pulled her shaking hand back away from the book and grasped Rory's left arm. "Rory," she muttered through clenched teeth. "It's him, the Wolf of Badenoch."

Rory grunted in response and placed his right hand on the hilt of his sword. Leaning close to Abby's ear, he whispered, "Be prepared to grab the book and run, A-by. But only when I say."

The Wolf cackled as he jumped down into the chamber with a thud. "I'm afraid there shall be no runnin'.'" He circled the outer wall of the room with deliberate steps. Reaching up, he passed a hand through the flames of the closest torch. Unscathed by the fire, he sneered at the unwelcome party. "In fact, ye shall make exquisite additions to me collection."

Abby's eyes opened wide as she realized what the Wolf meant. She looked to the passageway with horror— the passageway leading to the chamber of corpses.

With a ghoulish chuckle, the Wolf contemplated Abby's expression. "Aye, that's correct, Lass. Ye shall fit in nicely with the others," he said, turning his head and waving an arm toward the doorway. "Although," he continued with a gruff boom, snapping his head toward Finlay, "what to do with the filthy beast." He paused to scratch his chin for show. "Perhaps it shall make a fine meal or two."

A powerful rumble rippled through the air. Finlay snarled; the sound emanating from his core evolved into a deep, menacing growl. He bared his teeth at the Wolf and strode forward as he entered Abby's mind. *Remain behind me at all times, child. When the moment is right, grab the book and the boy. We must leave this place.*

The Wolf answered Finlay's roar by beating his chest with one fist and stepping toward the pedestal. He opened his arms wide, arched his back, and released a deafening howl, craning his head toward the ceiling.

Abby, Rory, and Finlay froze, all recognizing the familiar wail at once.

"Nnn, no," Abby sputtered. Her stomach twisted. "It. It can't be," she said in disbelief, looking to Rory.

Rory drew his sword in response while pushing Abby behind him with his free hand. "Stay back, A-by. I do no' know what devilry this is, but I shall protect ye."

The Wolf's howl trailed to nothing, leaving an eerie silence in the chamber. He lowered his head to reveal burning, yellow eyes and elongated incisors and canines. As he unclenched his fists, Abby's eye locked on the tips of his fingers—those too appeared longer and sharper than humanly possible. Fear enveloped Abby as she looked on. It was now clear how the Wolf of Badenoch acquired his name and reputation. His already massive form seemed to swell before them as he held his hands out to either side, fingers splayed, beckoning a battle.

"The book," Abby mumbled to herself as she looked to the pedestal. She stared at the book with determination. Her eyes shifted to Rory, and then to Finlay, envisioning the path she would take. *Grab the book, grab Rory, grab Finlay. Then we're out of this nightmare.*

Hearing her thoughts, Finlay shot a glance over his shoulder, urging Abby to stop. *No, Lass.* He cried. *Not yet.*

Abby cinched her pack, and as fast as she could, lunged for the pedestal, arms outstretched.

The Wolf roared at the sight of Abby's fingers wrapping around the Book of Shay. He crouched low, then leaped high into the air, over the heads of his invaders. Deliberately, he raked the stone ceiling with his claws, sending an ear-piercing screech throughout the chamber. He landed with a forceful thump and whipped around to glare at the young thief before him. Abby's heart raced as she glanced over her shoulder at the Wolf. She turned, knees weak, as the Wolf stood to his full height. "Thief," he hissed.

Abby tried to back away from the beast, only to find her path blocked by the pedestal. She gulped, realizing the magnitude of her error.

The Wolf took one long stride forward. "All thieves shall die," he screamed, lashing out at Abby with his claws.

Chaos filled the chamber as a searing pain ripped through the inside of Abby's right thigh.

Rory cried out. A fury of flames exploded from his sword, filling the room.

Finlay bellowed a mixture of pain and intense anger. He launched himself through the air at the Wolf, landing inches away. Finlay snapped, snarled, and latched onto the Wolf's forearm. Not a second later, the blood curdling howls and growls stopped. Finlay and the Wolf disappeared.

"Finlay," Abby cried out as she slumped to the ground, the Book of Shay clasped tight to her chest.

Rory rushed to Abby, sheathing his sword. He scooped her up into his arms and propped her against the pedestal. He pulled at his braids in dismay. "No, no, no, no, no," he wailed at what lay before him. Blood soaked Abby's pant leg at a steady and alarming rate.

"Rory," Abby whispered, struggling to raise her eyes. "I don't feel so good. Keep the book safe," she mumbled, attempting to hold out the treasure.

Rory removed the tome from her arms and set it to her side. As he did, Abby's eyes shut, and her head rolled back.

"A-by! A-by!" Rory sobbed. "So much blood. Must stop the blood."

As Rory cried out and worked feverishly to cut a strip of wool from his tunic, Abby became aware of her body. Though she slumped in pain and darkness, she felt a brightness to her surroundings. With effort, Abby opened her eyes. She wavered at the image before her. She now looked down upon herself and Rory. *Wha...what the heck? What's happening?*

Rory wrapped a section of his tunic around Abby's leg just above the wound. He pulled the strip taut and tied it off in a knot, then applied a second section of tunic to the wound itself and applied pressure. "A-by!" he wailed, "please wake up, A-by."

Abby reached down toward the Scotsman and called out to him. *Rory! Don't cry, I'm right here.* After a moment, Abby realized she could not speak. Terror swelled throughout her mind as she watched Rory attend to her motionless body, oblivious to her form overhead. *Am, am I dead?* Abby raised her hands in front of her face and attempted to pinch one with the other. She froze when her hands passed through each other. *Wait a minute,* Abby thought after a second attempt. *This feels just like that dream I had when we escaped the mountain.* Relief rushed through her mind. *That's it. I'm dreaming again. No way I'm dead.*

As Abby continued to analyze her situation, a far off noise caught her attention. *What was that?* She whirled her head around, attempting to pinpoint the location. Blocking out the sounds of Rory below her, she held her breath, listening for the noise to repeat. *There,* she sucked in a deep breath when the roar of Finlay's rage again reached her ear. *Finlay. He needs me. But where?* Concentrating on the dog, Abby felt herself float upward. *Whoa, weird.* Reaching the ceiling, Abby continued to float upward through the stone. She pinched her eyes tight, unable to believe what was happening; she was floating out of the castle.

Cracking an eye open, the Wolf's lair appeared smaller from above than Abby would have imagined. Darkness cloaked much of the structure, but Abby had a strange feeling if she concentrated hard enough, she could see through the stones to Rory and herself. *Later. I should try that later.*

Reluctantly looking away from the castle, Abby tuned her ears and searched for Finlay. To her left, close by the faerie pool, a streak of movement caught her eye; a savage roar followed the motion. Abby whirled toward the frightening sounds. Finlay and the Wolf circled one another at the water's edge, each one trying to anticipate the other's next move. The Wolf lunged and swiped at the dog with his right arm, missing narrowly. Finlay jumped back into a defensive stance and snarled.

Abby called out to her white warrior. *Finlay! Be careful.* When no response came from the dog, Abby panicked. *Can't he hear me? He should be able to hear me.* Trying again, Abby focused her thoughts. *Finlay! I'm here. Please be careful.* Again, the dog continued to circle his adversary, waiting for the Wolf to lower his guard. A knot formed in Abby's throat. *He really can't hear me. Maybe I am dead!*

Finlay came to a halt, the faerie pool behind him. He crouched low, shifting his full weight onto his hind legs, preparing to attack. The Wolf bared his teeth, sensing his opponent's intentions. He hunched low to the ground, rocking back and forth with a crazed look. For minutes Abby watched on. Neither canine seemed willing to attack. But, the Wolf's patience soon grew thin. He rocketed himself through the air at Finlay, signaling his intentions with a hair-raising wail. Anticipating the Wolf's move, Finlay shifted his weight to his left side, and then sprang to his right, away from the beast's path.

The Wolf flew past the now empty space and somersaulted into the faerie pool. He jumped up and wheeled around with a roar, the shallow waters splashing in his wake. Running full force, he barreled toward Finlay, his claws outstretched, searching for soft flesh. Abby cried out, fearful for her magical friend. Even from where she was, she could see the uncontrollable rage in the Wolf's eyes.

Finlay stretched to his full height as he turned to face the Wolf. His hackles rose as he stood patiently with not even the quiver of a single muscle as he awaited the right moment.

Abby screamed to herself. *What is he doing! That dog will get himself killed if he just stands there. Fight back, fuzzball!*

The Wolf continued his charge. His arms swung wildly as he closed the space between them. Finlay leaned forward, his body tense, standing still until the last possible moment. When the Wolf overtook him, Finlay lashed out, clamping onto the man's right arm. The Wolf screamed in pain, then reached across his body with his left arm, slashing at Finlay's midsection. The Wolf's claws struck as Finlay disappeared.

Seconds later, Finlay reappeared on the other side of the Wolf, arm in mouth, causing the Wolf's body to spin side over side in the air as Finlay released his grip on the beast. The Wolf flopped to the ground, landing on his stomach with a surprised groan. Finlay wasted no time in pouncing onto the man's back, his girth smashing the Wolf's chest into the hard ground. The Wolf attempted to rise, pushing up with his arms, but Finlay's mass proved too much for him. When that didn't work, the Wolf reached behind him with both hands and searched the air for any vulnerable piece of the dog with which he might connect. Finlay stomped on the Wolf's back in response, moving his left foreleg out of reach not a moment too soon. His right leg, however, did not fare as well. The Wolf's claws sank into the lower part of Finlay's foreleg. The dog howled as pain coursed through his leg. Pleased, the Wolf cackled, squeezing harder.

Abby sobbed when Finlay continued to howl, his leg now streaked with blood. Never had she feared for his life. *Finlay! Do something!*

For a moment, the dog looked into the night sky. Abby drew in a breath, wondering if he had heard her pleadings. Then in a single, swift movement, Finlay whipped his head toward the Wolf of Badenoch and chomped onto the back of his neck. Finlay closed his eyes as the Wolf flailed his legs and his free arm in protest. The sound of bones crushing reached Abby's ears. Then all was silent.

The Wolf's limbs went limp, allowing Finlay to extricate his leg from the beast's claws. His lifeless body laid still, a shell of the monstrous soul it once held. Abby raised a hand to cover her mouth, feeling shocked at the sight and Finlay's actions, yet grateful for her white warrior's safety.

Finlay stepped from the man's back, favoring his wounded leg. He eyed the Wolf's body as he circled it twice, then plopped to the ground where he licked his wounds.

Abby choked back a tear watching her warrior clean the blood from his now imperfect coat. She became entranced with the rhythm of his tongue, shutting out everything else around her. Moments later, a faint noise startled her, followed by a strange movement near the Wolf's body. Finlay, oblivious to both, continued tending to his wound. Abby's mouth dropped open, neither understanding, nor quite believing what she was witnessing.

Above the Wolf of Badenoch's body, a fuzzy and shadowed form appeared to pull itself free from the corpse. The empty form hovered above the ground as if discovering its surroundings for the first time. After a brief pause, it swiveled around until it faced the dog, then shot backward in the air before an ominous wail filled the air. "Murderer!" it screamed.

Abby felt her insides tremble. At the same instant, Finlay jerked his head up, trying to pinpoint the source of the familiar cry. Finlay jumped to his feet and growled. The shadow shot toward the dog, flying above him in a repeated figure eight. "Murderer!" it continued to wail and hiss. Finlay snorted defiantly, realizing he was no longer in danger. He strode forward to the Wolf's body. After sniffing and nudging it with his nose, he dragged the corpse toward the faerie pool. The shadow shrieked in protest when the dog pulled the body into the water. Finlay backed into the pool several feet and released the creature's remains. Turning himself around, he gave the Wolf a determined push with his muzzle and trotted back to dry ground.

Abby watched in awe. *Rory. I've got to tell Rory what just happened.* Abby pulled her gaze from the shadow and looked to the castle. *But how do I get back?* Closing her eyes, Abby concentrated on Rory, envisioning him in her mind. To her surprise, she felt herself move. Sneaking a peek with one eye, she realized she was approaching the structure at an increasing rate. Abby squeezed her eyes tight again, focusing on Rory once more. Moments later, she felt herself come to a stop. Drawing a deep breath, Abby opened her eyes.

Rory knelt before her body, speaking in soft tones. "This is goin' to hurt, A-by," he said drawing his sword, "but I'm left with no choice. I must stop the bleedin'."

Abby willed herself to float closer. She cringed at the sight of herself, pale and tiny, her jeans a sea of red. *What's he going to do?*

Rory held the blade before him, his eyes serious. Seconds later, the engravings along the metal glowed a deep red. Rory readjusted his stance, removed the bandage, and lowered the blade to Abby's thigh.

Abby cringed as a soft sizzle filled the chamber. *He's cauterizing my leg! Gross, but genius.*

Rory pulled the metal from Abby's wound and ran his fingers around the site. Smiling, he whispered to his companion, "The bleedin' stopped, A-by. It's goin' to be alright."

Seeing the result, Rory commanded his sword to sleep. Unaware they were no longer in danger, Rory laid the weapon on the stone floor between Abby and himself.

He leaned in close to check for signs of life, placing his ear next to her mouth. After a long moment, he pulled away. Reaching up with his right hand, Rory brushed the curls from Abby's eyes.

"Please wake up, A-by," he sighed, moving to caress her cheek. When there was no response, Rory lowered his hand, resting it on the hilt of his sword. By reflex, his fingers wrapped themselves around the extension of his body. Rory shifted his attention back to the cauterized wound. He rested the palm of his left hand over the ravaged skin and choked back a sob. "Ye must wake, A-by. I do no' know what else to do." He drew a deep breath, his shoulders slumping in defeat. Looking upon Abby's still face, Rory whispered, "Me heart is full of love for ye, A-by." He craned his head toward his shoulder and wiped a single tear from his cheek. "I will no' bear losin' ye. Wake," he commanded, "ye must wake."

Abby floated closer to Rory and her still form. *What did he just say?*

Before Abby could contemplate Rory's admission, the engravings on his sword glowed a fierce red. Rory looked down, startled by the sudden awakening of his weapon. The sword's glow increased in intensity, causing Abby to shield her eyes. But she lowered her hand when she saw what followed. The golden drop of Myst's prophecy—her mother's amulet, still embedded in the hilt of the sword—

began to hum, to engulf the area with yellow light. From Abby's vantage, the light seemed to pulse. As she floated closer for a better look, the light shot out from the hilt, traveling along Rory's arm, across his back, and down his left side to the hand now massaging the wound in her thigh.

Rory looked from the hilt to Abby's leg. His left hand, now engulfed in the warm yellow light, pulsed in unison with the hilt of the sword. The light expanded with a burst, engulfing both Rory and Abby.

Abby's jaw dropped. *Rory!* She screamed to herself. *What's happening?* She floated closer, sensing an odd, yet familiar tug at her abdomen. Falling forward, she felt herself yanked into the field of yellow. Then a wave of blackness washed over her.

✳✳✳

Abby opened her eyes and jerked her head back against the harsh stone of the pedestal. She reached up, pushing Rory's expectant face from her own. "Rory," she groaned, "what are you doing."

"A-by!" Rory cried. "Yer alive."

Taking a moment to digest Rory's words, Abby lifted her hands in front of her face. Pinching herself, she sighed. "I knew it. It was only a dream." Replaying the scene in her head, Abby sat up with a jolt and reached for her right thigh. She sucked in a deep breath of disbelief, her fingers stopping short. A makeshift tourniquet adorned her leg, just above a jagged hole in her blood-soaked jeans. Abby fumbled for words.

"It, it was real?" she choked. "But," Abby paused, looking back to her leg. Her eyes grew big. "Wait a second," she drawled. Abby inspected her leg, pulling back the ragged edges of the material. Her skin appeared soft, free from injury and blood. She raised her head to gaze at Rory; the goofy grin stretching across his face caused her to suppress a giggle. "But how?" were the only words Abby could form.

"I healed ye, A-by," Rory proclaimed. "I do no' understand how, but," he reached down to squeeze her hand, "I have ye back. Only this matters."

Abby released Rory's hand and worked the knot on the scrap of tunic tied around her leg. "Rory, I," Abby trailed off, feeling dumbfounded.

"What is it, A-by?" Rory said with concern. "Are ye feelin' pained?"

Abby considered the question for a moment as she finished removing the wrap on her leg. "No," she replied, looking up to meet Rory's eyes. "Actually, I've never felt so good, that I can remember anyway. It's just," she paused, "this will probably sound weird, but, I watched everything happen."

"What do ye mean, A-by?" Rory asked, overwhelmed with confusion. "Yer eyes were shut. I'd say ye had no sense about ye."

Abby let out a long breath and motioned for Rory to help her to her feet. "I don't know how to explain it, but, I was floating in the air," she pointed a finger toward the ceiling of the chamber. "I was up there and could see and hear everything going on." She paused, thinking back to a recent book she read. "It was like I was having an out-of-body experience or something." Abby sighed upon seeing Rory's blank stare. "I know, I know, it sounds confusing. I thought I was dreaming, but now I'm not so sure." Abby furrowed her brow as she continued. "I watched you heal me, Rory. Your sword glowed, then the amulet went crazy and blasted yellow light along your body all the way to your left hand. Then," she trailed off, pointing to her thigh, "this."

Rory grunted, considering her story, only to be cut short by Abby's rush of excitement.

"Finlay!" Abby squealed. "Oh my gosh, Rory, you won't believe what happened," she rambled. "I floated outside the castle, and Finlay, he was out there by the faerie pool fighting the Wolf!" Abby paused long enough to take in a deep breath. "It was a horrible fight." Abby stretched her arms wide and high, pretending to have claws. "I thought Finlay was a goner, but then, Finlay killed him!" Abby's face turned serious. "But, I mean, he had to; he had no choice." Abby wrapped her arms around her chest, giving herself a protective hug. "The scariest thing happened after that, though."

Rory did nothing to hide his worry. "Tell me, A-by, what frightened ye?"

Abby shivered as she thought about the ghostly form that materialized from the Wolf's dead body. "Well, remember the wailing thing that chased us in the forest, and then seemed to follow us back in time?"

A mixture of dread and concern washed across Rory's face. "Aye, A-by, would be hard to forget."

"It sounds unbelievable, but," Abby lowered her voice to a whisper and peered around the chamber, half expecting someone to be listening in, "I'm pretty sure it was the ghost of the Wolf."

Rory tilted his head. "Ghost? Did ye actually see it, A-by?"

"I swear it, Rory. If only you'd been there," Abby said, "as soon as Finlay killed him, this creepy black shadow thing peeled from his body. Then it started howling and flying all around Finlay, but he acted like he couldn't see it. And, it sounded like the thing that chased us." Abby paused, tapping a finger against her chin. "You know, I bet his ghost has been hanging around the forest for hundreds of years. It probably recognized us in my time." Abby's eyes grew big. "That's why it called us murderers and thieves!"

Rory nodded his head, "Seems a reasonable explanation, A-by. If ye say ye saw it, I believe ye." He looked around the chamber and pointed to the Book of Shay. "Ye best secure the book in yer bag, A-by. Then let us find Finlay. We should stay here no longer."

Abby nodded at Rory's logic, then squatted, grabbing her backpack and slipping the book into its largest pouch. As she zipped the bag shut, a welcome warmth washed over her. "Finlay!" Abby exclaimed as she jumped up and whirled around to find her white warrior standing mere inches away. She pulled his muzzle to her face, rubbing her cheek against his, but gasped as she glanced at his foreleg. "You're still bleeding," she cried.

A confused grumble entered Abby's mind. *What do you mean 'still,' child? You could not have known of my injury.*

Abby released her hold on the dog and bent to inspect his wound. "Like I was telling Rory," she replied, "when the Wolf slashed my leg, I must have passed out, and I think I had an out-of-body experience." She looked up to meet Finlay's eye. "I could float around and see things, like a ghost, I guess, but I was still alive." Abby stood straight as she continued. "I saw you clobber that nasty Wolf. I was even calling out to you, but you acted like you couldn't hear me."

Finlay snorted and shifted his weight to his hind legs. *What you say confuses me, Lass, allow me time to consider its meaning.* Pausing for a moment to reflect, he rumbled through Abby's mind again. *This does explain the overwhelming sensation I had that you were near. Indeed, I did not hear you, but now I know it was your presence I felt. Why and how you experienced this, I do not know. Perhaps in time, the meaning will become clear.* Finlay lowered his head and sniffed Abby's leg. *How is it you are no longer injured, Lass? I feared the worst.*

Abby smiled at Rory as she answered. "You probably won't believe it, but Rory healed me," she shrugged, "or at least his sword did." Abby waved a dismissive hand through the air. "I don't care how he did it, just that he did."

Finlay stepped toward the Scotsman, lowering his head into a deep bow. *Tell Rory I am forever grateful. I am twice now in his debt.* Rory took a cautionary step back, unsure of Finlay's action.

Abby giggled. "It's okay, Rory, Finlay's just saying 'thanks' for saving me." Abby paused, realizing her oversight. "Hey! You should heal Finlay," she said, pointing to the dog's injured leg. "That's got to hurt."

Finlay huffed as he straightened to his full height, holding his foreleg aloft. *My needs are of no concern right now. Your father's safety must be realized. We must leave at once.*

"No way, fuzzball," Abby said, rolling her eyes. "Sure, we need to get out of here and save my dad, but you can't go around with gross, bloody holes in your leg!" She turned to Rory, jerking a thumb toward the dog. "He's being stubborn now. Thinks it's okay to leave his leg like that."

Rory grimaced as he leaned in to examine Finlay's wounds. "Aye, A-by. It will no' do to leave his leg as it is." He paused, uncertainty filling his eyes. "But I'm no' sure how I even healed ye. I'm afraid I may no' be able to do it again," he admitted.

"You have to at least try, Rory," Abby replied with a softened voice, "you'll never know if you don't. And have more confidence in yourself. I think you can do it."

Rory's face flushed. Whether from embarrassment or pride, Abby was uncertain. He grunted with a smile and stepped close to the dog. Kneeling next to Finlay's leg, Rory locked eyes with the powerful canine before him. "I must place me hand upon your leg."

Finlay nodded, but Rory glanced to Abby for affirmation.

Abby giggled. "It's okay, Rory, go ahead, he's not going to eat you."

Rory looked back to the wound with determination. Holding his sword low, he placed his left hand over the damaged area of Finlay's leg. Relaxing his shoulders, Rory stared at the sword. When nothing happened, he reasserted his grip on the hilt and readjusted the placement of his hand. "It's no' working," he said, frustrated.

"Well," Abby blurted when Rory turned to look at her, "you were pretty emotional when you healed me, maybe that's what it takes." Seeing Rory's eyes widen larger than she thought possible, Abby gulped. *Oh geez. I pretty much just admitted to hearing what he said earlier, and from the look on his face, he meant it.* Abby felt her cheeks flush. *He...he really loves me?*

Rory turned quickly back to Finlay's leg. "Aye, A-by," he said, clearing his throat as a distraction, "this could be, but I do no' have a strong connection with him."

Abby pushed her thoughts of the Scotsman aside and focused, "So think about how much the fur face means to me. I'd be devastated if the Wolf had done to him what he did to the Wolf. Use that as your source of emotion."

Rory tightened his forehead and nodded. Concentrating, he closed his eyes and lowered his head.

Finlay blinked at Abby. *We are wasting time, Lass.*

Abby scrunched her face in return. *Just a second! Give him a chance.*

As the thought rolled from her mind, a brilliant blast of yellow exploded from the sword, traveling along Rory's body. A tingling excitement encompassed Abby seeing the power flow from Rory's sword first hand. "Wow!" she exclaimed when the light retreated to its resting place. "Cool, Rory," Abby beamed. "I knew you could do it."

Rory pulled his hand from the dog's leg, not convinced he had succeeded. When he peeled the last finger away, a wide grin spread across his face. There were no longer any remnants of the Wolf's blow.

Finlay sniffed his leg, snorted approval, and lowered his head in a long bow. This time, Rory needed no translation to understand the dog's gratitude.

Finlay stood tall and stamped his forelegs. *Now we must leave before we are discovered again.*

No arguments here, Abby thought, swinging her pack into place and cinching the straps. She turned to Rory as he sheathed his sword. "Ready to go save my dad?"

"Aye," Rory nodded, reaching for Abby's hand.

Abby interlocked her fingers with Rory's, taking care not to lose grip. "Alright, let's go." Abby chewed at the corner of her lip. "I guess you should take us back to the morning after we left. Don't know how all this time hopping impacts things, but we'd better at least try to keep it in line."

Finlay snorted. *Aye. As you wish, little one.* The dog tilted his head, winking playfully as he searched Abby's mind. *And Lass, I told you he fancies you.*

Abby groaned as she sunk her hand into Finlay's fur, wishing for parental control over what thoughts her magical dog could and could not access. *Just take us home!*

9

*A*bby tapped on the locked door to the shop, concerned the disheveled appearance of both herself and Rory would draw unwanted attention. A pair of aged eyes peered through the side window, and moments later, the door to Fletcher's Finds swung open. Mrs. MacTavish, Agatha, Victoria, and Sage stood in an anxious group just inside the door. As four sets of apprehensive eyes took in the sight before them, a collective din filled the room. Victoria rushed forward and patted Abby from head to toe.

"Oh my sweet," she cried, stepping back. "What happened? Are you hurt?" She ushered the group inside as she continued her motherly concern. "You, you're covered in blood." Victoria raised a hand, holding the back of it to her forehead as if she were flushed. "And your pants. Why are they shredded?" Her eyes widened when she took in the state of Rory's tunic. "Rory! Your shirt." The spectacle proved too much for Victoria; she leaned against the front counter for support. "What on earth happened to you both?" she asked, drawing in a calming breath. "I knew I shouldn't have allowed you children to go off on your own."

Abby stopped herself from her typical, defiant eye roll. "Mom," she replied soothingly, "it's okay. We're okay."

Sage snorted at her sister's declaration. "Well, it certainly looks like you weren't okay at some point." Sage crossed her arms. "Mind explaining why there's blood all over your jeans?"

Abby tensed her shoulders, uncertain how much she should reveal. "Well. Okay. You're right. We ran into some trouble," she paused before continuing, "but Finlay and Rory kept me safe."

Sage tapped a foot in response.

Abby ignored her sister's reaction and continued, swinging her backpack from her shoulder. "But most importantly," she said, placing the bag on the floor and unzipping the main pouch, "we found this." Abby pulled the Book of Shay from her backpack and held its golden cover proudly out for everyone to see. As Abby hoped, attention shifted from her ruined clothes to the book.

"Oh, dearie me," Mrs. MacTavish exclaimed. "May I?" she asked, motioning with her hands.

Abby nodded and handed the book to the shopkeeper.

Mrs. MacTavish shuffled off around the counter, moved the keyboard aside, and placed the book in front of the computer screen. She studied the ornate cover as Abby, Sage, Victoria, and Agatha crowded in around her. Rory stretched his lean frame over the counter to observe from a distance while Finlay hovered behind Abby. Abby glanced over her shoulder with a smile and reached absentmindedly behind her to tickle Finlay's chest.

The shopkeeper opened the cover and began to flip the first few pages. An intricate border, mirroring the elements of the tree on the cover, adorned each of the pages, which were otherwise devoid of any script. The group fell silent when Mrs. MacTavish turned the next page. A lavish tree with grand roots etched in metallic gold commanded their attention. The roots encompassed an elegant script below the base of the tree. Abby leaned in, squinting at the foreign writing. "I've never seen words like that," she said, looking from one group member to the next. "Can anybody read it?"

One by one, each onlooker agreed they could not decipher the strange writing.

Mrs. MacTavish flipped through the pages again, albeit at a faster rate. The unusual script continued throughout the book, accompanied by drawings of random trees, plants, and animals.

Abby sighed, "So much for figuring out what's so special about this book."

"Speaking of that," Sage interjected, "have we forgotten we need to respond to the kidnapper's email?"

Abby yawned, the impact of her most recent adventure taking its toll on her system. "Ah, geez," she mumbled, "I'd better do it right away."

"I got this, Abby," Sage replied, after scrutinizing her sister's exhausted state. "You need to clean yourself up and take a nap." She gave Rory a quick once-over. "Same with your friend. Let's get some of Dad's clothes for him."

Abby sighed. As much as she hated to agree with her sister, Sage was right. She and Rory looked a fright. Fresh clothes and a quick nap were sound advice. "I guess you're right, but only if Rory's okay with it," she replied, looking to the Scotsman.

Rory shrugged and examined himself. He grimaced and his eyes grew large as he noticed for the first time the bloody handprints smeared along the front of his tunic. Rory raised his head. "Aye. Would be an honor if yer faither might have somethin' to share with me." He paused, doubt filling his eyes. "That is if ye're certain he would voice no distaste."

Abby snorted. "Trust me. Dad will not mind." Slipping an arm around her mother's waist, Abby pressed in for a brief hug. "Want to go to the cottage with us, maybe help Rory find some clothes?"

Victoria rubbed her daughter's arm. "Of course, my sweet," she said, with an added squeeze to Abby's shoulder, "let's get the pair of you cleaned up."

Abby released her embrace and motioned for Finlay to scoot out of the way. As she and her mother rounded the counter, Agatha stepped in line behind them. "I shall help ye with the boy. Experience says an extra set of hands won't hurt," she said, winking at Rory.

Abby giggled, thinking back to their ordeal in the cave. The memory of Rory in a dress was one she would not soon forget.

"Come on." Abby tugged at Rory's elbow as she headed toward the door. "We'll pick out some clothes for you; then we can take turns at a shower. I'll show you how to work the faucets." Rory simply nodded with a blank expression.

Abby paused before stepping out into the morning sun. "Keep that book safe no matter what, Sage. And swear you'll come get me the second you hear anything."

Sage clicked away on the keyboard. "Already sending a reply. Just go get some sleep," she said, raising her eyes from the monitor, "Mrs. MacTavish and I will take care of everything."

✳✳✳

Once she freshened up, Abby pulled on a set of her softest lounge wear and tumbled onto her bunkie-board bed. Sinking into her pillow, she fluffed her comforter, tucking it under her chin. Finlay curled himself into an over-sized ball at the foot of the bed with a soft sigh. In the distance, Abby could hear the grumblings of Rory as her mother and Agatha attempted to find something of her father's that might fit his lean frame. *Wonder if Dad still has that outfit he wore when we went to the Minnesota Renaissance Fair last year.* With that as a last thought, Abby drifted off into a deep and tranquil sleep.

After what seemed like mere moments, Abby awoke to the sound of someone calling her name, and the sensation of someone kneeling on her mattress. She cracked an eye open and groaned. Rory sat on the edge of the bed, leaning over her with an anxious look. "Ugh," she mumbled. "What d'ya want, Rory, and why are you in my room?"

"Apologies for wakin' ye, A-by, but ye must dress yerself." Rory motioned toward the bookstore. "There is news about yer faither. The others request yer presence."

Abby sat up, casting her blankets aside. She rolled from the bed and stood, combing fingers through her chestnut curls. "Well, what'd they say?"

Rory shook his head. "Nothin' more, A-by. Was only told to fetch ye."

Abby paused to clear her mind. As she did, she realized Rory looked different. She chuckled. "Guess you're a better fit for my dad's clothes than I thought."

Rory looked at his waist and fiddled with the leather straps of his scabbard, ensuring it was secure. He lifted his head with a grin and posed, hands on hips. "What do ye think, A-by? Was wary at first but am most humbled for the new clothin'."

Abby giggled at Rory's expression. His scabbard cinched a beige, silken tunic at the waist. Billowing arms and a v-cut neck completed the look Abby would expect to see on the upper half of a medieval Scotsman. But, his bottom half told a different story. Her father's khaki utility pants, with two side pockets on each pant leg, were perhaps an inch too short for Rory's long legs, but she thought no one would notice, as he was wearing them over his hunting boots. "Not bad, Rory," Abby acknowledged. "But I need you to leave now," she added, gesturing toward the door.

Rory let his arms go limp at his sides, the smallest of frowns forming at the corners of his mouth.

Abby held back a snort. "Rory. I have to change clothes. You don't think I'm going to do that while you watch, do you?"

Rory's face flushed. "Oh. Aye," he replied, failing to hide his embarrassment. "I shall wait for ye across the way then, A-by."

As Abby watched Rory turn to leave, a soft yawn and smacking of lips startled her. She turned to see Finlay stand, stretch, and shake the sleep from his body. He was so quiet, she had forgotten her white warrior kept watch over her. "You too, fuzzball," she said, reaching out to stroke his lush coat, "a girl needs her privacy sometimes."

Finlay snorted with a low bow. *As you wish, Lass.* Then with a crackle of the air, he disappeared.

✱✱✱

Abby stared at the computer screen; her heart raced as she read the words aloud for the third time. "Bring the book to the following location at 9:00 pm on this night: N56 58'36.04" W3 47'23.77". Send anyone but the youngest child, and the Keeper of Books dies. Send any enforcers, and the Keeper of Books dies. Any foolery, and the Keeper of Books dies."

No one spoke, the words weighing heavy.

"Anyone else find the wording of this message odd?" Sage questioned, breaking the silence.

"Aye, perhaps so," Mrs. MacTavish agreed. "I imagine the scoundrel is referrin' to the police constables when they say not to bring any enforcers. Quite peculiar if ye ask me."

Victoria moved to stand beside Abby at the computer. "And to demand my youngest be the only one to deliver the book. They're out of their minds if they think I'm going to send Abby off by herself into harm's way. It's absurd."

Abby sighed, bringing her brows together. "Well, regardless, we need to figure out what these numbers mean. I think it's a GPS location." With several clicks of the mouse, she opened the Google Earth app and copy/pasted what she hoped were longitude and latitude coordinates. The picture of the globe rotated and zoomed in, a red placement marker indicating her goal. She hovered the mouse over the marker. "Huh. Says it's a place called Airehart Falls."

Victoria leaned in. "Are there any pictures?"

"Sure I can find some on the Internet," Abby replied as she minimized the app and Googled the name. "There," she said, clicking on the images link and selecting the first picture.

A modest waterfall tumbled thirty feet below to a murky, green lagoon. Unforgiving crags lined either side of the pool while jagged rocks jutted randomly from the cliff face visible in the photograph. A footbridge spanning from cliff to cliff allowed travelers to view the waterfall straight on, and from a safe distance. It was a view Abby felt she could appreciate, were it under different circumstances.

Letting a deep breath out, Abby called to Finlay. *Come check out this picture. I'll need you to take me there.*

Finlay rounded the counter, holding his head just over those of Abby and her mother. *Your elders will not allow this, young one. Do not pretend you did not hear your mother's wishes.*

Abby groaned softly. *Yeah, I heard her. But how else does she expect to save Dad? Besides, I'm not going alone. You and Rory are coming with me.*

Finlay puffed hot air against the back of Abby's head. *Do not dismiss the warning of the message. I fear the presence of the boy and myself will jeopardize the safety of your father. Take great care in the plan you devise.*

Abby reached back to ruffle Finlay's chest. *It's simple. The three of us go early, check the place out from a distance where we're sure no one will see you. There's got to be some places to hide around there. When it hits 9:00 pm, I'll make the trade. The book for my dad. You guys will be there to cover my back, in case anything goes wrong. And if it comes to that, we'll figure things out. It's the only way. It will work.*

Finlay shifted his weight from paw to paw. *I do not favor dismissing the wishes of your mother, Lass. But with present complexity, there may be no other solution.*

Satisfied with her idea, Abby broached the matter with her mother. "So, Mom," she began, turning to Victoria. "Would you agree it sounds like if we don't follow what the email says, Dad will get hurt?"

Victoria was silent for a moment. "Well," she replied slowly, "yes. It's a serious and complicated situation."

"Right," Abby nodded, "so we should do what they say." Abby straightened her shoulders, "I'll deliver the book."

Sounds of disapproval from the elder women filled the room, causing Abby to sigh.

"Just wait," Abby implored, "hear me out for a second."

With a stern look, Victoria placed a hand on Abby's. "Alright. Tell me your thoughts, young lady, though I expect I will not like them one bit."

Excitement churned in Abby's stomach—the chance to save her father. She just needed her mom to trust her abilities. "I'll take the book and swap it for Dad. But,"

Abby explained, anticipating her mother's objections, "I won't be alone. Rory and Finlay will go too."

Victoria frowned. "Then your father will be in danger as the message says you must go alone."

"I know," Abby replied, "but they'll hide out of the way somewhere. The kidnapper will never see them. Look," she said, pointing to the computer screen. Abby opened a second picture of the falls. "See here, in the background? There's lots of hills around the waterfall—plenty of places for them to duck out of the way."

Victoria released a long, slow breath. "I don't like this, and it's against my better judgment," she said, looking to Rory and then to Finlay, "but it seems the three of you are quite capable of taking care of yourselves."

Abby's heart skipped a beat. "So you're good with this then?"

Sage interjected, "Mom. Really?"

Victoria raised a hand, stopping Sage short. "We have little choice. If this is how it needs to happen to bring my dear Jonathon back, then I," she paused, "we must put our faith in Abby again. She is a strong, young woman, in every capacity." Victoria concluded with a grin directed at her youngest, "She did, after all, save me."

"Aye," Agatha agreed. "Let us not forget Abby saved many from those wretched faerie brothers."

"And she returned with the Book of Shay," Mrs. MacTavish added. "As dangerous as it may be, and as much as me better sense tells me, I have faith in the lass to bring our dear Mr. Fletcher home."

Rory cleared his throat and gestured toward Victoria. "I shall see no harm comes to yer daughter, and trust yer husband shall return to his family," Rory crossed an arm over his chest, "to this I swear."

"Well," Mrs. MacTavish said with a curt nod, "let us not worry on this any further. All will be well, Victoria, as what must be done must be done. Now," she turned her attention to Abby and Rory, "let's get ye young 'uns fed. Would be wrong to send you off without a proper meal."

Abby smiled as her mother stepped away to aid Mrs. MacTavish. *Well, that was way easier than I thought,* Abby giggled to herself.

Finlay brushed up against Abby's backside. *Do not be so quick to celebrate, Lass. We do not know what dangers await us.*

Yeah, yeah. You're right, but at least we can prepare ourselves a little bit. Abby motioned for Rory to join her at the computer. "Let's check out the terrain with Google Earth," she said as he rounded the counter and slipped past Finlay. "You've definitely seen nothing like this, Rory, it's really cool."

As Abby explained what they were looking at, Mrs. MacTavish distracted them with an aromatic plate of fresh scones. "Here ye are, Dearies. I'll have mince and tatties ready for ye in a wee bit." She shuffled off to her private quarters but paused to turn back. "And for you too," she said, pointing to Finlay. "We shall keep ye well fed. Don't need ye huntin' any of the local's sheep." Mrs. MacTavish chuckled to herself as she disappeared into the back room.

Abby snorted at Finlay. Popping a chunk of scone into her mouth, she continued pointing out areas around the waterfall. Through her mouthful of warm delight, she mumbled, "We'll leave at 8:00pm sharp."

10

*T*onight more than ever, Abby felt grateful for the rolling hills, rocky outcrops, and deep valleys of the land she now called home. She instructed Finlay to transport them one-half mile north of the waterfall. They would hike along the stream until the cascade was in sight, then investigate the surrounding landscape for the best hiding place.

The group traveled in silence for a half hour, each lost in their own thoughts. At the sound of water crashing upon rocks, Abby raised her hand as she came to an abrupt stop and whispered over her shoulder, "Hold up, guys. I think we're close."

"Aye, A-by, we must be wary with our movements now."

Finlay brushed along Abby's leg and crouched to the ground. He lifted his muzzle upward and sniffed. After several moments, he entered Abby's mind. *He is here, Lass. Close. I detect his scent.*

Abby's stomach lurched. *My dad. I need to see my dad.* Abby rushed forward, intent on climbing the closest hill.

Rory reached out and grabbed Abby by the elbow, bringing her to a halt. "What are ye doin', A-by? We must no' move with haste."

Abby groaned, knowing Rory was correct. "Finlay says he can smell my dad. We need to get to higher ground. I have to see him," she cried, "I need to know he's okay."

"Very well then, Lass," Rory replied, examining the area around them. "There," he said, pointing to a rocky hill ahead and to their left. "We shall survey from atop that ridge. Follow me," he directed to both Abby and Finlay.

Rory hunched and moved in silence from one thicket to the next until they stood at the base of the intended hill. Abby could see it would be the perfect hiding place. The sides of the ridge curved back toward them, creating a protective barrier, a half-moon to shelter the group. The crest of the hill appeared to level out just enough to allow a secure spot to lie flat.

Abby smiled as she began to climb. "Good choice, Rory."

Rory grunted and stepped ahead of Abby, testing each foothold, showing the safest route to take. Finlay followed close behind with careful movements. Rory reached the top first, stretching a firm hand for Abby to grasp.

Pulling herself to the crest, Abby laid flat next to Rory and peeked over to view the stream. The sun was just making its descent beneath the horizon to their right, providing sufficient light for Abby to follow the flow of the swift water until it tumbled below to its fate in the waiting ravine. Remembering the bridge in the photos, Abby raised her chin until her eyes locked onto the structure spanning the chasm. "What the..." Abby squinted, daring to raise her head higher. She clamped a distraught hand over her mouth. "No," she sobbed, pulling her hand away, "it can't be."

"What is it, A-by?" Rory asked, straining his eyes in the same direction, "what do ye see?"

Abby slipped an arm from her backpack, rolled to her side, and slid the pack in front of her. She rummaged through a small pouch, producing a pair of compact binoculars. Lifting the oculars to her eyes, she replied, "It's my dad. They've tied him to the bridge." The words stuck in her throat. "To the outside of the railing! He's, he's just hanging there!" Abby passed the binoculars to Rory. "Here, look."

Hesitantly, Rory accepted the field glasses and mimicked Abby's prior actions. Upon placing the lenses to his eyes, he jerked his head back in disbelief, grunted, and peered through them again. "Aye, A-by, it is so. It appears his arms and legs are each lashed to the bridge." With an amazed look, Rory handed the binoculars back to Abby.

Finlay, having stayed back from the crest for lack of space, inched his way to the top of the hill and squeezed in next to Abby. He stretched his neck just enough to allow him a view of the situation. Blinking rapidly several times, he snorted his disfavor. *This will complicate matters, Lass.*

Abby secured her bag to her back again, moving as if to slide her way down the hill. "I have to get down there. I can't leave him like that."

Rory caught hold of Abby's backpack, stopping her in place. "Be sensible, Lass. There are unseen dangers here. Ye must have yer head about ye."

Abby growled deep in her throat at herself. "You're right," she replied, swiveling back around to face the bridge. "Smart to survey the area first," she continued, looking through the binoculars. "Maybe I can find where the bad guy is hiding."

As Abby explored the terrain with her field glasses, Finlay lifted his head and tested the air again. After several moments, the dog let out a frustrated sigh. *It is strange, child. I detect no other human scent beyond that of your father. Not now, and none that have traversed this land in recent times.*

Abby lowered her binoculars. "Weird." She leaned her head toward Rory. "Finlay just said he doesn't smell anyone besides my dad." She handed the lenses to Rory again. "Tell me what you think. I didn't see anyone anywhere. Granted, there are lots of places to hide down there, but still." Abby pulled her phone briefly out of her hoodie pocket to check the time. "And it's almost 9:00; you'd think whoever set this up would be waiting by the bridge."

"Aye, A-by. I agree with yer assessment. I see no movement." Rory handed the binoculars back to Abby. With a quick nod, Abby swiveled her bag to the front and stored the precious tool.

"Okay," Abby's voice turned serious. "I'm going down." Hesitating, she rubbed her chin. "Hmm. Maybe I can even free him before anyone shows up, or at least get him off that railing. That can't feel good. I'll set the book out on the bridge where it's visible, so if someone's watching, they'll hopefully understand I'm not trying anything funny, like a show of good faith."

Rory placed a gentle hand on Abby's shoulder. "Move wisely, A-by. If ye fear yer in danger, tell Finlay so he may bring me to yer side." Rory paused, a thought coming to mind. "A-by, what if Finlay took us to yer faither's side right this moment, before any foe appears? We could free him and be gone, book and all!"

Uncertainty filled Abby's eyes. "I don't know, Rory." She glanced back to her father's wriggling form. "It's too risky. I'm supposed to go alone. If the kidnapper shows up before we free him, they could shoot him, or us, if they have a gun that is. I think the smart thing to do is follow their instructions. It's probably the only way we all get out of here in one piece, and honestly, I don't care about the stupid book. They can have it. I just want my dad back."

Rory lowered his head with a bob. "If this is what ye wish, A-by, I will abide by it." He placed his hand on hers and squeezed it. "Please be careful, Lass."

"Don't worry. I promise to be careful." Abby's face lit up. "Hey," she said removing the binoculars from her bag again and passing them back to Rory. "You can keep watch for me. If you see anyone coming, tell Finlay, and he can relay it to me. At least that way, no one will sneak up on me."

Finlay snorted. *Excellent idea, Lass. I will be by your side the moment anything appears awry.* Nudging his head against her face, he added. *And please do as the boy asks. Be careful and think before you act.*

Abby crinkled her nose at the dog and ran her hands through his coat. "I swear to you both," she declared, "I will be careful." She stopped to roll her eyes. "But now we're just wasting time." Abby adjusted her pack and looked to the base of the hill. "I have to go," she said, sidestepping her way down the ridge. With careful steps, Abby reached the bottom. She glanced back to the top and returned Rory's brief nod.

Hunching over, Abby made her way around the right side of the hill. Her eyes in constant movement, she scanned the terrain ahead for any sign of life. She followed the stream, using what clumps of bushes she could as temporary cover. The sound of crashing water intensified as she approached the cliff. Abby stopped and squatted behind a large boulder to plan her route. She estimated her father was one hundred feet from her, but she'd need to travel twice as far to skirt around the ravine and cross part of the bridge. Identifying several spots to hide her presence, Abby drew in a deep breath to calm her racing heart. *You can do this, Abby.*

With her eyes fixed on a dense group of bushes in the distance, Abby sprang from her concealment and ran in a half crouch as fast as she could. Taking longer than she cared for, Abby pushed into the thicket, hands in front of her face. Once finding an open section within the bushes, she leaned over, palms on knees, and worked to control her breathing. Feeling collected, Abby stood tall and pushed her way through to the edge of the underbrush. She could see her father clearly now, and her lips quivered in reaction to his appearance. He looked tired, his skin paler than usual, a smudge of dirt on his cheek. He jerked his lean frame against the bindings and issued a sigh of defeat, lowering his chin to his chest.

Abby stepped from the bushes and squatted to the ground. Her eyes darted in all directions—still no sign of the kidnapper. *Hmm. Maybe I don't need to hide.* Abby continued crouching, contemplating her best move. *He looks miserable. He needs to know I'm here.* Hoping her father would hear her, she pursed her lips to mimic the call of a Northern Cardinal, one of their favorite birds; they'd practice imitating its call together when she was little. She looked on in anticipation after the last sweet sound left her lips, but there was no response from her father. He hung inert, his chin resting on his chest. Abby cocked an ear toward the falls, deciding the noise of the water must have drowned out her signal. She puckered her lips a second time and whistled the melodic call with greater force. This time, her father's head snapped up as he recognized the bird call. Looking to the left, he searched the landscape. Abby repeated the call in brief, knowing her father's thoughts; Cardinals are sometimes difficult to spot, regardless of their striking plumage. Her tactic worked. Jonathon Fletcher jerked his head to the right and began scanning the trees and bushes. When his eyes reached the thicket where Abby crouched, she flapped her arms. As she hoped, her movement proved enough to catch his attention.

Jonathon stretched his head toward Abby as if to confirm his youngest stood before him. His eyes grew large, fear evident within them. He repeated the word 'no' as Abby wiggled her fingers at him to say hello. She took a last glance around her and sprinted toward the bridge, her legs in high gear. Pumping her arms, Abby rounded the foot of the bridge and continued to head toward her father, her footfalls echoing throughout the chasm. She skidded to a halt upon reaching him. "Dad!"

"No! No, Abs, no," he cried in response. "This is no good, kiddo. You're in danger. You must hide. Now!"

Abby rolled her eyes and gestured at his bound limbs. "Well, this is no good either. I'm here to free you." Abby's expression brightened at a single thought tucked away in her mind. *Mom.* Her stomach danced with a mixture of nerves and excitement. She reached up to test the straps around her father's right arm. "Dad," she blurted, "there's something I have to tell you. You will not believe this, but Mom..."

Finlay rumbled into Abby's mind, cutting her announcement short, and overwhelming her with a sense of urgency she'd never experienced. *Lass. Behind you. You are no longer alone.*

11

*A*bby's stomach lurched; she indeed sensed the presence of another on the bridge. She dropped her hands from the railing and rotated her body to the right, fear consuming her as she imagined a giant troll considering her for his next snack. When her eyes beheld the strange form before her, she jerked back, pushing herself against the rail.

Ten feet to her left, in the middle of the bridge, stood a tall, spindly woman. Everything about her was odd, or off, in Abby's eyes. She wore a metallic bodysuit, like something Abby would expect to see on a trapeze artist. The material enhanced her muscular, yet lanky frame. The stranger's hair, cropped short and sleek, glimmered an opal white in the setting sun. Her high cheekbones and strong jawline drew Abby's attention from her eyes for a moment. *Her eyes,* Abby thought as she stared in wonderment. She strained to determine the color of the woman's eyes. They seemed to shift throughout the spectrum. Abby froze, confused as to who, or what, stood in front of her.

The bizarre figure cracked her knuckles in turn as she examined the girl. Starting at Abby's boots, she lifted her chin, taking in every aspect of the newcomer. When her eyes alighted upon the golden curl in Abby's hair, she stepped back with a piercing hiss. "Manta," she spat, disgusted. The woman advanced, bringing herself several feet closer to Abby and her father. "What is your kind doing here? I should dispatch you at once."

Abby pressed her head close to her father's and whispered out the side of her mouth. "Who is she, Dad? What the heck is she talking about?"

Jonathon wrenched his head as far as he could, seeking out the woman. "Mallena," he addressed without wavering, "come now, there's no need for violence." He paused and jerked his head toward Abby. "This is my youngest, Abby, as you requested."

Mallena took an apprehensive step toward her prisoner, refusing to move her gaze from Abby's hair. Abby groaned to herself. *What is it with these creeps and my golden curl?*

"Abby, is it?" Mallena uttered, pulling a strange, curved blade from seemingly nowhere. "Stand over there," she directed, pointing away from and to the left of Jonathon.

Abby glanced at her dad, and upon seeing his slight nod, moved in the general direction Mallena indicated.

"Farther," barked the woman, displeased with where Abby planted her feet.

Abby cringed, scooting farther from her father.

"Good," Mallena said. "Now show me the book," she demanded, touching the end of her short, sickle-shaped blade to the tip of a finger. "For your father's sake, you had best brought the book."

"Dad?" Abby called out, her voice wavering.

"Of course she has the book," Jonathon retorted. "Show her the book, Abs," he replied, turning his head to find her. Jonathon nodded encouragingly. "Go on, kiddo, do as Mallena says and everything will be fine."

Abby looked back and forth between her father and Mallena. "O, okay then," she said, fixing on their adversary. "It's in my bag," she explained, pointing to her back, "so I'm going to slide it off my shoulders and set it down in front of me." Abby paused for a moment, then did as she described, all the while keeping constant watch on Mallena. With the backpack propped in front of her on the bridge, Abby unzipped the main pouch. She retrieved the Book of Shay and stood straight, holding it cover-out.

"See," she said, "the book."

Mallena's freakish eyes flashed an array of green. She hissed with approval and pointed at the bridge with her blade. "There. Set it there. Then return to where you stand," she ordered.

"Go ahead, Abs, do what she says," Jonathon said, relief evident in his voice.

Abby nodded her understanding, stepping forward to place the book where instructed. Once done, she walked backward to her bag and shouldered it.

Mallena pointed her blade at Abby. "Do not move." Lowering her weapon, Mallena streaked forward, scooped up the book, and streaked back to where she stood originally. She stroked the cover, lost in thought. "Shay," she cooed. Pulling her gaze away, she stared at Abby with cold, hard eyes. "Now what to do with you, Manta?"

Abby fought to control the frustration building inside her. *Why does she keep calling me that? And why doesn't she leave? She got what she wanted. Take the dumb book and go already.*

A welcome tingling washed through Abby's mind. *Tread carefully, Lass. Mind your thoughts and stay alert. I do not know what this creature is, but human she is not, of this I am certain.*

Mallena advanced toward Abby, her intentions becoming more apparent with every step. She twirled her weapon in front of her, clucking to herself.

Abby's knees quivered. She shuffled her feet backward and called out with her mind. *Finlay, I don't like this.*

"Yes," Mallena cackled, her eyes a strange, fiery crimson. "I don't believe you will leave here." The creature darted toward Abby, but a crackling in the air brought her to a stop.

Finlay and Rory roared onto the bridge, materializing behind Abby. Finlay stepped to Abby's side, his hackles raised and his teeth bared. A low growl emanated from deep within his chest.

Mallena shrieked at the sudden appearance. "More of your kind?" she spat. "How is this so?" She narrowed her eyes and glanced behind her at the helpless figure strapped to the bridge. She sneered, repeating familiar words. "Any trickery and the Keeper of Books dies." Mallena bolted to Jonathon, raising her blade.

Abby cried out and rushed toward her father. "Nooo!"

Rory drew his sword and chased after Abby, sending flames into the approaching night sky.

The air sizzled again as Finlay disappeared. Materializing to the right of Mallena, he prepared to clamp onto her arm.

But the collective effort was moments too late. In one fluid motion, Mallena struck out with her blade, first severing the straps on Jonathon's left leg, then left arm, then right arm. She swiped at the bindings around his right leg, but missed.

Jonathon wasn't expecting the sudden lack of tension on his aching limbs. With a surprised howl, he lurched forward, away from the bridge.

Mallena capitalized on the moment of ensuing chaos. She turned and sprang onto the opposite railing, clutching the book tight to her chest. Without a final look behind her, she squatted and rocketed herself toward the face of the cliff. She glided effortlessly to the rocky wall, securing a hold with only her free hand. Using the momentum of her swinging body, she flipped herself to solid ground atop the cliff. With two bounds, she disappeared around the nearest knoll.

Jonathon continued falling forward. Abby and Rory reached out for him, desperate to connect with any appendage. Abby screamed when they weren't fast enough.

A sickening crack filled the air, causing Abby's stomach to twist. Jonathon now dangled from the bridge, the strap around his right ankle saving him from plummeting head first into the lagoon. He cried out in agonizing pain and fell silent.

"Dad! Dad!" Abby wailed in between sobs. When her father didn't answer, she clutched Rory's tunic. "We have to pull him up. Now!"

Rory sheathed his sword as he contemplated the situation. He rubbed his chin for a moment and nodded to himself. "I shall climb down for him, A-by," he declared, unbuckling his sheath and placing his sword on the bridge. Pushing up the sleeves of his tunic, he gripped the rail.

"What? Are you crazy Rory? You might fall." Abby pulled at her hair. "There has to be a safer way," she lowered her voice to a whisper, "but I'm not sure how."

"I shall bring him to ye, A-by. Ye have me word. No further harm shall come his way," Rory said, as he straddled the railing.

Finlay nudged Abby in the back. *Let him do as he will, child. I see no other options. Let him see you trust his actions.*

Of course, you're right, Abby sighed. She strode forward to the rail as Rory swung himself over. "I trust you, Rory," she said, forcing a small smile. "Tell me how to help."

Rory suppressed a grand grin. "Get down on yer belly, A-by, in front of the lashings which bind yer faither's foot," he instructed without hesitation. "I shall lower meself to the bottom of the bridge. When I get there, I want ye to reach in between the lowest slats with yer left arm and loop yer elbow with me elbow."

Abby nodded, crouching down and sprawling herself out onto the walkway. She tilted her head up and watched as Rory lowered himself cautiously, board by board, until he was eye level with Abby. She drew a determined breath and, reaching her left arm through the bottom opening as far as she could, she hooked elbows with the Scotsman. Pulling her forearm toward her, she gripped the top of the lowest slat with the tips of her fingers. "Now what, Rory?"

Rory braced himself and released his left hand from the safety of the structure. He looked upon Jonathon's dangling form and attempted to reach the man's left hand. He grunted, wishing his own arms were several inches longer. "Sir Fletcher," he called, "ye must wake. Ye must give me yer hand."

Jonathon let out a weak moan.

"Dad," Abby yelled. "Listen to me. The voice you heard is my friend, Rory. He's going to pull you up, but he can't do it without your help. Try to reach his hand, Dad. But you've got to do it right away, I'm the only thing keeping Rory from falling, and he's getting heavy."

At the sound of his daughter's voice, Jonathon turned his head and looked up. His face was turning beet red; Abby feared he might lose consciousness.

Abby's stomach churned. "He needs motivation," she whispered to herself. "Dad?" she called. "Dad. You need to get home right away," Abby continued with a touch of authority. "You'll regret it if you don't. It's Mom." She paused for effect. "Dad. Mom's alive, and home, safe. She's waiting for you."

A sharp inhale came from below. "Victoria?" Jonathon croaked, his voice rimmed with a mixture of pain and elation. Turning his head again, he searched the sky until he locked eyes with Rory.

Rory nodded, motioning with his free hand. "She speaks the truth, Sir. I have seen her me-self."

Determination flowed across Jonathon's face. Twisting his torso, he raised his left arm behind him as high as he could, stretching with what little energy he could muster. And it was just enough.

Rory hooked several of Jonathon's fingers with his own and worked his hand into a wrist lock on the man's arm. When he felt confident his grasp would suffice, he looked up at Abby. "A-by, ye must free the binding on yer faither's leg. When ye do, do not let yer hold on me arm weaken or we shall both be doomed."

Abby gulped, the tension on her appendage becoming unbearable. "Uh, okay. But what happens then? How are you going to pull him up? I don't think he'll be able to climb on his own."

Rory bit the corner of his lip, his face lighting up. "Easy, A-by. As soon as ye release the bindin', grab hold of yer dog. Tell him to use his magic and place us on the bridge where we may attend to yer faither."

Abby nodded, appreciating Rory's quick wit. "Hear that, Finlay?" Abby called over her shoulder. "I need you next to me so I can grab your leg."

Finlay shook his body and moved to stand to Abby's right, parallel with the rail. *Aye, child. As long as your father's leg is free from the bridge, the suggestion is sound. But make haste, for the boy appears to be struggling.*

Abby glanced at Rory. His face showed evidence of great strain; veins along his temples bulged while his flesh turned a hue of purple-red. Abby focused on the rope attached to the wood. The thick fiber snaked its way around the lowest slat multiple times and trailed to Jonathon's ankle where it resulted in the same. Two knots, one on the wood and one on Jonathon's ankle, secured him to the structure. Abby studied the rope bound to the bridge before working the knot with her right hand.

"Hurry, A-by," Rory urged, amidst groans from Jonathon.

"I, I can't get it with one hand," Abby cried. She continued to struggle, tears forming in the corners of her eyes.

Finlay lowered his head, nudging Abby's hand from the slat. *I shall remedy this, Lass.*

Abby jerked her fingers away once she realized Finlay's intentions. He ripped into the rope with his right canine and lurched back before he gnawed with his incisors. He paused to smack his lips and peep through the barrier, then continued gnawing at the rope.

"It's working," Abby called out excitedly. "Just hold on, Dad, we're almost there."

With a final snort and shake of his head, Finlay severed the fibrous prison. As the rope curled back on itself, Finlay lurched his head toward Abby's hand. *Now, Lass!*

Abby grasped Finlay's ear and held her breath, hoping four bodies would end up back on the bridge. The familiar sensation of teleportation washed across Abby's body and in a blink, she found herself flopped upon the walkway. She raised her head to see Rory and her father still clasped together at the wrist, stretched out next to one another several feet away. Finlay stood over her. She could feel his concern. *Best to tend to your father's injury, Lass. I sense it to be serious.*

Abby scrambled to her father who laid flat on his back. It was clear to Abby he felt disoriented and confused with the sudden change of location. He lifted his head and considered the fiery, redheaded young man releasing his wrist.

"Huh, how'd we get on the bridge, Abs?" Jonathon asked, propping himself up on his elbows. Before anyone could consider how to answer, Abby's father noticed at once the enormous, snowy-white wolfhound trotting toward him. "Whoa. That's one big pup." Jonathon continued to stare, with part wonderment and part apprehension. "Please tell me you're acquainted with it and its sizable teeth, kiddo."

Abby snorted as she kneeled next to her father. "No worries, Dad, his name's Finlay. He's my new dog," she stated proudly.

Jonathon's eyes widened as he sat up and untied the remaining rope from his leg. "Your new dog? I don't recall discussing this, Abs."

Abby giggled. "Yup. Mom said I could keep him."

Jonathon's breath caught. "Victoria," her name trailed from his mouth, nearly inaudible. "So I wasn't hallucinating? I figured with all the blood rushing to my head I must've heard you wrong." He scooped up his daughter's hands, clasping them inside his own. "I knew it! I knew she wasn't dead. But how? Tell me everything, Abs." He paused. "Better yet, help me up and take me to her!"

Abby slipped her hands free and shifted to examine her father's ankle. "I don't know, Dad," she said, hiking up his pant leg. "Are you sure you can even walk? Your ankle looks swollen."

Jonathon attempted to rotate his foot. He sucked in a deep breath and released it slowly, combined with a soft moan. Raising his hands to either side, he motioned for help to stand. "Only one way to find out."

Rory and Abby scurried to offer their support. Each took an arm, and they hoisted Jonathon to his feet. Abby's father smiled at her as he balanced on his left leg and turned toward Rory. "Thanks," he said. "Rory, is it?"

Rory bowed with dramatic flair. "Aye. At yer service, Sir."

Jonathon smiled with curiosity at the young Scotsman. "Well then, let's get away from this miserable bridge," he said, taking a cautious step forward. Jonathon placed his full weight on his injured leg, only to draw it up with a painful exclamation. He gritted his teeth. "I believe my ankle is broken." He frowned with a sigh, "Sorry, Abs. Looks like I will slow our departure."

Sadness filled Abby. She hated seeing her father in pain. A realization came to her as she mulled over their current predicament. She gasped, turning to Rory. "Rory! You can heal him."

"Heal me? That's an astonishing statement," Jonathon said. "What's gotten into you, kiddo?"

Abby groaned to herself, knowing a long explanation was at hand. Would he believe the whole of her fantastic tale? "Dad, maybe you should lean against the side of the bridge for a bit." Abby stepped to the rail and patted it. "C'mere, I'll tell you a story," she encouraged, "but you've got to hear me out and not interrupt, okay? No matter how unbelievable it sounds, which it will, I guarantee it."

Jonathon chuckled at his daughter and hopped to the rail. "Very well, Abs. Let's hear this story of yours." He paused to smile. "It best be a good one."

Abby relaxed her shoulders and took a deep breath. "Okay. I'll sum this up as best I can," she replied, looking over her shoulder in the direction Mallena disappeared. "Don't want to chance that creepy whatever-she-is thing coming back."

Rory retrieved his sword, strapping the sheath to his waist while Abby retold their adventure.

"So Finlay here," she gestured to the dog, "used to be green and gooey looking, but that was because he was being held prisoner by two evil faerie brothers named Mavis and Tavis. See, Finlay has magical powers, and the brothers made him kidnap girls with golden curls," she explained, twisting her own curl around a finger. "Finlay came to me with a message. He said 'The Red King must set me free.'" Abby tapped her forehead with both index fingers. "We can talk to each other in our heads.

Telepathy, right?" She watched her father's changing expression as she continued. "Finlay can also travel through space and time, and when I found an old scroll in a cave in Caledonia, he took me back to Rory's time. I'm guessing the early 1300's."

Rory fidgeted as Abby caught her breath before continuing. "Someone stole Rory's father's sword," she said, pointing toward Rory's sheath, "and I agreed to help him find it, if he'd help me find the Red King. The sword was easy enough to track down, didn't take us long to get it back. But then I remembered the scroll, and Rory translated it for me. Turns out it was an ancient prophecy. And then these grimy thieves kidnapped me and took me to Mavis and Tavis. And, you won't believe this, Dad, but that's where I found Mom!" Abby sucked in another breath as excitement pulsed through her. "This whole time that we thought she was dead, she was trapped in a horrible cave in the past. She didn't fall into the Well of Fair Maidens after all!" She motioned to her white warrior. "Finlay saved her from hitting her head on it, but ended up kidnapping her in the process." Abby stopped, a serious look on her face. "He didn't have a choice, though. He had to do the faeries' bidding. And we've all forgiven him already, so don't be mad at him, Dad." She smiled at Finlay and wrinkled her nose. "Anyway, it turns out Rory is descended from the Red

King. So, he's the one I needed to find. Once he believed in himself, we were able to imprison the faeries inside the cave wall by placing Mrs. MacTavish's amulet—you know, the one she gave to Mom and then Mom gave to Sage—in a special indentation on Rory's sword." Abby thumbed where the necklace had hung at her throat, thinking back to the moment her sister passed it on to her. "After that, Finlay brought us home: me, Mom, Rory, Agatha—she's one of Mom's friends from the cave—and, oh yeah, Sage. Finlay had to bring Sage to the cave too, but she can tell you all about it." Abby stopped to suck in a giant breath, releasing it with an exaggerated sigh. "And there you have it." She pointed to Finlay and said, "magical dog," and then to Rory, "boy with magical sword who's related to the Red King."

Jonathon leaned against the rail in silence, contemplating what Abby hoped he wouldn't think to be an outlandish and improbable story. "The Red King," he said, astonished. He stared at Rory, studying his sword, then moved his gaze to Abby and spoke. "So it's true then? The Prophecy of Myst? The Red King?"

Abby opened her mouth to reply but clamped it shut, confused. "Well," she said eventually, "yes, it's all true, just as I've told it."

Jonathon reached out and placed a firm hand on Abby's shoulder. "The book," he warned, "we must get the Book of Shay back!"

Abby stood stunned. "What? I don't understand? What's the book got to do with anything? I flipped through it, and it's just a bunch of drawings of trees and animals with strange writing."

Jonathon glanced down and grimaced. He sucked in a calming breath before replying. "It was long rumored the Book of Shay contains secrets about the Red King, about his origins, perhaps, although the details are unclear. I'd been searching for it myself. I thought, well, I thought it might contain clues to finding your mother." He paused, allowing his eyes to drift to Rory's sword. "And if all is as you say, Abs," he said, connecting with his daughter's eyes again, "well, we simply cannot allow Mallena to keep it. My gut tells me there's something greater at play here."

Abby stared into the twilight, contemplating her father's words. *Could there really be secrets about the Red King in the book?* She glanced at Rory, wondering if he now regretted giving it up to save her father.

Jonathon hopped on his left leg, readjusting his stance. "Speaking of bones, my ankle is in need of a doctor."

Abby groaned, touching Rory's elbow. "I should've asked you to heal him while I talked. We're wasting time now, especially if we have to chase after the book again." She motioned to her father's ankle. "Would you mind trying?"

Rory nodded as he unsheathed his sword.

Jonathon pressed back against the rail, uncertain why the Scotsman drew his weapon.

Seeing her father's misgivings, Abby stood close beside him. "It's okay, Dad. Trust me on this. Rory will fix you up, but he's got to put his hand on your ankle for the magic to work."

Rory squatted in front of Jonathon's right leg, reaching his left hand toward the man's ankle. He glanced up at Abby and her father. His expression did nothing to hide his nervousness. Only after an encouraging nod from Abby did he continue. Rory looked back to the injury and cupped his hand around Jonathon's swollen ankle. He laid the sword flat on the bridge and gripped the hilt. Closing his eyes, Rory breathed deep and concentrated.

After a quiet minute, Jonathon nudged his daughter. "Nothing's happening, Abs," he whispered in her ear. "You sure about this?"

"Yes, I'm sure," she whispered back, "give him a chance."

Hearing the soft murmurs above him, Rory relaxed his posture and opened his eyes. He looked up at the pair, frustrated. "It's no' workin'. And I do no' know why."

"Try again, Rory," Abby replied with a cheery smile, "remember to find an emotional connection, like last time."

Rory bobbed his head. "Aye, Lass, I have no' forgotten. I shall try again."

Placing his hand back onto Jonathon's ankle, Rory again relaxed into a state of silent focus.

Abby released a tense breath after another unsuccessful minute. "It's not working, Rory. Are you sure you're concentrating hard enough?"

Rory's shoulders slumped as he removed his hand from Jonathon's leg. He stood, his face flushed. "Me humble apologies, Sir," he said, bowing his head. "I have failed ye." He sheathed his sword and turned to Abby with a frown. "I did nothin' different, A-by. I do no' understand."

Abby sighed, trying to hide her disappointment.

Sensing her mixed emotions, Finlay entered her mind. *There are always things which will remain a mystery. Be patient, child.*

Heeding Finlay's words, Abby met Rory's eyes and smiled. "It's okay, Rory. Maybe you need more practice."

She glanced at her dad. "Time for a trip to a hospital. The book will have to wait."

Jonathon shook his head. "Home first, then the hospital. If you recall," he said, winking at Abby, "I'd like to see my wife and oldest daughter." Turning toward Finlay, he eyed the wolfhound with a childlike curiosity. "Is your dog going to show me a trick and take us there?"

Abby snorted, motioning for Rory to take her hand. "It's a trick all right. I'll even let you initiate it." Abby intertwined the fingers of her free hand with those of her father.

Though exhausted, Jonathon's eyes twinkled with excitement. "Let me guess. I say a magical phrase?"

Abby grinned. "Nope, even easier. Just reach out and touch him, but don't let go."

Jonathon stretched his hand toward Finlay's chest, pausing as a thought came to mind. "You never mentioned how you found the book."

Abby tensed inside, calling out to Finlay to step into her father's grasp. "You don't want to know."

12

*A*bby requested Finlay transport them to outside the shop entrance at the current time. It was nearing 10:00 pm and Abby knew all would be quiet on the street. As she expected, there were lights on inside the bookstore. "Rory," she whispered, "help my dad walk, will you?" Rory nodded, positioned himself on Jonathon's ailing side, and offered his frame as support, wrapping his arm around Jonathon's back.

Abby tapped on the window to alert the occupants of their arrival. The door swung open; Mrs. MacTavish stood at the threshold, her eyes growing large. "Oh dearie me," she exclaimed, "Jonathon, you're injured!" She waved her hands excitedly, directing the group into the shop. Abby and Finlay stood aside, allowing Rory to guide Jonathon through the entrance. Following close behind, Abby surveyed the street before shutting and locking the door.

She turned to find Mrs. MacTavish encouraging her father to sit in a chair she had placed in front of him.

Sage popped her head out of the back storeroom. "Dad?" she called uncertainly as she continued to make her way up front. Seeing her father, she rushed to the chair and kneeled in front of him. "You're hurt! What happened?"

Jonathon squeezed his older daughter's shoulder, winking as he replied. "Just a scratch. Can't even feel it anymore."

Sage stared at her father's oversized ankle. "Dad. Be serious, that's more than a scratch. You need an x-ray. We should take you to the hospital."

Jonathon sighed. "Yes, the hospital is on my to-do list. But first," he said, peering to every corner of the shop, "I understand there's someone important waiting to see me." He squeezed Sage's shoulder again. "Where is she, Sage?" He questioned, his voice turning serious. "Where's your mother?"

Sage's eyes filled with warmth. "She's resting in Mrs. MacTavish's room. Her friend Agatha is watching over her." She glanced toward the room. "Want me to wake her up?"

Jonathon shook his head. "No, no. As eager as I am to see Victoria, let's allow her to sleep as much..."

A soft squeak, followed by unintelligible words mixed with sobs, caused every head to turn to its source.

Victoria filled the doorway to Mrs. MacTavish's private quarters. A shaking hand covered her mouth while tears spilled from her eyes. She rushed forward, rounding the front counter, stopping several feet in front of her husband. Her tears subsided, but a flow of emotion consumed her eyes—joy, uncertainty, a hint of fear.

Jonathon straightened up in the chair, clearing the lump from his throat. "My sweet Victoria. I never stopped believing. Hoping. Wishing. Never." He beckoned her with raised arms. "My love."

Victoria sobbed again as she flung herself into his arms, murmuring terms of endearment. To allow for a private reunion, the others retreated to the back of the shop.

Abby watched on, nodding her head and releasing a sigh. "I've never seen Dad this happy, even with a hurt foot."

Mrs. MacTavish dabbed at the corners of her eyes with her kerchief. "Of all things, I'd never imagine seein' such a sight. But tell us, Lass," she whispered, leaning toward Abby, "what happened to yer father? And what of his kidnapper?"

Abby closed her eyes for a moment, envisioning her father dangling from the bridge. Shivers shot along her spine. "His kidnapper. Well, I'm not sure how to describe her."

Agatha huffed. "A woman did this to him?"

Abby looked to Finlay, remembering his words. "Female's probably a better description, and her name is Mallena. Finlay doesn't think she's human. I guess he couldn't smell her, and she was pretty odd looking." She shrugged before continuing. "Anyway, Mallena strapped Dad to the outside of the bridge overlooking the waterfall. After I gave her the book, she intended to kill me, so Finlay and Rory had no choice but to help. That really boiled her blood. She freaked out and slashed the ropes holding Dad to the bridge, but missed the last one tied to his right ankle." Abby gestured toward her father, "that's how he hurt it. We're lucky, though, if Mallena hadn't missed that last rope..." Abby trailed off into silence as she watched her parents embrace.

"We need to go to the hospital," Sage said with a stern voice. "What if his ankle's broken?"

The shopkeeper nodded. "Aye, Sage, we best be gettin' him looked after."

Abby snorted. "Good luck getting him to go. He told me we have to get the book back. Plus," she said, pointing to her parents with a smile, "I don't think they'll be willing to let go of each other."

"What? Get the book back?" Sage tightened her lips while shaking her head. "Guess it shouldn't surprise me he'd say that, but it's ridiculous considering what just happened." Sage stomped toward the front of the shop. "Get the book back," she grumbled. Upon approaching her parents, Sage cleared her throat in an exaggerated manner. "Mom, sorry to interrupt, but we need to take Dad to the hospital. Like now."

Jonathon rubbed his wife's back as she removed her face from the curve of his neck. Victoria, looking relaxed in her husband's lap, wiped the remnants of the last tears from her eyes. "Yes, yes of course," she said, standing and smoothing her clothes. She leaned over to examine Jonathon's injury. "Oh, my love, it must be frightfully painful. Can you walk on it?"

Jonathon shook his head in response and motioned for Victoria to help him stand. Rising from the chair, he stroked her cheek with the back of his hand. "No, my love, but I imagine I can withstand the most brutal of miseries now that I have you back."

Sage rolled her eyes. "Don't be so corny, Dad. Come on," she said, sliding her shoulder into the pit of his arm, "I'm driving. Mom, you can sit in the back seat with Dad, help prop his foot up and keep it stable." Sage jerked her head toward the main door to the bookstore. "Mrs.

MacTavish, feel like joining us? Help me keep these two lovebirds in line?"

Mrs. MacTavish toddled to the front of the store, removing her apron. "Aye, would be an honor to do so. But what about the others?" she questioned, motioning behind her.

Sage shrugged. "Have the dog take them there—can only fit four in the car."

"No need, no need," Jonathon said, shaking his head. "There's something far more important than them being bored to death at the hospital. They need to secure the Book of Shay. It's imperative."

"But we don't even know where Mallena went," Abby blurted, joining her elders.

Jonathon grinned at his youngest. "Ah, but there's where you're wrong, Abs. We do know where Mallena went."

Abby crinkled her nose. "We do? How so?"

"After she nabbed me, she forced me to give up my smartphone." Jonathon glared at the memory. "She moved away from me and placed a call. Guess she thought I couldn't hear her. A fortunate miscalculation on her part." Jonathon grunted before continuing. "You'll find her in the Cave of Lost Souls. Google it. If I recall, it's quite close to the waterfall."

"Cave of Lost Souls? Why's she going there?" Abby asked, confused.

"She's meeting Aillig Ratchet, a renowned archaeologist with expertise in deciphering ancient writings." Jonathon ran a hand through his mussed hair. "Apparently, Mallena thinks the Book of Shay holds a secret. She mumbled something about finding her way to the greatest of treasures." Jonathon shook his head and rubbed his eyes. "I don't have a clue what she was referring to, but I still believe there's a connection between the book and Red King." Jonathon locked eyes with Rory. "We can't let her keep it."

Abby tapped her chin. "Secret. Treasure." Her eyes widened. "Dad. The scroll. I didn't tell you about the scroll." Abby jerked her bag from her back and rummaged for her copy of the translated writing. Pulling the paper from her backpack, she looked excitedly to her father. "Listen to this, Dad." She cleared her throat and read.

Where the land and sky meet

Among the ancient pine

Near the faerie pool

The Wolf's lair ye shall find

And within his stone haven

A sacred book doth dwell

The secret it holds

It shan't likely tell

But hold no despair
Do not doubt thine eye
For the Rose of Shaeron
Will show its true guise

A treasure so grand
Protected through time
Until blood of like blood
Reveals what's inside

"The first part isn't important anymore," Abby said, searching her father's eyes, "but it says it right there, secret and treasure. Maybe Mallena is right?"

Jonathon rubbed the back of his head, deep in thought. After a moment, he motioned to Abby for the paper. "Can I hold on to that, Abs? I'd like to study it," he said, skimming over the verses. "There is always more to things than what we first think. Perhaps an answer will come to me. But in the meantime," he directed, reaching out a hand and squeezing the top of Abby's head, "you must retrieve the book."

Victoria let out a frustrated sigh. "My love, I can't bear the idea of sending our daughter into the face of danger again. I don't know how much more my heart can take. I fear one of these times she won't return."

Jonathon moved his hand from the top of Abby's head to his wife's cheek. "She will return." He pulled his eyes away from Victoria's and considered his daughter's companions. "Mallena won't dare harm her now."

Agatha shuffled forward and touched Victoria's back. "My dearest friend," she said softly, "I shall go with Abby, keepin' her best interests in mind. Let yer heart rest easy. It has been through enough of late."

Victoria closed her eyes and nodded acceptance. "Very well then." Turning to her youngest, she took a deep breath and stood straight. "Mind what Agatha tells you, my sweet." Victoria leaned in, giving Abby a quick hug. "Now go get that book as your father asks. Just promise to be careful."

Abby sighed inside. *I wish they'd realize I can handle myself.* She stifled a snort. *Well, mostly, wolves excluded.* Abby looked to her parents, pushing the memory of The Wolf to the back of her mind. "Mom, Dad," she said, her heart soaring to address them together, "don't worry. We'll be fine, book included. Hopefully we'll be back by the time you're done at the hospital." Abby glanced at her father's ankle. "I see a boot cast in your future."

"Come on," Sage groaned, "we're all wasting time." She swiveled toward the door, giving her father no choice but to hobble along.

Jonathon twisted his head around to find Abby. "Get that book, Abs, just mind your steps to doing so." He stretched his neck even farther and made eye contact with Rory, looking as if to say something. Jonathon paused, then simply nodded at the Scotsman.

Rory grunted, returning the nod as Sage and Jonathon made their way outside, followed by Victoria and Mrs. MacTavish. The shopkeeper stopped, turning back to grasp Rory's hand. "See to the lass, my young kin," she whispered, "keep her safe. Keep yerself safe." With a wink, she bustled out the door, closing it behind her.

"A-by," Rory urged, "we best find the location of the cave."

"Right," Abby replied as she secured her bag to her back. "That should be easy enough."

For the next several minutes, Abby, Rory, and Agatha stood huddled around the computer screen. Finlay paced behind the group until Abby called out to him. "Hey, Finlay. Come look at this map."

Finlay rotated his girth toward the monitor. With a puff of hot air, he leaned forward and rested his chin on Abby's shoulder. *Aye, Lass. What does your mysterious contraption say?*

Abby giggled to herself. "See this here," she said, zooming in with Google Earth. She pointed to the screen, "that's where Airehart Falls is, and that," she continued, panning the view to the right and tapping her finger on the display, "is where the Cave of Lost Souls is. Not that far from the waterfall. I'm betting it didn't take Mallena long to get there."

Finlay rubbed his muzzle against Abby's cheek. *I shall take us south of the cave. If I'm interpreting this magical picture as truth, there shall be plenty of cover to hide our approach. We do not know what awaits us. We must take great care.*

Abby nodded, considering his words. "Smart thinking, Finlay." She turned her head, first to Agatha, and then to Rory. "Finlay thinks we should approach from here," she said, pointing to an area south of the cave. "Looks like there's plenty of trees and spots to hide so Mallena and this Aillig won't see us coming."

"Very well, Lass," Agatha said. "How shall we prepare?"

Abby shrugged. "Prepare? Don't think there's time for that. It's late and we're all tired," she replied with a nervous chuckle. "What better way to start another adventure, eh?" Abby motioned for Rory to take Agatha's hand, then slipped her own fingers in between his. "Let's get that book," she said, placing her hand upon Finlay's head.

13

"*T*here," Abby whispered, pointing through a dense clump of bushes. The night sky offered no cover to the group. Any clouds had rolled out, allowing the moon to illuminate their surroundings. They hid at the opening of a ravine. Towering crags rose to either side, affording limited access to the gorge. A dark hole consumed the cliff face ahead and to their right. A soft, orange glow deep within, coupled with the occasional dance of shadows, assured Abby they were in the correct place. The unnerving name swirled through her mind. *The Cave of Lost Souls.*

Finlay nudged Abby's back. *Let us move with caution, Lass. Haste is not our friend this eve.*

Abby slunk low to the ground, peeking around a bush. *Don't worry, fuzz face. I won't go rushing in. Learned my lesson with The Wolf.* Abby turned her head, placing a finger to her mouth, encouraging everyone to be as quiet as possible. She strained her ears and looked back to her companions. "I can hear Mallena." Abby directed her ear at the cave again and nodded. "Yep, that's her, sounds like she's talking to a guy. Must be Aillig."

Rory peered around the opposite side of the thicket. Studying the terrain for several moments, he squatted and turned back toward Abby. "Would be smart to approach from both sides, A-by. Ye go with Finlay and Agatha shall accompany me."

Abby chewed the corner of her mouth, considering the Scotsman's suggestion. "Okay," she replied. "If you guys sneak your way up the ravine on this side and double back along the opposite wall, hopefully they won't see or hear you." Abby glanced up at her dog. "Finlay and I will wait for a minute, then work our way to the closest side of the cave." Abby grimaced, thinking about Finlay's girth and brilliant, white coat. "Sometimes I wish you could turn invisible," she groaned.

"There's a simpler way," Agatha whispered, leaning in close to Abby. "No need for all the sneakin' around." She straightened and pointed to the dog. "Best if Finlay takes us to where ye like. No sound. No movement."

Abby palmed her forehead. "Of course. I'm overthinking it." She smiled at her elder, "Brilliant idea, Agatha." Abby scooted herself backward behind the cover of the thicket before standing to brush debris from her clothing. "Got that Finlay?"

The dog bowed his head in acknowledgment. *Aye, Lass. Tell Agatha and the boy to place their hands upon me now.*

Abby motioned to Agatha and Rory. "Whenever you're ready, Finlay says to grab hold of him."

Agatha wrung her hands in anticipation and moved to stand next to Rory. The pair nodded at each other, placing their hands on Finlay's flank. Finlay bowed his head at Abby and seconds later, the three disappeared.

Abby scrambled to the left side of the bushes, squatted, and scanned the opposite cliff face for signs of movement. She sighed relief when she saw Rory and Agatha flattening themselves against the ragged surface. When they were ten feet from the cave opening, Rory paused, pointing to Abby. He placed a hand palm-out in the air as if to say they would stay still. Abby exaggerated a nod while giving him two thumbs up. She called out in her mind. *Where are you?*

A soft snort startled Abby, causing her to jerk her head over her shoulder. *For as big as you are, I'm amazed how sneaky you can be sometimes.*

Finlay crouched low to the ground behind the thicket. A low rumble rolled from his chest. *And I'm amazed how unaware of your surroundings you can be sometimes.*

Abby crawled to the dog's side. *Ha ha, fuzzball.* She snickered, sinking her face into his lush coat. "Alright," she whispered, grasping onto his back, "let's do this."

The transition in space was instantaneous as usual, but something seemed different to Abby this time. She almost felt as if she were one with the dog in movement. Leaving the thought behind, Abby studied their position. Finlay placed them equidistant from the cave opening as Rory and Agatha. Abby stepped in front of the dog. *Let me go first. I can keep to the shadows easier.*

Finlay snorted agreement as Abby slipped past him and pressed herself against the cliff face. She signaled to Rory and crept toward the cave opening. Voices shaped into words the closer Abby moved.

"You said you could decipher anything," Mallena roared with a crackly hiss.

"Yes, yes," replied an aged man, "I know what I said, but this," he paused, uncertainty consuming his voice, "this is different."

Abby froze. She stared at Rory and held a silencing finger to her mouth. She called out to Finlay as the conversation in the cave continued. *That must be Aillig. Let's hope it's just the two of them. I don't think I've heard any other voices.*

Finlay lifted his snout in the air and drew in quiet breaths. After several moments, he grumbled into Abby's head. *I detect only one person, the man. I am perplexed why Mallena still holds no scent.*

Abby shrugged. *Well at least it's just the two of them, we'll worry about her oddness later. Or not at all. Let's remember our purpose here. All that matters is the book. If my Dad says it's that important, we can't leave here without it.*

Finlay rubbed his muzzle against Abby's arm. *And leave here with the book we shall, Lass.*

Warmth filled Abby. She knew the amazing creature crouched behind her would always fight for her, protect her. She smiled as she continued to creep forward toward the cave entrance. Without warning, Mallena's voice drew near. Abby froze again, holding her breath. After a moment of shouting, Mallena's odd vocalizations diminished into the depths of the cave. Abby tightened her lips as she listened to the rise and fall of Mallena's rant. *She must be pacing back and forth.* Abby glanced back at Finlay. *As soon as it sounds like she's farthest away from the entrance, let's see if we can sneak in.*

The uncertainties before us play to our disadvantage, child. It is likely there will not be any cloaking of our presence. Finlay pawed at the ground. *But we have little choice. I shall follow your lead.*

Abby nodded, then waved to get Rory's attention. She pretended to draw a sword from her hip and pointed to the Scotsman, hoping he would understand her intention. Smiling when he obliged, Abby held a hand up and mouthed the word 'wait.' Rory saluted in return, sword at ready.

Edging her way within several feet of the entrance, Abby tilted her head to study the sounds emanating from the cavern. Both voices were of equal, distant volume, filling Abby with a hopeful rush. She looked to Rory, holding up three fingers and began a silent countdown to one.

"Go," she whispered, tucking the last finger to her fist.

Two by two, the group eased toward the opening, stopping just before its boundary. Abby peered into the cave and sighed. *So much for the perfect sneak attack.* Finlay's speculation proved true. The cavern would not allow for an unannounced entry. Its smooth, rounded walls extended thirty feet into the base of the precipice. It reminded Abby of a fishbowl. So much so, she concluded someone carved out the cavern by hand, but for what purpose, she was unsure. *Don't think we want to find out why it's called The Cave of Lost Souls.* She shrugged off the thought, taking stock of what she saw.

A small fire flickered several feet from the back wall of the cave. With her back to the entrance, Mallena towered over a man of slight build sitting cross-legged on the ground, who appeared to be cradling the Book of Shay in his lap. A worn, leather satchel lay to his left, and miscellaneous items sprawled to his right on the cave floor. The man, who Abby assumed to be Aillig Ratchet, hunched over the book. He held a magnifying glass in one hand and stroked a manicured handlebar mustache with the other. Though he sat with his profile turned to the entrance, Aillig showed no signs of noticing the quartet now entering the cavern. Transfixed by the ancient text, he whispered to himself, flipping from page to page. Mallena crossed her arms and tapped her foot.

"Well," she demanded, making her impatience clear.

"A moment, a moment," Aillig replied without removing his eyes from the pages.

Abby held her breath as she motioned for Rory and Agatha to continue creeping forward. Twenty feet away. Fifteen feet away. Ten feet from their adversary. Abby raised a hand for everyone to halt. Finlay stepped to her side as Rory readied himself in a defensive stance. Her knees quivered in anticipation. Releasing a silent, deep breath, Abby called out, "Hey! Mallena."

Mallena's head jerked up at the sound of her name. She jumped into the air, whirling around and landing in a crouched position. Her eyes flickered a wild array of colors as she examined the group before her. "Manta!" she spat venomously. "Come for the book, have you?"

"Quit calling me that," Abby growled, "and yes, we're taking the book. You're not meant to have it."

Mallena rocked back and forth on the balls of her feet. "Is that so? We will see, now won't we?" Before anyone could react, Mallena sprang high into the air and latched onto the ceiling of the cave with both hands. After dangling for an instant, she swung herself forward until her feet also contacted the ceiling. She released her hands, and in an act unbelievable to all who watched, she pushed off, somersaulted through the air, and landed behind the stunned travelers.

What the heck is she? Abby screamed in her mind as she spun around, tracking Mallena's movements.

The creature stretched to her full height, curved blade in hand. "I should have taken care of you the first time." Her voice boiled as she glared at Abby.

Finlay's hackles rose. He growled, positioning himself in front of Abby. *Stay behind me, Lass.*

Rory summoned the power of his sword, sending flames smashing into the ceiling of the cavern.

Mallena hissed at the flames, taking a step back. Looking from Rory to Finlay, to Abby, to Agatha, her face quivered uncontrollably.

Abby squinted, then rubbed her eyes, trying to decipher what she was seeing. *Uh. What's wrong with her? It's like her face is out of focus or something.*

With a final shake of her head, Mallena's face came to a rest. She narrowed her eyes at the group and cackled. "It remains a mystery how you have come to be here, Manta," she paused, whirling her peculiar blade in her hand, "but my kind will always be a step ahead." As she hissed her last words, Mallena streaked forward, grabbing Agatha by the arm.

Agatha cried out when Mallena backed away from the group with her, one arm secured under Agatha's armpits, and the other pressing her weapon to the old woman's throat.

"Leave her alone!" Abby screamed, moving as if to run toward the mysterious creature.

"Do not test me, Manta," Mallena asserted, directing pressure to Agatha's neck.

Agatha hardened her face. "No worries, Lass. This will sort itself out, ye'll see."

Mallena snorted, tightening her grip on Agatha's torso. "Silence crone or those will be your last words."

Finlay growled, shaking the chamber as Rory adjusted the grip on his sword. No one moved for fear of the repercussions.

"Good," Mallena sneered. "Now that I have your attention, this is what you will do." Mallena backed herself and Agatha toward the nearest wall, then flattened against it. "Your band of filth will leave here at once, or the witch dies. You shall return to where you came from, or the witch dies. If you impede my course in any manner, the witch dies." Mallena nicked at Agatha's wrinkled flesh with the tip of her blade, causing a single drop of red to appear on her pale skin. "Understood?"

"Enough!" roared an unexpected voice from the back of the cave.

Abby whipped around, surprised by the outcry. She scrunched her face at the scene before her.

Aillig Ratchet stood to his full five feet. Legs spread wide and arms extended over the fire, he held the book over the hungry flames. "Mallena," he threatened, "leave the old gal be, or I swear I will destroy the book."

Momentary silence filled the chamber as all eyes turned to watch the fire's flames stretch toward the old tome.

"You wouldn't dare, Ratchet," Mallena said, her voice dripping with malice.

"Oh, but yes, yes, you know it to be true." Aillig paused, not moving his eyes from Agatha and the knife at her neck. "Consider your next move carefully, Mallena."

Glaring at the old archaeologist, Mallena growled. Deciding the threat not to be a bluff, she released her grip on Agatha and shoved the old woman away.

Agatha stumbled forward, unable to catch her balance and toppled to the ground with a groan.

Abby watched in disbelief as Agatha lay in a heap. She wanted to rush to her side but feared how Mallena might react. As she contemplated what to do, Abby felt a steamy puff of dog breath against her cheek and looked to her side. In one moment, Finlay's grand stance filled her view, and in the next, he was gone. Abby blinked, looking around the cavern. *Where'd he go?*

Moments later, Finlay reappeared by Mallena's side, causing her to jump back. In one swift movement Finlay latched onto Mallena's arm, and in an instant, they disappeared.

The threat nullified, Abby rushed to Agatha. "Are you okay?" she asked, helping the old woman to her feet.

"Aye, Lass," Agatha replied, wiping debris from her clothing. "Will take more than that to keep these old bones down."

Abby smiled with relief and watched as Rory quenched the magic of his sword. Sheathing his blade, he stepped forward and rubbed Agatha's back. "I'm relieved no harm came to ye, Agatha." Rory paused to look around the chamber. "Where do ye suppose he took that beastly creature, A-by?"

Abby shrugged. "Who knows, but the farther—"

Finlay cut Abby's thought short, reappearing near the fire.

"Finlay!" Abby rushed to the dog's side. "Where'd you take her? What'd you do to her?" she asked.

Finlay appeared to grin. *I dropped her deep inside Caledonia, among the maze of tunnels.*

Abby snorted while trying to suppress a belly laugh. "Oh man, Finlay says he took Mallena to see Mavis and Tavis. Good luck finding her way out of there."

Agatha smoothed her smock. "Too bad those brothers are imprisoned, it would serve her justly to deal with the likes of them."

The sound of a clearing throat interrupted the group's discussion over Mallena's suitable fate. All fell silent, turning their attention toward the source.

Aillig Ratchet stood opposite the fire clutching the Book of Shay to his chest. He raised an eyebrow and reached up with a bony finger to readjust the wire-rim glasses on the bridge of his nose.

"Curious, curious," he stated, studying each member of the group one by one. He rounded the fire, inching toward Finlay, holding his breath as he did. "Remarkable," he whispered after a long moment. "Is he," Aillig paused, pointing to the dog while addressing Abby, "is this magnificent creature capable of," he paused again, deciding if his next words would be met with reason, "teleportation? And," he continued with more reluctance, "are you able to communicate with it?"

Abby smiled on the inside, proud someone referred to her Finlay as magnificent, but she felt caution rise within. Though Aillig in a sense saved Agatha, he was a stranger to them, and he currently possessed the book. She reached out to Finlay. *What's your vibe with this guy? Can we trust him? He's already seen your ability and the power of Rory's sword. I hope he wasn't serious about burning the book. We don't want to test him.*

Finlay blinked acknowledgment as he took one step forward and lowered his head near that of Aillig's. The dog scrutinized the old man with each sniff; Aillig stood motionless, in awe of the interaction. Swinging his head toward Abby, he bowed in a nod. *I sense no ill intentions. I believe him to be trustworthy, but be cautious what secrets you divulge, child.*

Abby reached out to ruffle Finlay's fur and nodded. "Yes," she replied, turning to Aillig. "What you've asked is true. His name is Finlay and we can understand each other. Don't know how or why, but he can also teleport anywhere or time he wants," she boasted.

Aillig stroked the curl of his mustache. "Fascinating, fascinating," he replied as he continued staring at Finlay. "And might I inquire your names, young lady?"

"I'm Abby, and this is Rory and Agatha," she said, pointing to her companions.

"I see, I see," Aillig replied with a bow. "My name is Aillig Ratchet, renowned archaeologist," he said with a hint of self-importance. "Now, if I understand correctly, you've come seeking the book?"

Abby nodded. "That's right, Mr. Ratchet. That creepy whatever-she-is Mallena threatened to kill my dad if we didn't bring her the book. We made the trade, but my dad insisted we get it back. It contains information we need."

Aillig stood silent for a moment as he stroked the cover of the book with a thumb. "How are you so certain it contains something you desire? Even I cannot decipher the scriptures contained within. It's an oddity, I tell you, an oddity."

Abby sighed, unsure of how much more she should reveal. "My father believes there's something important about the Red King in it. So..." she trailed off, "...we need to figure out what it says."

Aillig's eyes grew large. "The Red King? And what would you know of him?"

"Well—" Abby began, only to be outspoken by Rory.

"I am Rory MacKay of the clan MacKay," he said, stepping forward, hand on his hilt. "The blood of the Red King flows within me. I am his true heir."

"Unbelievable, unbelievable," Aillig said with wonderment as he scooted away from Finlay and rounded the opposite side of the fire to inspect Rory up close.

"Fascinating," he whispered. "Then is that," he questioned, pointing to Rory's sword, "the fabled weapon created by Sylvan Myst?"

Rory cleared his throat, surprised by the knowledge of the old man before him. "Aye, it is the one."

Aillig stumbled backward and plopped to the cave floor. He sat stunned, taking in the strangers' words, stroking the cover of the book. "Utterly amazing," he murmured to himself. "Then let us further investigate the scriptures within this most mysterious artifact," he said, motioning for everyone to gather around him.

Abby took an eager seat to the left of the archaeologist while Rory and Agatha observed from behind. Finlay positioned himself on the opposite side of the fire and curled up into a giant ball. Abby smiled at her dog as she pulled her attention back to the book and quirky man stationed next to her. She considered Aillig's reaction to Rory. It was obvious he knew much more than he was willing to reveal, but Abby dared not question him, at least not while he held the book.

"You see," Aillig pointed to the first page of mysterious writing, "in all my days, throughout all my discoveries, I've encountered nothing like this. It is both amazing and baffling."

A stray thought itched at Abby's mind as she stared at the senseless writing. She caught her breath, eager to share her idea with Rory. He met her eyes, mouthing the word 'what?' Abby motioned for him to come close. When he leaned over, she whispered in his ear. Rory straightened and considered her words before nodding agreement. Abby's eyes twinkled in the firelight as Rory dug in the utility pocket of his pants and pulled out his copy of the scroll's translation. He glanced from the old man to the scroll, and with a shrug, passed it to Abby.

"Here," she said, handing the paper to the archaeologist. "Maybe this will mean something to you."

Aillig accepted the sheet, curiosity filling his eyes. "What have we here?" he questioned, unfolding it and glancing at Abby.

"We found it in my dad's bookstore. It's a riddle about the book."

Aillig's face flushed with excitement. His eyes darted to the cryptic verses.

Abby fidgeted, hoping he could make more sense of it than she.

"The Rose of Shaeron, the Rose of Shaeron." Aillig's jaw gaped after whispering the words. He turned to Abby, his face serious. "It's a palimpsest."

Abby scratched her head. "A palimp-what?"

"A palimpsest, this book is a palimpsest," the man sighed upon her confusion. "Easiest to think of it as an ancient way of recycling. When supplies were short, scripture was scraped, or washed away from the parchment for reuse. Often bits of the prior writing remain. Normally I use a special UV light to decipher the hidden text." Aillig pushed his glasses high on his bridge and twirled his mustache around a finger.

Agatha cleared her throat and bent down to tap Aillig on the shoulder. "But how do ye know this book is such a thing?"

Aillig held up the paper with the riddle. "Simple. This states the Rose of Shaeron will reveal the book's hidden secret."

"But," Abby interjected, "that makes little sense. We don't even know what the Rose of Shaeron is, so how do you figure the book is a pamp-liset based on that?"

Aillig shook his head with frustration. "Palimpsest, palimpsest. And you're assuming incorrectly about the Rose of Shaeron. It's a sacred stone made from rose quartz. Ancient texts allude to the bearer of the stone possessing an enhanced quality of insight. In this case, it takes the place of a UV light. I believe it will reveal the hidden messages of the book. It makes perfect sense."

Abby motioned to Aillig for the copy of the riddle. She pinched at her upper lip while skimming through the pertinent verses again.

And within his stone haven

A sacred book doth dwell

The secret it holds

It shan't likely tell

But hold no despair

Do not doubt thine eye

For the Rose of Shaeron

Will show its true guise

She rubbed her forehead, wishing things weren't so ambiguous. *I suppose he could be right. Based on the riddle, I guess there could be writing we can't see. And it sure sounds like the Rose of Shaeron will reveal it.* Abby groaned as she tucked the paper into her bag. "Okay. So say you're right, where do we find this stone?"

Aillig removed his glasses to rub his eyes. He then sighed, replacing his spectacles. "That, young lady, is our limiting factor."

Abby jerked her head back in response. "What's that supposed to mean?"

Aillig stared into the fire before responding. "The Rose of Sharon was spoken of during the reign of the Red King. Scriptures indicate it was hidden away in an unknown place of worship. Purportedly, when moonlight streamed through it at just the right angle, the stone would engulf the area in brilliant rays of rosy red. I imagine it to be a spectacular..."

A dramatic thud silenced the chamber, sending Abby's heart pounding. She leaned forward to look past the old man. Agatha sat to the right in a disheveled heap, staring into the fire. With glazed eyes, she reached into the air and stretched her fingers for an invisible unknown. "I see it now, a pink sea washin' over me," she said in a trance before a hushed silence.

Abby scrambled to her elder's side, plopping down next to her and placing a hand on her shoulder. "Hey," she said with a gentle shake, "tell us what you remember. You know something about the stone?"

At the sound of Abby's voice, Agatha nodded before running a hand down her face. "Aye," she said, turning to Abby. "I was just a wee one, but I remember it now." Agatha wrung her hands before continuing. "Do ye recall me sayin' I had seen the Red King with me own eyes?"

Abby thought back to the moment Agatha first met Rory. The old woman looked as if the dead had risen. "Yep, sure do."

Excitement flushed across Agatha's face. "The Rose of Shaeron," she paused to nod toward Aillig, "it's true what the gentleman says, was the centerpiece of our sacred lands. I can see the brilliant, rosy glow now," she said, staring at the cave wall beyond the fire. Meeting Abby's eyes again, she shrugged, "But I only remember bits of it. As I said, I was just a wee lass."

"It's okay, Agatha. The fact you even know about it is, well..." Abby trailed off, shaking her head in amazement. She looked from Agatha to Rory to Finlay. A sense of something more than coincidence welled inside her. "It's amazing," Abby said, squeezing the old woman's shoulder. "Can you remember anything about where the stone was kept or where you saw it? Maybe there was a secret hiding spot or building or something?"

"Oh, aye. I know precisely where those from my village safeguarded the stone." Agatha stopped to suck in a deep breath, bringing herself back to the present as Rory and Aillig moved closer, determined not to miss a word the old woman spoke.

Abby glanced annoyingly at the others for disturbing Agatha's thoughts. "Go on," she encouraged.

"To the west of the Well of Fair Maidens, just beyond the outskirts of the black forest, me kinfolk discovered a magical valley. And in this valley," she whispered, drawing all ears closer to her, even those of the dog, "was the most mysterious and mystical hollow. I best describe it as constructed from trees ripped straight from the ground, root and all. In me days as a wee one, I'd have said giants were responsible for such a sight. But magic, magic was surely at use." Agatha motioned with her hands as she depicted the scene. "The trees were stacked one upon the other, largest at the bottom, smallest on top. Two towerin' stacks met, treetop-to-treetop, forming what looked like a sliver of moon, were they curved. But the most curious thing was the roots. The roots of each tree intertwined with the next, climbin' higher and higher, makin' their way up atop the towers to meet in the middle. There the roots from each grand stack twisted together, bindin' them against all forces. From this fusion, thirteen, thick braids of root spiraled to the ground, creatin' a kind of protected chamber. Was here they hid the Rose of Shaeron."

The group sat silently until Aillig spoke next, his voice filled with anticipation. "Then we must go to this place," he declared, looking first to Abby, and then to Finlay.

"Can he," he questioned, pointing to the dog, "take us there?" Aillig gulped, eager for a response.

Abby nodded with apprehension. "Well, yeah, Finlay could, but he has to either have been there already or see a picture of the location. Otherwise, who knows where we'd end up," she said with a shrug. "I kind of doubt he has any clue where this magical valley is."

Finlay stood, stretched, and shook his body in dramatic fashion. He tilted his head at Abby and entered her mind as his movements transfixed all eyes. *Do not presume so hastily, child. I know the location of this tower of trees.*

Abby snorted, "Huh. Figures." She looked around at the expectant eyes, forgetting they weren't able to hear the dog. "Oh, sorry. Finlay says he knows where it is."

Agatha clapped her hands together but stopped short. "Is he most certain? It was so very long ago. And what if it no longer stands?"

Finlay's chest rumbled. *Do not be alarmed, Lass, I will be back in a moment.* Before Abby could reply, Finlay's massive form disappeared.

All but Abby gasped when the dog reappeared moments later. He bowed before the group. *The structure stands strong.*

Without breaking eye contact with the dog, Abby relayed his statement, then drilled him with questions. *And how exactly do you know about this place, and why didn't you say anything before about the Rose of Shaeron? Are you holding out on us?*

Finlay appeared to smile at the strong-minded teenager before landing a strategic, sloppy lick square on her nose.

"Yuck!" Abby declared, wiping her nose on her hoodie sleeve.

Finlay's chest rumbled with laughter. *You are quick to presume the truth, child. I, in fact, have no knowledge of this sacred stone. I did, however, come upon a peculiar structure made of woven trees during my imprisonment.*

Only once pure chance led me there, but its uniqueness remained ingrained in my mind.

Oh. Abby blushed. *Sorry, fuzz face, I should know better by now.* She buried her face in Finlay's thick coat. *You'll never do me wrong.*

"Are you having a conversation?" Aillig blurted. "Yes, yes it appears you are. Please, young lady, what does this magnificent creature have to say?"

Before addressing the historian, Abby reached out to Finlay. *There's something weird about this guy I can't figure out. We should have asked him how he got mixed up with Mallena.*

"I was just asking Finlay how he knew about the place Agatha described," she said straightforwardly after turning to Aillig. Abby glanced at Rory and Agatha. "He said he found it one day when he was out searching," she paused, thinking cautious words would be best, "you know... while doing that job for Mavis and Tavis." Her companions nodded slowly, noticing her reluctance to reveal too much.

Aillig appeared confused but then seemed to accept the response, "I see, I see. Well then, are we in agreement we should leave at once? I am not at ease remaining in this place."

Rory grunted and extended a hand to help Agatha up from the cave floor. She smoothed her smock and clasped her hands together. "I am most eager to see the lands of me kin again."

"Okay then," Abby said, looking over her shoulder at Finlay.

Her white warrior bowed in response. *You know what to do, Lass.*

"Alright, make sure you've got everything you came with." Abby circled the fire, leaning over to grab her bag. She lifted her head and eyed Aillig.

Stroking the cover of the book, the old man caught Abby's eye. He froze briefly, holding her gaze. With no warning, he held the Book of Shay out with both hands. "You should take this, young lady. A gesture of trust."

Abby reached out to accept the book, tucking it into the main pouch of her bag. "Thanks. My dad will appreciate it."

Aillig nodded as he gathered his tools, slipping them into his satchel. "Well then, what's the routine? How does the dog work his magic?"

Abby secured her bag on her back and motioned for Aillig to follow her. "By touch," she said, stopping next to Finlay. "We'll all hold hands; then I'll grab onto him. All you need to concentrate on is not letting go. Easy, right?"

"Yes, yes. Easy," replied Aillig with a hint of impatience. He looked from hand to hand.

Seeing his uncertainty, Agatha reached out and offered her left hand. "There ye are. Grab hold." With an added wink, she said, "We'll be there before you can say palimpsest."

Abby snorted as she interlaced her fingers with Rory's, an action she began to find comfort in. A goofy grin spread across Rory's face. To hide his delight, he jerked his head toward Agatha and offered his free hand. When the awkward chain of travelers linked, Abby nodded to Finlay. "Hope everyone's ready, no turning back now!"

14

*A*bby swiveled her head in all directions. It was astonishing. Never had she witnessed anything like the grand structure before her. Everything Agatha described to them in the cave held true over the centuries. Standing at the cusp of the hollow, Abby realized the shape of the structure reminded her of a baseball field. Naked treetops wove their branches together permanently at what would be home plate. The stunned companions stood in the outfield.

Finlay crept forward. *Stay put, child.*

Abby held her arms out, signaling for the others to stay back.

The dog strode toward the darkened apex. Though the moon hung high to the east, the pinnacle of the towering complex cast shadows upon everything within its breadth. Finlay lifted his nose to the night sky, paused, and sniffed the ground. Repeating this routine, he stopped within ten feet of the strange weaving of roots at the center which seemed to form a tubular chamber. He swung his head back, calling to Abby. *You may approach. I detect no danger.*

Abby lowered her arms. "Finlay says it's safe. Let's go."

Aillig rushed forward the moment Abby spoke, ignoring the others.

"Okay," Abby drawled, rolling her eyes.

Rory drew his sword, calling forth a soft glow to illuminate their path. "I shall guide yer way," he whispered, glancing to Agatha and Abby. He paused, noticing Agatha's hesitation. "What troubles ye, Agatha?" he asked, stepping close to the old woman and placing a hand on her shoulder.

Agatha sighed. "Oh, is nothin' bad. I-I just," she stuttered, "I never thought I'd see me kin's most sacred of places again." She sucked in a deep breath. "And the stone. So many memories are whirlin' in me head now. Could it truly still be here?"

Abby leaned in toward the pair. "I can only imagine how it must feel for you to come back here after, well, hundreds of years, Agatha. I'll be kind of surprised if someone hasn't stolen the stone, but there's only one way to find out," she said with an encouraging smile.

Agatha nodded, stepping forward to follow Rory. The three weaved their way through clumps of overgrowth.

The further into the hollow they traveled, the more fire Rory commanded from his sword. As they approached the center, Abby could see Aillig pacing back and forth several feet from the assemblage of roots. She called out to Finlay. *What's he doing?*

I believe he's contemplating how to gain access. He reeks of fear. I am troubled and confused by this as I detect no danger.

"Psstt, Aillig," Abby whispered. "Slow down there; we need to be cautious."

Aillig whirled around to face the group. He reached to readjust his glasses. "Yes, yes. Of course. I apologize for my haste. I admit excitement clouded my judgment," he said, hugging his satchel tight to his chest.

A brief feeling of suspicion washed over Abby. Shaking it off, she joined Finlay in his careful inspection of the strange roots. Abby squinted into the dark, motioning for Rory to step closer. "See if you can find a way in. I bet that's where the Rose of Shaeron is hidden. Maybe there's a wide enough gap somewhere to squeeze through."

Rory grunted as he guided his sword around the roots. With the blade at a safe distance, he made his way behind the four-foot-wide structure, disappearing from sight.

After several moments of silence, Abby called out to him. "Rory? Everything okay?" Butterflies assaulted her gut when no response came. *Something's happened.* She summoned her courage and rushed around the braided roots just as Rory called out to his companions.

"Back here," he said, "I've found somethin'."

"Answer me next time, Rory," Abby said once she reached his side, "you had me worried for a second."

Rory frowned in response. "Me apologies, A-by." Shifting his eyes from hers, he pointed straight ahead. "But look."

Abby followed the line of the Scotsman's finger. "Whoa. Wild," she said as Aillig, Agatha, and Finlay approached.

The woven roots spun to the ground a generous ten feet from the face of the two walls of trees, affording comfortable space for the onlookers. Everyone stared with wonder. The weaving of roots formed a tight, intricate pattern. It was difficult for Abby not to view the structure as a work of art. She found the purpose of the millennium-old wood a complete mystery, and one she hoped she wouldn't have to deduce.

In the center of the roots, a passageway just taller than Rory led into the chamber. It reminded Abby of a rotted out tree, yet one not created by the wear of time. "Hey," she said, leaning toward the opening, straining her eyes. "It looks like there's something in there, almost hovering a few feet off the ground."

Aillig inched closer to the opening. "Why yes, yes, I agree. How curious."

Abby considered the flaming tongues flickering along Rory's sword. *He can't go sticking that inside the hole. Don't want to torch the trees.* Nodding to herself, she swung her backpack forward and retrieved a flashlight. Securing her pack, Abby shined the light into the chamber. Varied exclamations filled the air when the beam illuminated a single root dangling in the center of the structure. The end of the root proved the source of the group's surprise. Looped into a circle parallel with the ground, it secured a gem aloft the forest floor.

"The Rose of Shaeron. It must be!" Aillig cried. Before anyone could react, the old man rushed toward the opening. He stumbled upon reaching the aperture and placed his hand on the ancient wood to steady himself. The moment his flesh brushed the roots, the ground began to rumble.

Panic rushed through Abby's innards as she stepped forward instinctively and yanked Aillig away from the structure. It seemed the entire world shook, first as a gentle caution, then as an ominous warning. "Everybody back," Abby yelled, "get back to the clearing," she added, pushing the old man out and around the roots. Rory guided a rattled Agatha in front of him while Finlay teleported a safe distance to stand in wait of his companions.

The group huddled in the middle of the hollow. Abby grasped at her dog, taking comfort in his muscular form. *Finlay! What's happening?*

Finlay's hackles rose as he sniffed the air. *I do not know, child. But it seems the historian has disrupted the balance of something powerful.*

Abby narrowed her eyes while glancing at the old man. *Apparently!* She looked to the ground, concentrating on the vibration assaulting her feet. "Hey. I think it's letting up." Murmurs of agreement met her ears, silenced in the next moment by a new noise.

Though the ground no longer shook, the towers of trees shifted with loud cracks, pops, and groans. Rory met Abby's eyes, a blank and confused stare shared between them. Abby shined her light along the trees to her left, and then to her right. "What the..."

Unseen roots poked from the core of the towers, undulating to the ground and releasing from their source with a stiff plop. Twelve masses, spread along the two towers, swirled and flowed, stretching upward and taking form. Abby focused her light on one of the oddities. "Whoa..." She continued shining the beam on what appeared to be the malformed shape of a head. "It, it looks like a person made of wood," she said. As if in response, wood-grained eyes flicked open. Abby jumped back, flipping her flashlight off and tightening her grasp on Finlay, "Did you guys see that?"

The sound of intensifying pops, snaps, and scrapes filled the hollow. Abby strained her eyes from the forms at one tower to the other. Her chest tightened and her hands quivered. Fearful of what she might see, Abby raised her light to find the woody creature again. Sucking in a breath, she turned on the flashlight. Exclamations of surprise rang in unison from the huddled group. The bizarre creation stood not six feet away. Abby swung the light from side to side. The twelve figures—the men of wood—formed a semi-circle around the frightened travelers, who now all pressed their backs against Finlay. Abby called out to her dog. *Maybe this would be a good time for you to get us out of here?*

Finlay snorted and swayed his head. *Calm your nerves, child, and trust in my words. Something here is familiar but what I know not. I sense no malicious intent. No harm shall come to us.*

Hope you know what you're talking about. Abby pulled her mind from the dog and whispered, "Finlay says not to be scared. Try to stay calm." On her left, Rory squeezed her arm in reply, and to her right, Abby felt Aillig attempting to wedge his body in between Finlay and herself. She elbowed his feeble attempt at hiding. He grunted with an 'oof' and shrunk begrudgingly back to stand next to Agatha, in full view of the beings before them.

The sound of disjointed whispers filled the air, commanding absolute attention from those who listened. The whispers continued, rising into a unified, scratchy voice. "Who is this that awakens our sleep?"

Abby gulped. No one dared be the first to respond.

"Who is this that stands before us?" commanded the twelve figures as one.

In her peripheral, Abby noticed Rory tense, as if preparing to step forward. Unexpectedly to her, she cleared her own throat to reply. "Uh, Sirs, we, we're sorry we woke you. We didn't know anyone was, uh, sleeping." Abby considered her words. "We were looking for something important and should have been more careful."

Unified whispers swirled through the air. "The Rose, the Rose, the Rose," they chanted. As the whispers drifted away, a soft, pink glow filled the hollow. Slipping her flashlight into her hoodie pocket, Abby studied the strange forms. Though lacking fully formed appendages, the creatures took on a humanoid shape.

"Bizarre," Abby mouthed to herself. Becoming uncomfortable with the growing silence, Abby cleared her throat again. "Sirs, may we inquire who you are?" she asked, half expecting no answer considering she had skirted around the very question.

To Abby's surprise, whispers filled the air again until a single voice boomed. "We are the end. We are the beginning. We are the many. We are the few. We are the one," the voice paused as the figures seemed to bow, "We, are Mantara," they finished with an airy breath.

Finlay quivered in response. Abby glanced back at him. *What? What is it Finlay?*

The dog shifted weight, stomping his front legs back and forth. *I...I'm not sure, Lass.*

Abby turned back to the beings now identified as Mantara. She questioned everything about them but knew one thing for certain; they guarded the Rose of Shaeron. She ran a hand through her curls. *I suppose they won't let us just take it.*

As Abby wandered through her own thoughts, Aillig cleared his throat and stepped forward two paces. "With respect, Mantara," the old man said with a curt bow, "I ask your permission to retrieve the Rose of Shaeron. I believe in good conscience it will answer a mystery," he said, turning to sweep an arm at those behind him, "which we wish to resolve."

Abby fumed silently at the archaeologist. *Who does he think he is? He doesn't speak for us!* Abby glanced at

Rory, relieved to see a similar sentiment. The Scotsman wrinkled an eyebrow and crossed his arms.

A low rumble rolled from one earthy being to the next. "Only those of the Origin may unite with the Rose. Do you claim to be so?"

Aillig sputtered at the response and in his confusion, stepped back to stand between Abby and Agatha again. He clutched his satchel tight and shrugged as Abby caught his eye.

Abby readjusted her attention, roving her eyes along the curious forms, pondering what they meant by the Origin. Taking a determined breath, she resolved to find the answer. "Sirs," she said, "I'm afraid I'm confused. What is the Origin?"

No response came for several, heart-stopping moments. Abby held her breath, wondering if perhaps she spoke too forthright. Just as she contemplated repeating her question, the twelve figures shook. "The Origin is for us to determine," the voice asserted. Then from each being, a slender, lone root protruded out of its base and snaked along the ground. The roots met as one and continued zigzagging toward the startled group.

Agatha flinched when the root slithered to a stop in front of her. Like a rising serpent, the root swayed in the air, directing its gnarled tip at the old woman's leg. To everyone's shock, the root shot forward and latched onto

Agatha's calf. It twisted around and around, stopping only when it contacted skin. Agatha drew in a startled breath but looked to Abby and mouthed she was unharmed. Suddenly, the root released its grasp and spiraled back to the ground. "Not of the Origin," the raspy voice said.

When the root slid sideways, stopping in front of Aillig, Abby whispered in his ear. "Pull your pant leg up to expose your skin." Aillig watched the root with apprehension and nodded at Abby's suggestion. He stretched a hand down to hike up his trousers. The root bobbed in the air, then rocketed forward to wrap around the exposed skin, causing Aillig to flinch. The old man released his grip and squeezed his eyes shut. In moments, the root dropped to the ground. "Not of the Origin," repeated the voice.

Knowing what to expect, Abby pulled her jeans up to her knee and waited patiently for the phrase she knew would come. The root coiled around her leg, and to Abby's dismay, did not release after brief inspection. She breathed deep, pushing back the bit of panic she felt brewing inside. *Just stay calm. Any second and it will move on to Rory. Then we've got to figure out how to get to the gemstone. This isn't going to work.* The tension around Abby's leg subsided, interrupting her thoughts. She looked down to watch the root flop to the ground. "Not of the Origin," said the voice.

Abby sighed relief as she concentrated on Rory. The Scotsman broke the pattern by kneeling and pushing up a sleeve of his tunic. He extended his forearm while locking his eyes on the root. The woody appendage seemed to bow before stretching toward the awaiting flesh, but in a swift movement taking all by surprise, the root tilted its tip toward Finlay and rose into the air. Hovering above Rory's head, the root leveled itself with Finlay's eye. For a long minute, it swayed back and forth as if in deep contemplation. Whether pleased with its deduction or not, the head of the snake-limb lowered itself to inspect Rory's forearm. Without further hesitation, it curled around the Scotsman's limb. The instant the root made contact, the pink glow in the hollow intensified. The group watched with wonder. "Rory," Abby exclaimed, pointing to his scabbard, "your sword. Look!"

As soon as Abby spoke, the root withdrew its grasp. With haste, it separated into twelve and returned to its respective cores. The tree men rumbled before ringing out in unison. "You are the end. You are the beginning. You are the many. You are the few. You are the one. You, are of the Origin. Step forward and name yourself."

Stunned, Abby met Rory's eyes. A mixture of confusion and excitement flashed across his face.

Swallowing hard, Rory placed a hand on his hilt. The blade pulsed a vibrant red, visible at the opening of the sheath. He looked back to Abby, filled his lungs, and stepped forward, drawing his sword in one fluid movement. Kneeling, Rory plunged the tip into the forest floor. He spoke with pride, gazing from one woody form to the next. "I am Rory MacKay of the clan MacKay, the rightful heir to the Red King."

A wild wind whipped through the hollow causing Abby to lean against Finlay's grand stature for support. The tree men began to splinter, crack, and wail, sliding rapidly toward one another. They collided with such force the ground rumbled and the towers shook. Abby feared the massive structures would not survive the assault, envisioning those dear to her squashed flat by the ancient trees. Moments later the shaking stopped, relieving her fears. She watched on as the tree men appeared to meld into one giant blob of wood. The form flowed into the air as it took a new shape. All jaws stood agape when the wood came to an end; before them stood an enormous figure. There was no mistaking its identity. Its long wooden braids, the broad shoulders, the knightly stature, the hand on its hilt. Abby squeaked in amazement. "Rory. It's, it's you! But older, maybe."

Rory bowed his head and placed a hand over his heart. "Me kin," he whispered to himself, "the Red King."

The figure creaked and groaned, drawing a wooden sword and falling to one knee with a rattling thud. "Our King," it said, eyes settling on Rory as it crossed a bulky arm over its chest. "Long have we endured the demand of humankind. Long have we protected the Rose. Long have we awaited your return." The being swooped its arm from its chest toward the resting place of the Rose. The roots forming the chamber unwound, climbing higher and higher toward the top of the towers, revealing the lone tendril suspending the Rose of Shaeron. "That which is yours to take, our King," the wooden man said, "protect it as we have."

Rory glanced over his shoulder at Abby, then rose and sheathed his sword. He paused and again turned to look at Abby. She nodded, made a shooing motion with her hands, and mouthed the word 'go.' Rory drew a deep breath and stared at the gemstone. As he strode past the Mantara, the being lowered its head. Whispers filled the air as Rory approached the dangling root. "The Rose, the Rose, the Rose." The Scotsman slowed his pace, coming to a halt several feet from the stone. He tilted his head curiously to examine the Rose. Abby sensed he was contemplating his actions to come. He raised his right hand and stepped forward a pace, stretching his fingers and hovering them above the stone. Abby called out in her mind when he paused again. *Just grab it, Rory!* As if hearing her plea, Rory plucked the Rose of Shaeron from its resting place.

A brilliant blast shot from Rory's hand and filled the hollow with a hazy warmth. A pulsing orb of pink soon enveloped him. Abby covered her mouth, overwhelmed by the beauty of the Rose and its display. She ran toward Rory, stopping near the vibrant field surrounding him. He stood tall with the Rose raised in front of him. Abby watched as a myriad of emotions filled his face. He spoke no words as he stared in amazement at the stone. Then with a final pulse, the orb of light faded, and the Rose ceased to glow. Rory stumbled backward, taking a moment to gain his feet. He looked again to the stone gripped in his hand.

"Unbelievable," he whispered.

Abby rushed to his side, placing one hand on his back, the other on his arm. "Rory? Are you okay?" Abby asked, meeting his eyes. "What was unbelievable?"

"I could see them. Well, only in brief."

"See who, Rory?"

"Those who came before, in the hollow." He rubbed a hand across his face. "Was almost like I was seein' through another's eyes. His eyes," he said with emphasis.

"The Red King," Abby said without question. "Memories maybe?"

"Aye, A-by, perhaps." Rory gestured toward Agatha. "There was a wee lass in many of these images."

"Yeah, and?" Abby said.

"She bore a golden curl in her hair, A-by." Rory stared at Agatha as the old woman approached. "Was Agatha. I'm certain of it. Many times her face flashed before me, then everythin' went black. The images stopped."

Agatha tilted her head up to stare deep into the Scotsman's eyes. "Ye are truly his kin. I see him when I gaze upon ye, just as I gazed upon him when I was a wee lass, as you say. Ye speak the truth. It was I ye witnessed. I remember now me folk would usher me here every time the moon hung full above. The Red King would appear wieldin' the Rose of Shaeron, baskin' us in its radiant glow. I never understood what was takin' place, but I had no care when I could dance and play in the light of the stone. Then, sadly, one moon after another passed when the Red King was no' to be seen."

Abby grimaced. "Mavis and Tavis." She darted her eyes between Agatha and Rory. "That must have been when those creeps killed him."

Rory nodded. "Aye, what ye say is sensible. And when he did no' return, the Mantara protected the Rose." Rory unrolled his fingers to reveal the stone. "Protected it until one day his kin would reclaim it." Rory lifted his head and glanced around until he locked eyes with Finlay. For a fleeting moment, a peculiar look crossed his face. "I also," he began to say, pausing, "ah, is of no importance now. We possess the Rose, let us determine the mystery of the book."

Aillig sprang forward to eye the stone. "Yes, yes, let us not forget our purpose here." He motioned to Abby. "Young lady, would you be so kind as to produce the book for us?"

Abby held back a glare as she glanced at Aillig, swinging her backpack in front of her. "Sure, I'm on it." Abby retrieved the book, letting her bag flop to the ground. She waved an arm for everyone to join her as she plunked to the forest floor and crossed her legs.

Rory mimicked Abby's action and settled himself to her left, while Aillig stooped to her right and Agatha and Finlay peered over their shoulders. Abby laid the book in her lap and opened the cover. As she did, the now familiar whispers swirled throughout the hollow. The wooden giant rose with a rough groan. "The Book of Shay," it purred.

Abby felt goosebumps form along her spine. Controlling a brief shiver, she flipped to the first page of unintelligible writing. "So now what?" she said to no one in particular.

"The Rose of Shaeron," Aillig said, "I must use the stone."

Abby glanced warily at Rory as Aillig extended an open hand toward him. "May I?" he asked.

After a moment of consideration, Rory grunted and opened his fist to reveal the gem. Aillig stretched his hand forward, but when the tip of the old man's index finger touched the stone, a spark of pink light appeared to strike him. "Curses!" Aillig cried out, pulling his hand back to his chest. With a scowl, he sucked on the assaulted finger.

Serves him right, Abby thought to herself as she refrained from smiling. "I think Rory's the only one who can touch the stone," she said. "You know, the whole Origin thing?"

Aillig grimaced, pulling his finger from his mouth. "Very well then," he motioned toward the book, "let us delay no further."

Rory looked to Abby for approval and directed a curt nod Aillig's way. "Place the book in me lap, A-by, will be easier."

"Yeah, you're right," she said, setting the book on top of his crossed legs.

Rory smiled his thanks as he contemplated the first page of writing.

"Try laying the stone on the parchment," the archaeologist said.

Without moving his eyes, Rory nodded, adjusted his grip on the stone, and readied to place it on the page.

The scratchy voice of the Mantara whipped through the air. "That which you seek the pages do not contain."

"Nonsense," Aillig scoffed. "The book is a palimpsest. Go ahead young man, set the stone on the page. I have utmost confidence its secrets will be revealed."

Rory locked eyes with Abby. After a simultaneous shrug, he laid the Rose atop the writing.

"That which you seek is contained not within but without," boomed the Mantara.

Abby thought she sensed an edge of irritation in the ancient voice. She considered its words as Rory slid the stone experimentally across the page.

Rory frowned. "There's nothin' here."

Abby stared at the archaeologist in silence, watching as he removed his glasses to run a hand across his face and through his hair. "Well," she said with annoyance, turning back to Rory, "I bet if we figure out what the Mantara meant, we'll find our answer."

Rory nodded, then scooped up the stone and shut the cover.

Abby rubbed her chin. "I think the last bit it said was 'contained not within but without,' but that doesn't make much sense."

Rory stared at the cover. "Contained no' within but without," he repeated. The tension in Rory's face released and his eyes opened wide. "No' within but without."

"Yeah, I think we've established that," Abby said.

Rory opened the book again and pointed. "No' within the pages," he continued, closing the cover and running his hand along it, "but outside the pages."

"The cover," Abby said. "Of course! You're brilliant, Rory."

Rory grinned, making no attempt to hide his feelings over Abby's praise. He placed the stone atop the cover and slid it back and forth methodically, checking every inch. His grin turned to a frown when no secret writing appeared. He cleared his throat, doing his best to sound confident.

"Perhaps the backside," he said, flipping the book over. After a moment of hesitation, Rory lowered the stone toward the cover. When the smooth cut of the Rose fell flush with the binding, the stone glowed. Rory's hand shook with anticipation as he repeated the process of sliding the stone back and forth. Upon reaching the center of the cover, a refined script emblazoned in red appeared.

Abby scrambled for her backpack. "Rory, hold on a sec, let me grab my notepad and pencil." After retrieving them, Abby sidled up against the Scotsman again. "Can you read it?" she asked, looking at the cover to Rory and back.

Leaning forward, Rory readjusted his grasp on the stone. Contemplating the script, he nodded. "Aye, A-by."

Abby smiled. "Perfect. Remember to go slow so I can write it down."

Rory read each verse with a deliberate, slow pace, glancing from cover to notepad after completing each one, ensuring Abby ample time to transcribe.

> A ring of thirteen
> Standing tall through time
> The secret it bears
> Must come to rise
>
> For what lay within
> Erstwhile betrayed
> Will find its path home
> From that of Berry Brae

When the last verse rolled from his tongue, Rory gripped the stone tight in his palm. He closed his eyes, and an orb of pink haze enveloped him.

Abby looked at her companions. "What's he doing?" she whispered.

After several quiet moments, Rory's eyes shot open, and the stone went dark. "We must go there," he directed.

Abby scrunched her face. "Uh, go where?"

"Pay attention," Aillig sneered, pointing to Abby's notepad, "the location is before you, young lady."

Abby glared at the old man, drawing a deep breath to calm herself. *Think before you speak, Abby.* She cleared her throat and looked down at the phrases. "Would you care to enlighten us?"

Aillig twirled his mustache around his pinky before replying. "Clearly, yes clearly this is referring to the stone circle of Berry Brae, though I've not been there myself."

"Clearly, huh?" Abby said, doing her best not to imitate Aillig's smug composure as she pulled her phone from her hoodie pocket. "I'll just ask my friend Google about it—can't do much without a location." Abby powered the device on only to drop her hands with a groan. "Figures. No service," she said, waggling the phone in front of her before sliding it back in her pocket.

"We have no need," Rory said. "I have seen it, through the eyes of the Rose." He relaxed his hand and gazed at the stone. "I feel a remarkable force pullin' me there."

Whispers of the Mantara filled the hollow in their eerie fashion. "Go there, go there, go there you must."

Agatha stepped around Aillig and paced in front of those seated. "The lad may know the location of the circle, but we don't know how to get there. What do ye suppose we do?"

Abby nodded. "Exactly. We need Finlay to take us there, but his powers are only good if he's already been there or if he sees a picture of it. Having the location in your head," she said, pointing at Rory, "doesn't do us any good." Abby leaned back and looked up at her dog. "Berry Brae Circle. Been there by chance?"

Finlay scratched at the forest floor. *No, Lass. I wish I could say differently.*

Abby directed a thumb over her shoulder. "Says he hasn't been there. So we're stuck, unless..." Abby jumped up and took several steps toward the wooden creature. "Mantara, sir?" she asked, restraining herself from jumping back when the man of wood creaked to turn toward her. "My dog can take us to the circle with just a thought, but he doesn't know where it is. So I don't know what to do. Can you help us?"

The Mantara turned toward Finlay. "Help we will, go there you must." With a quaking thud, the Mantara stepped forward a pace and lowered an arm. "Be still," it said as a lone root flowed from its malformed limb and wrapped itself around Finlay's leg. Seconds later the dog bowed, the root withdrew, and the Mantara stood silent.

Abby ran to Finlay's side. "What happened? Are you okay?"

Finlay bobbed his head. *It was quite curious, child. When the Mantara touched me, an image of an old, stone circle filled my mind. No doubt, this is where we must go.*

Relief flooded Abby. "Finlay knows where to go," she said, turning to the group. "Do you think we should leave now?"

Aillig stood to stretch, exaggerating a yawn as he brought a hand to his mouth. "No, no, we must rest, don't you think?" he said, pushing up his glasses.

Rory lifted himself from the forest floor, stone in hand and book tucked under arm. He looked from face to face, studying the many droopy eyes before nodding in agreement. "Is best. We must sleep before movin' on."

Abby shrugged. "Fine by me. It is the middle of the night."

Rory turned and looked up at the Mantara, leveling his shoulders and pushing his chest out. "May we seek refuge here in yer hollow for the night? Our bones are weary, and we face an arduous journey upon daybreak."

The Mantara bowed. "You may rest to replenish your souls, but your journey must begin, and end, before the new dawn breaks."

Rory bowed. "We thank ye."

Abby looked around the hollow wondering where they might find comfort. She sighed. *Guess it's me and the backpack again.* She rubbed her neck, remembering the last time she used it as a pillow without success.

Just as the others searched for a soft place to lie down, the hollow rumbled. Roots streamed from the tower of trees, forming into five large hammocks, one of which seemed dog-sized. "Wicked," Abby mumbled to herself.

Whispers of the Mantara swirled around the travelers. "Sleep without fear. You will wake refreshed when it is time."

Abby exchanged glances with Agatha and Rory and shrugged. "Okay then," she said, walking up to the nearest hammock. She inspected its construction, surprised by its warmth when she tested its strength by pushing down on it with both hands. "Here goes," she said, rolling herself onto the root hammock. The moment she laid her head back, Abby felt a rush of peace and calm flow over her. Thinking of her parents as she closed her eyes, Abby fell instantly into a deep sleep.

✸✸✸

Abby bolted upright to the sounds of Rory grumbling. She felt surprisingly refreshed and checked her phone. *Huh. It's only been two hours, but I feel like I slept a full night.* She rubbed the sleep from her eyes and swung her legs to the ground. "Rory? What's wrong? You sound angry."

"He's gone, and the book too!" the Scotsman shouted.

Abby boosted herself off the hammock. "Whoa. Gone? Who's gone?"

Rory stomped around the hollow looking behind every bush. He threw his hands in the air and made his way back to Abby. "Aillig. He's taken the Book of Shay."

"You're sure the book's gone?"

"Aye, A-by. I laid it beside me while sleepin'. Was missin' when I awoke."

"Dirty rat," she said, her eyes narrowing. Abby turned in a circle, taking in a quick visual of the hollow. "Hey, wait a minute, where's Finlay?"

In response to the concern in Abby's voice, Agatha rolled from her hammock and worked the kinks from her aged body. "What's the commotion, Lass?" she asked, hobbling to stand next to Abby.

"The Book of Shay is missing," Abby replied. "Rory thinks Aillig made off with it. But," she frowned, "Finlay's gone too, and we can't do anything without him."

Agatha reached out to pat Abby's shoulder. "Perhaps yer fine hound went in search of the scoundrel. Surely he'll be back any moment. Don't trouble yerself, Lass."

"You're right," Abby said with a slow nod. "I should know not to worry about the fur ball. So," she continued, slapping her hands on the front of her thighs, "we better get ready to leave. Once Finlay graces us with his presence, we'll have to figure out what to do."

Abby watched Agatha and Rory go about their own business. Deep in thought, she collected her backpack, making sure everything was in order. *Dad would want me to go after the book again, but from what the Mantara said, we need to go to the circle.* Calmness washed over Abby, causing her to close her eyes and lift her head. "Finlay," she whispered before turning to her companions. "He's coming," she declared.

"What? Who's coming, A-by?"

"Finlay. He'll be here any second."

Rory looked up at Abby curiously as he straightened his pant legs. "How do ye know, A-by? Are ye usin' yer witchy powers again?" he asked with a wink.

Abby flared her nose at the Scotsman. "Funny. To answer your question, I'm not sure, I..."

Finlay's sudden appearance in the middle of the hollow cut Abby's explanation short. "Finlay!" Abby ran to her dog, stopping several feet in front of him. She slapped her hands on her hips. "Where have you been, Mister? We think that sneaky old man disappeared with the book."

Finlay shook his body and bobbed his head. *You are correct, Lass. Upon our deepest sleep, my senses alerted me that something was amiss, and I awoke only in time to see Aillig creeping from the hollow. I'm certain he clutched the book to his chest. I waited several minutes, then followed his scent.* Finlay paced circles around Abby before meshing with her mind again. *How long I followed him, I do not know. His path was erratic, but it seems he headed toward the Cave of Lost Souls.* Stopping in front of Abby, Finlay lowered his head to lock eyes with her. *Then suddenly, he was gone, including his smell.*

"Gone?" Abby asked, confused.

Finlay bobbed his head again. *Aye, Lass. As peculiar as it is. Gone. I have no reasoning. I checked the cave after his mysterious exit only to find it empty.*

Abby groaned and turned to relay Finlay's story to Agatha and Rory. At its end, they were as perplexed as her.

"We need the book, though, don't we, A-by? I fear our chances of findin' it now are lost."

Abby pondered their predicament just as the ground began to rumble. She latched on to Finlay and watched with large eyes as the earthly hammocks unraveled, losing shape. The roots wiggled in the air, retracting back to the towering stacks. When all was silent, the Mantara creaked to life, turning to face its audience. "To the circle, to the circle, to the circle."

Rory stepped forward and bowed before the oddity emulating his kin from long ago. "The Book of Shay has been taken from us. We are uncertain of completin' our journey without it."

The Mantara lifted an arm and pointed toward the Rose of Shaeron, the tip of which poked from the pouch secured at Rory's waist. "That which you need, that which you have." The creature lowered its arm. "To the circle," it repeated with urgency.

Rory reached down to stroke the top of the stone. Securing the pouch, he turned to face the others. "We need to go. Book or no book. Somethin' pulls at me, somethin' I can no' deny." The Scotsman approached Abby and Agatha, beckoning their grasp with both hands held open.

Abby scooped up Rory's hand and waited for Agatha to do the same. She glanced around the hollow, stopping one last time to stare at the Mantara. Shaking her head at the sight, she motioned for Finlay. "Everybody ready?" she asked, sinking her hand into Finlay's rich coat. Satisfied with the response, Abby nodded to the dog and closed her eyes. "Let's go."

15

*F*rom the base of the hill, Abby could see the silhouettes of tips of giant stones stretching toward the stars. Unlike in the hollow, there were no obstructions to the moon's glow. Their trek up the hillside would be unhindered. Abby slowed her climb to keep pace with Agatha. "Do you need a hand?" she asked, holding out an arm.

Agatha shooed her off with a smile. "Sweet of you, Lass, but this old woman will do just fine," she replied in between labored breaths.

"Alright then, if you're sure." Abby glanced up the hill to see Rory pumping his arms in unison with his long strides. She shook her head with a snort. "Always has to be first to the top," she said, reaching out to run the ends of her fingers along Finlay's coat. Abby watched Rory crest the ridge, stopping to stand with his hands balled up on either hip.

The Scotsman turned around and cupped his hands to his mouth. "Hurry, A-by!"

Abby rolled her eyes. "Maybe we should just do this the easy way, seeing how Mr. Antsy-Pants thinks we're too slow," she said after Rory called for them to quicken their pace a second time. Abby wiggled her fingers at Agatha, "take a little help?" The old woman nodded at the now welcome relief from the steep climb. Abby sunk her other hand into Finlay's coat, "To the top, if you would," she said in a stately voice.

The dog snorted, and in moments, they stood next to Rory. Lost in her thoughts, Abby surveyed the meadow before her. A ring of stones, double in circumference to the last stone circle, dappled the landscape to her left. A copse of hardwood trees encircled the rightmost edge of the ring, serving as what might be a privacy screen for potential, prying eyes.

Rory tugged on Abby's elbow, pulling her back to the moment. "Look, A-by," he said, pointing to the uppermost part of the nearest stone. "A hole."

Abby stood on her tiptoes and tilted her head back. "Hey, you're right. Just like the other circle." Abby counted the stones. "Twelve upright and one on its side. Also the same." She glanced at Rory. "Should we see if they all have holes?"

Rory nodded eagerly, taking off to the right around the outside of the circle. Abby followed suit, heading to the left. After checking several rocks, she stopped at the horizontal stone. Placing her hands on the cool surface, she smiled as Rory zipped around the remaining section of circle. "Holes?" she asked as he strolled to stand next to her.

"Aye, A-by. But one misses its top."

Abby shrugged. "Well, it's almost the same as the other circle. This one is spread out a lot more." Surprise filled Abby when she looked to the edge of the hill to see Finlay sniffing the air and Agatha having not moved. "Guys, over here," she said with a beckoning wave. "Come check out this flat one."

Finlay marched around the outer edge of the circle, lifting his nose high, then stuffing it into the long grasses with repeated snorts. Agatha strolled behind him, not once removing her eyes from the stones. "I've never witnessed such a thing," she said as she approached the flat stone. "A remarkable sight if I do say so."

Abby nodded. "Yeah, it's pretty cool. I think my dad said this kind is a recumbent stone circle, because of this one here," she said, patting the stone that lay on its side. "Recumbent, like it's sleeping." Abby glanced behind her when she felt abrupt pressure on the back of her leg.

"What're you doing?" she giggled, seeing her dog's nose still in overdrive.

Finlay hovered over Abby's shoulder and sniffed fervently along the flat face of the giant rock. *You will question what I say but know I have no answer.* He paused to turn his head toward Abby, bringing his eye within inches of her own. *I...I have been here before, long ago, but any memories elude me.*

Abby stifled a laugh. "Say what? If you can't remember it, how do you know?"

Finlay swung his nose back to the stone and continued his olfactory exploration. *I know because my scent is here, however faint, but with no doubt here.*

"Huh, weird." Abby rubbed her chin. "Guys, Finlay says even though he can't remember it, he's been here before; he can smell himself." As Rory and Agatha discussed this strange announcement, Abby stared out into the expanse of the ring of stones. "Hey," she said, realizing something looked strange. "Check out the middle of the circle. I didn't notice until now, but there's no grass. Kind of odd it would grow right up to the edge of the ring and stop."

Rory leaned forward against the stone's surface and squinted into the circle. "Aye, appears to be so, A-by."

Abby rounded the stone and motioned for the others to follow. "Let's look."

Agatha followed Abby as Rory skirted around the other side of the sleeping stone. Finlay trailed behind, intent on sampling every scent his nose detected. Abby stopped shy of the center of the circle and bent over, scooping up a handful of what she thought to be dirt. "Wild. It's like super fine sand, like from some exotic beach." Straightening herself, Abby released the contents from her hand, watching it fall back to its resting place.

"Hey Finlay," she said, turning to find her dog. To Abby's surprise, Finlay danced around one of the upright stones, his front paws pushing on its surface for support. The enormity of his form challenged the height of the stone, and Abby feared Finlay might knock it to the ground. To her relief, the dog pushed off, bringing his front end to the earth with a thump. Jogging to his side, Abby ran her hands through his coat and welcomed the warmth radiating from his massive form. "Come on," she said, turning back to the center of the ring, "I bet there's some good doggie smells for you over here."

Finlay nudged Abby's shoulder playfully as they strolled toward the middle of the stone circle. After several steps, Abby paused, sensing Finlay was no longer behind her. She twisted her head back to find the dog frozen in place. Abby whipped around. "Finlay! What's wrong?" She rushed to his side, inspecting him. "Hey," she said, snapping her fingers near his eye. "Earth to Finlay."

Finlay's body started to quiver. *I...something...*

"What, what is it? I can't help if you don't tell me what's wrong," Abby pleaded.

With effort, the dog took two more steps forward and erupted into a piercing howl. At the same moment, the ground within the centermost point of the ring began to shake. Abby's eyes darted around the circle, fearful the stones—all of them—would tumble where they pleased. Finlay's howling lingered, his body jerking until he collapsed with a dull thud. Though the howling diminished to a soft whimper, the sand continued to rumble. Abby yelled for Rory and Agatha to back away, to find a safe path to her side.

Rory led the old woman around the ring, wary of the giant stones. Relieved to have everyone in one spot, Abby hurried to Finlay's side. She crouched and choked back a tear. "Finlay," she whimpered, placing her hands on his chest, "what's happening to you? How do I help?" She glanced up and focused on the sand. The violent shaking subsided, but the area continued to protest, bubbling as if it were scalding water. "What the heck is going on?" she whispered, darting her eyes from dog to sand to dog.

"A-by, look!" Rory exclaimed as Agatha gasped and covered her mouth with both hands. "Looks like somethin' is risin' from the sand." Rory stepped toward Abby with wide eyes. "A-by, I sense a strong magic," he continued after a hard gulp, "me thinks this is what I felt callin' me."

Speechless, Abby, Rory, and Agatha watched with disbelief as an unknown form rose from the earth. As tense moments passed, all movement in the circle ceased. While stroking Finlay's neck, Abby squinted at the mysterious, dark figure. The glow from the moon illuminated familiar lines, showing off the bumps and curves of the prone shape. "What the..." Abby rubbed her eyes, skeptical of what she was seeing. "It, it looks like a mummy," she blurted, glancing up at the Scotsman.

Rory looked from the figure to Abby. "I must inspect it," he said, holding out a hand. "Come with me?"

Abby frowned when a mournful whimper erupted from Finlay's chest. "You go," she replied, tugging gently on the dog's ear, "I don't want to leave him."

Rory released a slow breath and nodded. "Will be only a moment," he said, motioning for Agatha to stay with Abby. Turning toward the center of the circle, Rory reached down to tighten the straps of his scabbard, then searched out the stone with his fingers, sighing when they made contact with the smooth gem. With cautious steps, Rory approached the motionless shape. A faint, pink glow pulsed with increasing intensity from the Rose as he drew near the dark figure. Rory stopped, loosened the drawstring on the pouch, and slipped the stone into his hand. Turning his focus back to the center of the circle, Rory raised the gem in the air, allowing its pink radiance to fill the area. The warmth from the Rose curled its way around the silent shape. In that instance, a blazing red aura threatened to burst through what appeared to be a pristine shroud encompassing a long body. Rory stumbled back.

"It can no' be," he said, drawing his sword. With stone in one hand and hilt in the other, the Scotsman inched toward the glowing form. Extending the tip of the sword to the shroud, Rory held his breath as he lifted a corner of the covering and peeled it back.

Even from afar, Abby could see the muscles tense throughout Rory's lean frame as he removed the ancient veil, letting it slip from the end of the sword and flutter to the ground. She echoed his sharp breath, watching Rory drop weapon and stone and crumble to his knees. Filled with worry, Abby looked from Finlay to Rory. She leaned close and kissed the dog's nose. "I'll be right back." Jumping up, Abby bolted to the center of the ring, skidding to a halt behind the Scotsman. "Whoa," she said, taking in the preserved form before her. "Is that..." she began to question.

"Aye," choked Rory, cutting Abby short. "The Red King."

"No way," Abby whispered. After many silent moments, she swung her backpack forward, retrieved the scroll's translation, and read the last verse to herself.

A treasure so grand
Protected through time
Until blood of like blood
Reveals what's inside

"It's just like the scroll says, Rory. He's been here, protected through time, waiting for you to find him, I guess." She paused to scratch her head. "But, I don't get it. Mavis and Tavis killed him near Caledonia. If I remember, they said they burned his body." Abby rounded Rory and leaned over his kin. "I don't see any evidence of burns, and it's weird," she said, looking back at Rory with wide eyes. "He looks like he's just sleeping."

Recovered from his initial shock, Rory retrieved his sword and slipped the stone back into its pouch. He moved to stand by Abby's side and gazed down upon the Red King with wonder. With arms crossed over one another on his chest, the Red King appeared to be at peace. "Yer right, A-by," he agreed, reaching down to hover a hand over that of his kin, "he seems to be only dreamin'." When Rory brushed his fingers against the Red

King's leathered skin, a ghostly voice floated through the air, carried by a gust of wind.

Abby and Rory stared blankly at each other. "Did you hear that?" Abby asked.

Rory nodded. "Aye, A-by. Me thinks it said to complete the circle."

"I think you're right. But what circle?" Abby shrugged as she stepped back from the eerie resting place. Glancing over her shoulder to find Finlay sitting upright, Abby ran back to her dog. "Finlay," she cried, wrapping her arms around his thick neck. She looked into his eyes. "What happened? And promise me you won't do that again." Without giving the dog a chance to reply, Abby pointed excitedly toward Rory. "You'll never believe what we found, who we found!"

Finlay groaned, burrowing his head into Abby's armpit. With a weak sigh, he meshed with her mind. *I was his as he was mine. As you are mine and I am yours.*

Abby pulled Finlay's head from the crook of her arm, bringing his eyes level with her own. She cocked her head to the side. *Wait. What? Did you say you knew him?*

Finlay released a long moan. *That is so, Lass. My very essence was bound to his. I was his guide, as now I am yours.*

Abby pulled her face back from the dog. *Guide? Bound to him? Okay, wait, back up here. You could talk with him like you do with me?*

The dog bowed its head.

And could you teleport him too?

Finlay again bowed his head. *Aye, Lass. What I have with you, I had with him. But, our connection is powerful, most unlike my prior binding.*

Abby eyed the dog. *I'm still confused, Finlay. If you were bound to the Red King, why didn't you remember? And how come you didn't know he was buried here? You said you've been here before. It doesn't make any sense.*

Finlay filled his deep chest with the still night's air. *Place your hands upon my head and ready your mind for a journey into the past.*

Abby breathed deep, thinking back to the first, and last, time Finlay shared images of the past with her. Steadying her hands, she sunk them into his fur behind either ear. With a jolt, bursts of memories appeared in rapid succession. A flash of red light, the Red King and Finlay standing in the middle of Berry Brae Circle. Sylvan Myst and his daughter Enya, the Red King's undying love for her. Mavis and Tavis, a gruesome battle. The form of the Red King, lifeless upon the Giant rock. Finlay wandering inside a cave, the faerie brothers entwining him with their magic.

Those images and more sent Abby sprawling backward. "Holy cow," she said, catching her breath as a myriad of emotions rattled her insides.

Finlay rose slowly, shaking the memories from his body. *Now do you understand, child?*

Abby nodded and rubbed her face. "It's almost too incredible to believe. But yes, I understand." She turned to find Agatha studying their exchange while Rory continued to stand over the remains of his long dead kin. Abby called out to him while motioning for Agatha to join her. "Hey Rory, better c'mere, you'll want to hear this."

Rory pulled his eyes from the man of legend and jogged to Abby's side. "What's wrong? Does somethin' trouble ye, A-by?"

Abby brushed a stray curl from her face. "Well, I wouldn't say I'm troubled, in fact, certain things make so much more sense now. But," she turned to glance at Finlay, "I'm left with more questions."

"Well on with ye then, Lass," Agatha urged with a smile, "let the boy and I discover those same questions."

Abby looked up at the moon, contemplating how best to explain her newfound understanding. "Okay, so you know how I said Finlay had been here before?" She paused, allowing her companions to nod. "Well, that's because he came here from another land with the Red King, through a portal of some kind."

"Oh my," Agatha said, raising a hand to her mouth.

"A por-tal?" Rory asked, stumbling over the word.

Abby refrained from giggling at the Scotsman. "Yes, a portal, like a passageway between two places. Anyway, Sylvan Myst summoned the Red King here and," she said, pointing to the dog, "Finlay came with him because he was his animal guide. The Red King had a connection with him, just like I do." Rory and Agatha stared curiously at the dog as Abby continued. "Apparently, in exchange for protecting the countryside of Caledonia from the faeries, the Red King demanded Sylvan Myst cast a powerful spell upon him and the sword. They agreed if the Red King died in Caledonia, his body would be transported here, preserved, to lie in wait for his unnamed kin to take him home. And I guess even though Mavis and Tavis thought they hid your sword," she said, gesturing at Rory, "it also found its way to a safe place, I'm guessing with Enya."

"Well what about yer magnificent dog then?" Agatha asked with a flick of her head toward Finlay.

"Aye, A-by," Rory agreed, "Does no' explain why he has no memory of such things."

Abby raised her hands palm out, "I know, I know," she said, turning to face Finlay. She ruffled his neck as she looked at him with uncertain eyes. "Here's where things aren't as clear. It seems the bond between an animal guide and its person severs upon death. And I think Sylvan Myst cast a spell on Finlay too, so that if the Red King died here, Finlay would have no memory of who he was or where he came from." Abby shrugged, "As kind of a protective measure. Protective of who or what, though, I'm not sure."

Rory paced in a wide arc. "So could it be, when we approached the restin' place of me kin," he said, looking over his shoulder at the Red King, "was enough to stir his memory? Perhaps break any remnants of Sylvan Myst's spell?"

Abby lifted a shoulder. "Your guess is as good as mine."

As the group continued to ponder the meaning of Finlay's memories, the dog crept toward the still form of the Red King. With a mournful whimper, he sniffed around the body, taking great care with his movements. After several moments of inspection, Finlay lifted his head and locked eyes with Abby. *We must take him home, now.*

Feeling the seriousness of Finlay's statement, Abby motioned for the other's attention. "Hey, Finlay says we need to take the Red King home, right away."

"But how?" Agatha asked. "We don't even know where he came from or how to get there."

"But we do," Rory said, raising a finger. "The por-tal."

"Rory's right, we need to find it, which I'm betting won't be easy." Abby turned in a slow circle, examining the stones. "I'm sure whoever made it wouldn't want just anybody stumbling through."

Agatha rubbed her temples. "Perhaps there's a clue of sorts contained within the ring," she suggested after a quiet moment.

Abby nodded. "I bet you're right. That's what I'd do if I wanted to hide something for a certain person to find." Abby turned to stare at the center of the ring. "But where?" she said, tapping her chin, "not anywhere obvious, that's for sure."

"Let us search the stones again," Rory said as he began strolling toward a megalith.

"Sounds good," Abby agreed. She glanced at Finlay who now lay next to the Red King. The dog let out a pitiful whimper. Feeling his sadness, she vowed to herself to cheer him up once they solved the mystery at hand. She released a slow breath as she turned her back to him and headed toward the nearest stone. Though the moon highlighted her surroundings, it did little to show any fine detail.

"Need some light," she whispered to herself, retrieving a flashlight from her bag. Abby investigated the surface of the rock, shining the light in every crevice. Finding nothing of significance at the first, she moved from stone to stone in a methodical search, ending at the recumbent slab with a frustrated sigh. Abby frowned as Rory and Agatha approached with similar facades. "Anything?" she asked, knowing the response. When both shook their heads in unison, Abby drummed her fingers on the stone. "We must be missing something." Feeling the need for a different vantage point, Abby boosted herself atop the rock and shined her light into the circle.

Rory raised a hand toward Abby. "May I?" he asked, wiggling his fingers at the flashlight. "Perhaps I overlooked somethin'."

"I doubt it, but why not," Abby said, handing the light to the Scotsman. She leaned back, resting her palms on the cool stone as Rory strode off to repeat his search. Pondering the circle, Abby ran a hand along the top of the stone, tracing an unusual groove absentmindedly with her forefinger.

Standing behind her, Agatha watched the curious movement of Abby's finger. "Lass? What did ye find there?"

Abby jerked back to reality. "Huh? I didn't find..." Her voice trailed off as she twisted to the side and examined the spot her hand had been. "Hey wait," she whispered, looking up at Agatha. "You're right. There's something here." Abby ran her palm flat over the area. "It looks like there's writing carved into the top, but it's so worn." Abby called over her shoulder to the Scotsman. "Hey Rory, we found something. Bring me the light, would you?"

Rory hurried back to the stone and extended the light to Abby. "What is it, A-by?"

"There's writing of some sort," Abby said without removing her eyes from the strange markings. "Hop up here, check it out."

Rory grunted, joining Abby atop the stone. He leaned back on one arm and ran a hand over the surface. "Aye, yer right, A-by. Is very old writin'."

"It's so faint, worn with time," Abby said, "I can't read it."

Rory studied the markings before breaking into a wide grin. "I have an idea, A-by," he said, lowering himself to the ground.

Abby called after the Scotsman as he headed toward the center of the circle. "An idea? Like what? And where are you going?"

Rory walked toward Finlay and his kin with soft footfalls. Finlay raised his head as the young man approached. Showing no interest in the current activities, the dog blinked several times, then lowered his head and shut his eyes. Rory dropped to one knee and scooped up a handful of sand. He returned to the slab, hands cupped against one another. "Give me yer hands, A-by."

Abby twisted around so she faced the center of the ring. She tilted her head, unsure, yet curious about Rory's plan. She placed the flashlight to one side, cupped her hands, and watched as Rory poured the sand into them before he hopped back onto the rock. "Now what?" she asked.

"Now," he said, leaning in to retrieve a handful of the sand, "the sand shall tell us the stone's secret."

After a moment of confusion, comprehension clicked in Abby's head. "Ooohh," she cooed, twisting around to watch as Rory spread the sand over the worn writing.

Rory straightened with a smile upon seeing the wonder in Abby's eyes. He cupped the bottom of her hands with his, nodding toward them. "I'll take the rest, A-by."

Abby released the sand into Rory's waiting hands. "Nice going, Smarty."

Rory's grin widened as he twisted back to the mysterious writing and poured the remains over the area. He began to brush away the top layer. Once satisfied with his progress, he sucked in a deep breath and blew away any loose grains of sand. He sat back, admiring his work.

"You did it, Rory!" Abby exclaimed, grabbing the light and focusing it on the sand. She looked down with amazement at four lines of script. "That's definitely not

English. But," she paused with uncertainty, "can you read it?"

"Aye, A-by, I can."

"Well," she said, poking him in the side, "what's it say? We don't have all night, you know."

Rory flashed a comical face at Abby, eliciting a giggle from her as he turned to focus on the sand script. After a moment of study, he cleared his throat and translated.

When the moon and rose meet

Upon the sleeping stone

Only then

Will the path home be shown

Abby's eyes brightened with recognition after Rory read the lines aloud a second time. "The moon and the rose." Abby looked from Agatha to Rory. "The rose. I bet it means the Rose of Shaeron. And," she paused, looking up into the sky, "I bet the moon is supposed to shine on it." Abby started searching the surface of the rock. "Here, help me look for a hole or something the Rose might fit in."

Agatha bustled to the side of the stone. "I'll search down here, Lass."

"Perfect," Abby said as she continued twisting this way and that. Finding nothing to either side of her, Abby scooted to the left to check the space on which she sat.

"Humph," she grunted in disappointment at her lack of success. "Any luck?" she asked, glancing over at Rory.

"No, Lass," he replied with a frown.

In the same moment, Agatha called. "Over here, Lass," she said, bobbing her head up and down over the edge of the stone. "I think I've found what yer seekin'."

Abby caught Rory's excited gaze and slid with him in unison from the rock. They raced around the obstacle, stopping to stand behind Agatha at the crown of the sleeping stone.

"Here," she said, pointing to a spot near the top of the rock.

Rory stepped forward, reaching an arm over Agatha's head. He felt slowly around the area. "Aye," he said, turning to look at Abby. "May I have some light, A-by?"

Abby nodded and shined the light to where Rory pointed. "Sure looks like a notch of some sort. See if the Rose will fit in it, Rory."

Following Abby's suggestion, Rory drew a deep breath and pulled the Rose from its pouch. Holding it in front of him, he considered its shape and that of the hole his fingers explored. He lifted it toward the stone, rotating it and tilting it at an angle. Without further hesitation, Rory slid it into the crevice and removed his hand.

The three stepped back, looking from the stone to the Rose to the moon. After several long moments of anticipation, the moon seemed to brighten in the sky and focus its rays upon the Rose. Abby whipped her head back toward the sleeping stone, which now pulsed a deep pink in kind with the Rose.

"Wild," she whispered, watching as the color of the gem deepened to a fiery red. She jumped back when twelve tendrils of the same, intense color shot out unexpectedly from the center of the Rose.

"Oh dearie me," Agatha exclaimed, stumbling back into the Scotsman.

"A-by, what's happenin'?"

Abby glanced at Rory from the corner of her eye. "I have no idea, but I bet we'll find out soon," she said, pointing at the twelve strings of light now swirling through the air, each toward a standing stone. Moments before the rays of light reached their prospective targets, a low grating reverberated throughout the circle. Abby craned her neck and directed the flashlight beam onto one of the stones. "You guys, the rocks. I think they're turning!"

Each of the twelve stones pivoted with precision until the fiery, red rays pierced the holes at their apices, all save for one stone—the stone with the missing top. The last ray of light whirled round and round, searching for an unfindable goal.

Abby groaned. "That stone with no top," she said, turning to Rory and Agatha. "I don't think we can open the portal without it. What're we going to do?"

Before anyone could respond, a loud crashing and crunching emanated from the copse of hardwood. Abby spun around and shined her light beyond the stones. "What the heck?" she mumbled, searching the row of trees. Her body tensed as the racket drew nearer, increasing in intensity, until at the last moment, when Abby feared what her light might reveal, out stepped the giant buck.

16

"Seriously? That deer is following us," Abby said, lowering her light and turning to stare at Rory. "That's the third time." She narrowed her eyes after glancing back at the animal. "I'm beginning to think it's not a coincidence." Abby continued her rant, oblivious to the movement of the buck until Agatha pointed past her shoulder with a startled look on her face.

Abby whirled around, following the direction of the old woman's finger. To her surprise, the giant deer entered the stone circle. With slow steps, two by two, the stag approached the Red King. He lowered his enormous antlers and smelled the noble remains with rapid sniffs and snorts.

As if jarred from a deep sleep, Finlay flicked his eyes open and bolted upright. Turning to stand nose to nose with the buck, he gazed into the newcomer's eyes. Abby tensed, uncertain of what was happening. Moments later, both Finlay and the deer raised their heads, then twisted to look at the huddled group.

Abby gulped, a strange sensation pulling her toward the center of the ring. She mouthed to Rory and Agatha to wait by the sleeping stone before ducking under the source of fiery rays and jogging to Finlay. She slowed to a stop next to her grand dog and reached out to him. *What's with the deer? This is the third time he's crept up on Rory and me.*

Finlay rubbed his muzzle along Abby's arm, releasing a long sigh. *He is of my kind.*

Abby tilted her head, eying the creature with uncertainty. *An animal guide? Well, where's its person, you know, the one it's bound too?*

Finlay stretched his frame, ending the action with a yawn. *This I do not know, Lass. We cannot communicate. I can only sense his nature, and he, mine.*

Abby turned to face the stag. *He talked to me before, in that creepy forest.*

Finlay cocked his head. *This is most unexpected. Are you certain, child?*

Abby snorted. *Um, yeah. Positive. He warned me about the Wolf, I didn't catch on though. But why'd you say that? Why's it unexpected? I can talk to you, so why would it be strange if I could talk to him?*

Finlay remained silent as he considered her words after which a gruff rumble rolled from his chest. *For all my knowledge, this is most curious. I have no answer, Lass. I know only that with which I was created. Guides have the ability to communicate only with those to whom they are bound.*

Well, that's weird... Abby started to reply, feeling a stabbing pain in her temple. She cried out, clamping a hand to the side of her head. To her relief, the discomfort subsided, replaced by a familiar tingling sensation. She flicked her eyes to the buck. "That's you doing that, isn't it?"

The deer moved its rack up and down several times in response before reaching out with its mind a second time. *Complete the circle.*

"Finlay," Abby said aloud, "he talked to me again. You couldn't hear him?"

The dog shook his head. *No, Lass. Tell me what he said.*

Abby stared up at the deer's impressive rack. "He, he said to complete the circle."

Upon Abby's relay of his message, the stag turned from the center of the ring. The creature twisted his neck to either side and stopped upon seeing the stone with the missing top. The deer trotted to the upright rock, released a long snort, and followed the whirling path of the homeless tendril with its snout. It called out to Abby again. *Complete the circle.*

"Complete the circle," Abby whispered, noting the deer's fascination with the swirling ray of red. "I wonder if he means we need to fix the broken stone?" she pondered, watching Rory and Agatha join her with apprehensive steps. "Hey," she said once they stood by her side, "you probably won't believe this, but Finlay says that deer is an animal guide too. And," she paused to run her hand through the dog's scruff, "it says we need to complete the circle. I think we have to fix the broken stone, but I'm not sure how."

With one hand on the hilt of his sword and one on a hip, Rory observed the peculiar actions of the buck. After quiet contemplation, the Scotsman turned to Abby. "To fix the stone, it must have a hole the same as the like," he said, swooping an arm towards a portion of the ring. "I have no' seen the missing piece, but," he paused, a look of enlightenment washing across his face, "A-by! Think back to the last time we saw this grand beast."

Abby tipped her head, pondering the Scotsman's directive. "Rory, you're a genius!" she exclaimed, hugging him from the side. "I forgot about the broken top in the other circle. It even had a hole in it. That's perfect. But," she scratched her temple, "that thing looked heavy. How the heck are we going to get it here, let alone stick it on top of the stone?"

Agatha wrung her kerchief in her hands. "I may be speakin' foolishly, but those are mighty strong lookin' antlers on that stag. Perhaps the beast could scoop it up and carry it on its head."

"Aye," Rory said, "but that may be the clearest part. How do we get it from there," he continued, pointing to a faraway place, "to here?"

Abby swiveled to smile at Finlay. "Easy. We have a magical transporter right here. But," her smiled diminished, "he hasn't been there before, so I'm not sure how he's supposed to find it."

The trio contemplated the problem, and just when Abby thought no solution would present itself, Rory squared his shoulders. "Your pic-ture, A-by," he said, pointing to her jacket.

Abby looked down at her waist, confused by the Scotsman's statement. Slipping her hand inside the pocket, recognition blazed on her face. "Of course. I took a picture of the forest map." Abby tapped into her image gallery and held the phone in front of Finlay. Zooming in and shifting the map to the area of the stone circle, Abby pointed to the screen and pulled her hand out of the way.

"See that spot where the trail splits and there are open hills to the right, with more forest to the left? That's the path that leads to the other ring of stones, and here," she said, readjusting the view, "is about where you met up with us outside of the tree line. Think you can find that?" she asked, sliding the map back to the split in the trail.

Finlay turned his muzzle, bringing his left eye within inches of the screen. He blinked rapidly before pulling his head back. The dog's uncertainty entered Abby's mind. *The safest route is to begin on the trail. My confidence in finding an open path outweighs dropping you into a dense forest. I believe you wouldn't appreciate ending up inside a tree.*

Abby snorted. *Uh, yeah. Let's not do that.* Putting her phone away, Abby turned her attention back to Rory and Agatha. "We should be good," she said with a buzz. "Finlay thinks he can find the path to the other circle. But," she slowed her excitement, "I'm not sure the deer will understand what we want him to do."

"Ye said it spoke to ye, A-by," Rory said, rubbing his chin. "Will it understand ye in return?"

"Only one way to find out," Abby replied, heading off toward the stag. She slowed her pace as she neared the animal, placing herself in its line of vision. When Abby came to a stop, it swung to face her.

"So, you can understand me, right?" Abby asked, meeting the creature's eyes.

The deer nodded its head with a snort.

"Great. So it's obvious you want us to fix this stone, but, we'll need your help to do it," Abby paused, studying the deer's facial expressions, "will you help?"

The deer nodded its head again but this time lowered itself into a bow, bending one of its front legs.

"Okay then, I'll take that as a yes." Abby tucked her hands into opposite armpits. "I have an idea that may or may not work, but it involves taking you back to that other stone circle. Finlay," she said, pointing to the dog, "will help with that, it's his specialty. Are you agreeable to this?"

The stag stood upright, jerking its head up and down to end by staring up at the top of the broken stone.

Abby leaned to the side for a better view of her dog. *Let's do this before this big guy changes his mind.*

Seconds later, Finlay appeared to Abby's left, causing her to jump and place a hand on her heart. "Maybe someday I'll get used to that."

The dog winked at her. *I doubt it.*

"Funny." Abby giggled, sticking her tongue out. After ruffling Finlay's fur, she turned toward Rory and Agatha. "You guys should stay here to protect the Rose. We'll be right back. I hope!"

Rory nodded approval and placed a comforting hand on Agatha's shoulder upon noticing her nervous movements. "All shall be well."

With a final wringing of her kerchief, Agatha placed it back into a pocket and smoothed her smock. "Be swift, Lass," she called out.

Abby gave thumbs up to her friends before shifting her attention back to the surreal animals in her presence. She stared up at the stag, absorbed in her own thoughts. *No worries, Abby. Just get this buck with the obnoxiously large antlers to scoop up a massive rock and somehow balance it on top of a stone to which it doesn't belong. What could go wrong?* Abby smiled nervously at herself, moving to stand between the dog and the deer. She stretched an arm to Finlay, placing a soft grip on his fur, then addressed the stag. "For Finlay to take us there, I'll have to touch you, okay?" she asked, inching her free hand toward the deer's flank.

The buck responded by moving its hind end closer to her.

Abby grinned. "Alright, once I touch you, don't move."

With a feigned nod, the deer stilled itself as Abby sunk her fingers into its course hide. With a nod to Finlay, Abby closed her eyes.

✳✳✳

The buck paused at the side of the trail, plucking several leaves from a woody bush. Abby stopped at the sound of crunching and glanced over her shoulder. *Really? We don't have time for any late night snacks.* Finlay sensed Abby's tension with the deer and swung his head back. A grumble rolled from the dog's chest after making eye contact with the buck who then swallowed its take, returned the snort, and continued trotting along the path.

Abby rolled her eyes as she turned her attention back to the trail. "It should be around here," she said, pointing off to the right. Knowing the way would be dark, Abby retrieved her light and searched for the elusive gap in the brush. "Here," she said, "see where Rory and I stomped the grasses?" Abby stepped off the trail and into the wood. "It's just a little ways in, you can see the stones up ahead."

In short order, Abby led the dog and deer to the center of the ring. She swung her light around, bringing it to a stop on the tumbled, stone top. Abby turned to the buck. "Do you think you can pick that up?" she asked, jiggling the beam of light over the rock. The deer scratched at the ground and waved its head before following the light's path.

Abby motioned for Finlay to join her at the stone. They both stopped several feet from the deer, watching it sniff the rock and attempt to push it with its nose. Finding this tactic would fail, the deer lowered its rack and shoved the tip of an antler beneath the stone. After several unsuccessful tries to move it even the slightest, the buck pried its antler free.

Finlay grumbled into Abby's mind. *This will never do. I have a solution.* Striding around the stag to the opposite side of the stone, Finlay dug into the ground with powerful, lively strokes. Both Abby and the deer backed away as dirt flew haphazardly into the air. The dog grunted with pleasure and soon Abby could no longer see his head. "Uh, Finlay," she said, shining the light in his direction, "mind telling me how a hole will help us move the stone?"

With a final fling of dirt, Finlay scooted backward and out of the hole. He shook the result of his work from his fur, ambled back to sit by Abby, and licked his paws. *Tell the stag to place his rack into the hole. I shall push the stone from the opposite end. Then we must be on our way. The night grows short.*

"Alrighty, if you think that'll work," she said, turning to address the deer. To Abby's surprise, the stag trotted to the hole, stopped square on, and peered into the dark pocket below the stone. Lifting its head, it seemed to consider its antlers and look back to the hole. With a final wave of its head, the deer lowered its rack into the crevice, calling out to Abby. *Complete the circle.*

"Huh, well what do you know," she murmured. Glancing at Finlay, Abby rolled her eyes as he continued to groom himself. "Ah, Finlay, he's waiting on you."

The dog quit mid-lick and stood. He approached the deer and with a calculated hop, pounced on the stone at an angle. The thinned ground beneath the rock succumbed to the force of Finlay's weight, allowing the broken top to slide into the bowl of the stag's rack with a dull thump.

With the added weight of the rock, the deer's head lowered further into the hole. Abby feared its girth would prove too much for the animal, but soon the stag lifted its rack and stood straight. As it did, his antlers glowed a brilliant yellow. The radiance swirled in a circle to encompass the stone, relieving it of contact with the rack as it increased in speed with each turn. When the deer bobbed its head at Abby she gasped. The stone moved synchronously with the beast, floating within the curvature of its velvet covered bones.

"Whoa, how's it doing that?" she whispered, glancing at Finlay.

The dog bumped his head against her side. *All guides have a unique ability. Mine is movement through time and space. This appears to be his, perhaps a manipulation of objects.*

"Maybe I should ask him..."

If you ask him anything, child, start with his name. But be swift.

"Good point," she said, walking up to the deer and pocketing her light. Mesmerized by the floating rock, Abby pulled her attention back to the animal.

"Cool magic, Mr., ah, what's your name?" she stammered.

The deer tilted its head before working into Abby's mind. *Guido.*

"Wait, did you say Guido?" Abby asked with a quirky smile.

The deer bowed its head.

Abby choked back a laugh, knowing it would be immature and inappropriate to crack any mafia jokes. "Okay," she sang, releasing a calming breath. "So where's your person? The one you're bound to?"

Guido released a mournful moan. *Dead.*

Abby snapped her mouth shut. "Oh. Sorry," she said after a moment.

Guido scratched at the ground, impatient. *Complete the circle.*

"Right. You're right, Guido, we need to go." Abby sidled next to the deer and waved Finlay to her. When he was close enough, she sunk a hand into his coat and flattened the other against Guido. "Alright, let's complete that circle."

✳✳✳

Guido looked up to examine the rough top of the broken, upright stone. The deer circled the megalith several times, changing direction every few steps.

"What's it doin', A-by?"

"Not sure. Maybe he's trying to figure out how to attach the piece. And his name's Guido, by the way."

Rory grunted with a nod, turning his attention back to the magical creature.

Guido stopped with a snort, tilted his head down, and with a flick of his rack, released the stone top into the air. The yellow orb encapsulating the rock floated along, swirling and pulsing as it seemed to guide it to its new home. Guido's audience watched with amazement when the new top meshed seamlessly with the broken upright. The yellow radiance crept outward, engulfing the repaired stone. The megalith pulsed with great intensity but fizzled out to its natural state as the rock rotated, lining up with the rest of the circle. When the stone stopped moving, the lost, fiery tendril shot through the hole like an arrow.

Prior to that moment, Abby took no notice of where the red beams of light ended their paths. Her eyes grew large when she realized the rays looped overhead, high into the sky, meeting at a central point above the stone circle. The twelfth tendril soared into the air, corkscrewing as it went until commencing its union. With a fiery flash, the twelve rays twisted into one and rocketed toward the earth.

"Everybody back up," Abby yelled, motioning with her arms as the ray of light smashed into the ground several feet to the inside of the recumbent stone.

The force of the impact severed the connection between the rays, splitting them into individual balls of light. The tiny orbs lifted into the air, tracing an intricate pattern.

"Wicked," Abby breathed, "it looks like they're drawing a picture of something."

The orbs flitted back and forth, painting on a canvas of air, until meeting again in the center of their masterpiece to join as one. To everyone's surprise, the ball of light whisked up into the sky, stopping to dance above the sleeping stone. Plummeting toward the Rose of Shaeron, the gem swallowed the light.

Astonished, Abby watched as the Rose flickered out and became dormant. She pulled her eyes away to examine the creation shimmering vertically above the ground. Her jaw dropped. "You guys. It looks like the tree on the cover of the Book of Shay!"

Rory approached the glowing tree. "Must be the portal," he said, stretching a curious finger toward its surface.

Abby jumped to bat at his hand. "Rory! Don't touch it. At least, not yet. Not until we figure out what we're doing."

A moment later, both Finlay and Guido entered Abby's mind. *Home,* she heard in unison. A brief feeling of sadness welled up in Abby when she realized her dog might wish to return whence he came so long ago. Sucking in a deep breath, Abby tucked away her emotions just as Guido reached out to her again. *Complete the circle.*

Abby turned to find the deer. "But we did," she blurted.

Guido swung his head toward the Red King. *Complete the circle.*

Abby frowned, confused by his insistence. "It'd be helpful if you could speak more than three words at a time."

As Abby opened her mouth to question Guido further, a warm gust of wind rustled her hair. It rolled through the circle carrying the same, unknown voice. "Protect the Rose," it whispered, fading away as the wind diminished.

Abby, Rory, and Agatha swiveled their heads, searching for the source of the mysterious voice. "Protect the Rose," Abby repeated. "I think it wants you to take the stone again," she continued, turning to Rory. "Not sure what more we need it for, though," she added, shrugging.

Rory walked in a wide circle around the pulsing portal. "Its magic continues to pull me, A-by. I sense the Rose has a greater purpose," he said, stopping at the edge of the sleeping stone.

"But what of the portal?" Agatha asked. "Will it disappear if ye remove the Rose from the giant stone?"

Rory scratched his head, glancing repeatedly from the portal to the stone. "Nae," he said with conviction. "The Rose has recalled its magic. The por-tal is secure." Reaching up, Rory rubbed his fingers together. With a quick motion, he plucked the Rose from the sleeping stone and slipped it into his pouch. A smile spread across his face when he looked up to find the glowing tree intact.

"Well done, Lad," Agatha said. "Now how do ye suppose," she asked, walking to stand near the Red King, "he gets from here and through the portal?"

Rory looked blankly at Abby as she contemplated the question.

Without warning, a familiar, but unexpected voice broke the group's silence. "The protector doesn't, unless I go through first."

Startled, Abby twisted her head, searching for the crackly hiss that soon followed. She eyed the standing stone nearest Agatha with suspicion. The area around the rock appeared to go in and out of focus. "I think there's someone hiding back there," she said, pointing beyond the old woman.

Before Agatha could respond, Mallena and Aillig stepped out from behind the megalith. Mallena streaked forward and slipped an arm around Agatha's throat. "Seems it best I released you the last time," she droned in the old woman's ear, "I have a much better use for you now."

Once Abby realized what was happening, she tensed as if to run to Agatha's rescue, but Rory grabbed her by the elbow and swung her behind him. "No, Lass," he said, drawing his sword.

Finlay and Guido slunk to either side of Abby and Rory, the dog with his hackles alert and the deer in an obvious state of agitation.

Abby glared at the archaeologist, realizing he clutched the Book of Shay to his chest. "Thief," she spat, stepping to Rory's left, "sneaking off in the middle of the night. That wasn't yours to take," she finished with a stomp of her foot.

Aillig sneered in response. "Now, now, young lady, when it comes to it, I helped you obtain information you didn't even realize you needed. You likely wouldn't have found the portal on your own," he said, pointing his chin toward the fiery tree. "Consider the book repayment. It's of more value in my hands."

Abby's stomach lurched, and her shoulders tensed as a bead of sweat rolled along the contour of her spine. "We trusted you. And you, you," she stuttered, "teamed up with that thing."

"There, there, young lady. Let this be a lesson to you," he said with a biting tone. "As my dear father would say, never trust a Ratchet."

"Enough!" Mallena screeched as she produced her curved blade. "You will allow the historian and me to pass through the portal. If you resist, the crone dies."

Rory positioned himself in front of the tree, flames rolling from his sword. "I shall no' allow whatever lies beyond this por-tal to know yer foulness. Release our friend or I will be forced to harm ye." With a flick of his wrist, a single flame spiraled into the air.

Agatha whimpered and squeezed her eyes shut as Mallena shoved her forward. "I will spend no more of my days trapped in this hideous world," hissed the spindly creature, "now step aside, or the crone learns the true sting of my blade."

Finlay and Guido stalked the outer edges of the circle, positioning themselves behind Mallena. Aillig eyed the formidable animals and clutched the book even tighter to his chest as he cowered at Mallena's side. "Move quickly, move quickly," he warned, "the beasts intend to surround us."

Mallena glanced over her shoulder with a growl. "You choose not to heed my warning, and for that, the old hag will suffer." Pushing Agatha forward, closer and closer to the portal, Mallena released her arm from around the old woman's neck and latched onto her shoulder.

Abby sucked in a harsh breath and for the briefest of moments thought Mallena would release her elder from the threatening grasp. "Please, just let her go."

Mallena's eyes turned a blazing red as they narrowed. One corner of her mouth curled up into a forewarning grin. "I will not be denied," she asserted.

To Abby's horror, Mallena shoved Agatha forward, releasing her shoulder, and in the same moment caught the side of her neck with the tip of her blade. The knife ripped through the old woman's flesh as she fell forward.

Agatha shrieked and crumpled mere feet from Rory and Abby, her hand clasping her neck.

"Nooo!" Abby cried with horror, looking to Rory.

Face flushed, Rory charged toward Mallena and Aillig who were now angling for the portal. Abby reached out, grabbing his arm. "No, let them go, we have to help Agatha," she sobbed, falling to her knees in front of their elder.

Rory clenched his jaw, watching as their adversaries sprinted to a halt inches from the pulsing tree. "This isn't finished," he growled, turning to join Abby.

Finlay flashed to Abby's side. She looked up at him, her eyes filled with despair. "She's bleeding everywhere."

The dog swung his head toward the portal and lunged, releasing a powerful roar.

Abby followed Finlay's movement with her eyes. Mallena stepped into the portal, her hand wrapped around Aillig's wrist. In seconds, they both disappeared, engulfed by the fiery tree.

"Forget them," Abby called out to Finlay, before turning her attention back to Agatha. The old woman's eyes fluttered and her breathing slowed. "Rory, do something," she pleaded, "you have to save her."

Rory dropped to his knees, watching the flow of blood from between Agatha's fingers slow and her breath diminish. "No' again. So much blood." Finding his focus, Rory laid his sword in front of him and wrapped his fingers around the hilt. He then placed his other hand atop Agatha's and closed his eyes.

Abby shook her hands nervously, rocking back and forth. "You can do this, Rory, you have to do this," she whispered.

Rory rotated his neck and relaxed his shoulders, releasing a long breath when he felt the touch of Abby's hand on his shoulder. With renewed confidence, Rory readjusted his grip on the sword and in seconds, a yellow glow erupted from the hilt and traveled up his arm.

Abby pulled her hand back from Rory's shoulder, watching with relief as the healing light flowed through Agatha's wound. She shielded her eyes, the magic entrancing her; she couldn't help but peek through the slits in her fingers. "Whoa," Abby breathed when the light retreated to the sword. "You did it!" she exclaimed, wrapping her arms around the Scotsman's shoulders.

A wide smile stretched across Rory's face at the feel of Abby's embrace, followed by a release of tension when Agatha opened her eyes and brought herself to a sitting position.

"What's this?" the old woman said, touching her neck. "I thought that vile creature had brought me to me end."

Abby hopped up and extended a hand to Agatha. "Rory healed you," she said with pride, pulling her to her feet. "But," she frowned, glancing at the portal, "we let them get away, to whatever is through there."

Agatha stared at the young Scotsman and stroked her neck. "Remarkable, Lad. I'll be forever grateful to ye. I feel nearly young and spry." She shook her head with disbelief. "Amazin', Lad, amazin'."

While Abby and Agatha continued to praise Rory's actions, Finlay paced near the portal. With a final look at the tree, the dog strode to Abby's side. *Lass, the time is now. We must deliver the Red King home.*

Abby's smile wavered, remembering their sole purpose at the stone circle. *Right. That.* She touched both Rory and Agatha on the elbow. "We can't forget about the portal. We have to figure out how to get the Red King through it."

Rory's face turned serious while he sheathed his sword. "Aye, A-by. Finlay is right. We must take me kin hame, but I fear he is too much for me to carry."

Agatha spun, looking for the deer. "Perhaps that magnificent stag could do with the Red King what he did with the stone."

Rory nodded slowly. "Is clever thinkin', Agatha, could ye ask him, A-by?"

"Of course," Abby replied, "speaking of him, where the heck did he go?" She turned around several times before spotting the stag outside of the ring, rooting through the grass. Abby rolled her eyes. "Always with the eating," she muttered before calling out to him. "Hey, Guido!"

Guido lifted his head and continued chewing a mouthful of forage as he strolled back to the center of the ring. He stopped near the Red King's still form and reached out to Abby. *Home.*

"Right, he needs to go home. Do you think you could use your magic on him the way you did with the rock? Make him float through the portal?"

Guido sniffed at the body and bobbed his head up and down. *Home.*

"Good, but," Abby paused, looking at the portal, "where is home? What's it called?"

Shay. Home, Shay.

"Huh, like the book. The Land of Shay, I guess."

Guido waived his head in the air with a snort and lowered his nose to the Red King. *Lift.*

"Lift?" she asked, confused. "You mean you want us to lift the body?"

Guido bobbed his head again. *Lift.*

"Hey, Rory," she said, looking over to the Scotsman. "I think Guido needs us to lift the Red King for him to do his magic."

With a wrinkled brow, Rory strode to his kin. After circling the resting place several times, Rory stopped next to the Red King's shoulders. "We must be careful," he instructed. "Ye support his knees, and I shall lift here."

Abby walked around the body to stand on the opposite side as Rory. "Get ready, Guido," she said, glancing up at the deer. Watching as Rory slid his hands under his kin's back, Abby followed suit by scooping up his knees. "Okay, Rory, whenever you're ready."

Rory lifted the Red King's torso but soon lowered him to the ground. "I think we may need yer help, Agatha, if ye would join me on the other side?"

"Oh my," she said, shuffling to stand across from Rory. "I don't know how much help an old woman will be, but yes, anythin' ye require of me I shall try me best."

Rory smiled with a nod. "Do as I then," he said, sliding his hands underneath the body again. Once Agatha mimicked his motions, Rory signaled for Abby to lift. With effort, the trio supported the Red King several feet above the ground. Rory glanced at Abby. "Now what?"

Abby looked impatiently at the stag. "Uh, Guido, it's your turn now."

The deer snorted in rapid succession, tipping his rack toward the Red King. His antlers glowed a brilliant yellow and magic flowed from rack to body, swirling to engulf the Red King from head to toe. The deer lifted his head high and tilted an eye toward Abby. *Release.*

"Release?" Abby looked up, realizing the deer's meaning. "Let go of him, guys," she called out, pulling her own hands back to her side.

Exclamations of awe echoed throughout the ring as the three stepped back to witness the Red King's body hover above the ground. Guido snorted approval and trotted to stand before the nobleman's feet. He nudged at a boot with his nose, causing the body to float toward the tree. The deer blinked at Abby and pushed the Red King closer and closer to the portal. When the body floated to a stop just feet from the fiery tree, Guido strode to stand at its head. He turned back to stare at Abby. *Home. Now.* And with one last snort, Guido stepped through the pulsing gateway, leaving Abby stupefied.

"So that's it," Rory sounded, "we push him through the por-tal, we take him hame." The Scotsman paused, a look of recognition washing across his face. "To my hame, to his hame," he said, nodding toward Finlay.

Abby looked from Rory to Finlay before bursting into tears. She flung herself onto the dog. After a long sob, she pulled back to collect herself. "I know it's selfish," she choked, wiping her eyes on her sleeves, "but I don't want you to go. You, you can't," she begged.

Finlay lowered his head to Abby's level, nudging her cheek with his nose. *It is my home, child, and my duty to see the Red King returned. It is for me to go.* He swung his head toward Rory. *It is for Rory to go. And,* he turned back to Abby, touching her nose to nose, *it is for you to go, Lass.*

Abby stumbled back, her stomach churning and head whirling. "Me? It's for me to go?" She looked frantically to Rory and Agatha. "But, what about my family? I can't just leave them. They'll think I'm missing, or worse if I don't come home."

Rory reached out to take Abby by the hand. "I must go, A-by. There is no mistakin' the pull in me bones." He looked down in silence, stroking Abby's fingers with his thumb. "And there is no mistakin' the hole me heart will bear if I am made to part ways from ye. I do no' think I can do this without ye by me side, A-by. I can no' say why, but I sense yer path leads to Shay." Bending over, Rory lifted Abby's hand to his lips and placed a soft kiss atop. He hesitated for the briefest of moments before lowering her hand and standing tall.

Abby gulped, tingles washing along her arm in response to Rory's gentle touch. She raised her head to meet his eyes, and with a warm smile, Rory released his hold and looked to the portal.

Abby ran her fingers through her hair and paced, a multitude of thoughts racing through her mind. She couldn't bear to see Finlay go; her soul would break without him. And though she struggled to admit it to herself, she felt an undeniable connection to Rory, one which she didn't want to see severed. But her parents, her family, her home as she knew it—could she really walk away? Would she even be able to return? She palmed her temples and released an exhausted sigh.

"There, there now, Lassie," Agatha said with a comforting pat on Abby's back. "Calm yerself a moment." She pulled Abby around to meet her gaze. "This old woman knows a thing or two about decisions to test yer heart and I think ye know what path yer feet must follow." Agatha cupped Abby's hands in her own, giving them a quick squeeze. "Ye will never forgive yerself if ye part ways with yer two greatest loves," she whispered after leaning in close.

Abby pulled back from Agatha, her face blossoming a deep red. She opened her mouth to speak, but for lack of words snapped it shut. *My two greatest loves? Of course I love Finlay, but Rory? Is that what I'm feeling? I barely know him.*

Agatha chuckled at the young woman before her. "Follow yer heart, Lass. I will follow mine as well and see me way back to me dearest friend, yer mother. Fret not for their worries; I will see them taken away."

Abby looked to the ground and breathed deeply. "But, how will you get back to Kinloch-Rannoch? That is, if I don't go with you?"

Agatha smiled wryly. "I have feet, ye know. But why trouble yerself with such things, Lass? I've survived imprisonment and an attempt on me life. I could do for a long walk."

Abby turned to Finlay, then Rory, staring at them both in succession. "Thank you for your wisdom, Agatha," Abby called over her shoulder. "Tell my family I love them and I promise to come back."

Rory's face broke into an immediate grin at the sound of Abby's words. Watching as she turned to give Agatha one last hug, he extended a hand to her when she again met his eyes. "Are ye sure, A-by?"

Abby accepted his warm hand. "Of course I'm sure, Rory. I'm always up for a new adventure. Besides," she continued with a smile, "there's this book my dad expects me to return with."

Rory continued to grin as he led Abby to stand at the foot of his kin. He gave a gentle push, sending the Red King within inches of the glowing tree. Abby drew a deep breath while she contemplated what might lie beyond the portal, only to feel a wet tongue streak along her cheek. *Eww,* she giggled, reaching up to ruffle her dog's ear.

Finlay seemed to smile in return. *I knew you were a smart one, Lass.*

Butterflies tumbled in Abby's stomach as she looked at Rory. Exchanging a knowing nod, they pushed the Red

King in unison without looking back. "Alright," Abby said, "let's take him home."

To my readers:
Humble thanks for continuing
to follow Abby's adventure.
I found great joy in creating
the second installment of the
Red King Trilogy and hope you
look forward to the conclusion.

Coming Soon:
The Talisman of Darktree Hollow

If you enjoyed The Secret of Berry Brae Circle,
please consider leaving a review on Amazon.com
or your favorite online retailer

Visit me at:
redkingtrilogy.com
www.facebook.com/TheRedKingTrilogy
Twitter: @finlayforever

www.ingramcontent.com/pod-product-compliance
Lightning Source LLC
Chambersburg PA
CBHW031038120726
47905CB00007B/2239